First Paperback Edition 2010
Published in Canada
Book design: D.Grîn

 Cover art: David Aronson
www.alchemicalwedding.com

ISBN: 978-0-9810117-3-8

The Vicious Circulation of Dr. Catastrope:

A Polemical Ensemble

by

Kane X. Faucher

Starring:
Book 1: Dr. Lars-Frederik Catastrope
Book 2: Francois Coeurlourde
Book 3: Dr. Jonkil Calembour
Book 4: Vincent (Don Schixote)

The Vicious Circulation of Dr. Catastrope

Incipit Dedicatio

Written and presented by the stupendous and ever-charming subject to the Tin Crown, Monkane the Greek. A chronicle of spectacular subliminal petard and pish-tosh, a grounding element in the continued airy flights of Mankind and the loutishness of History, replete with the condemnable basenesses of our common kindred and kind, this species of vile pedantry, cowardice, and Woman. A tale of such shock and awe as to curl a pineapple or declare the rainbow-security systems Null and Void in this and every other Kingdom, hereafter known as the Waste-bin of Knowledge, or the Oily Semiotick of the Crowleyan Slaughterbench of Orgiastic Values. Anon!

Printed on this Day of Our Lord, Anno MMX, on the Month of Octanes Caesarea Poppea, Saint Flubbish Day, in the Shanty-House That Reason Built, next to Kibbler's Wharf, London Englapazoo!

Kane X Faucher

Book 1

Author's Prologue

By now, my inveterate boozehounds and whipperbang amphe-taminos, it is too late to follow that credo of *caveat evulgor*, which (in my intentionally confused Latin) means "publisher beware". It is far too late to retract this book, or just about any other that has made its rounds in the public, that good old-time feeling of etymology that states to publish is to make public, and so therefore to publish is to perish (say those who make the distinction between bios and graphe, life and death, and so the link is: to become public is to die, or to die in public, which may make suicide bombers authors—or publishers! It is vulgar to be public, and an embarrassment to make one's suicide a public event, submitted to their scrutiny, or to post upon billboards announcing such an event as a suicide and a publication). This author does not comply with all former criticisms of this text, its proliferating multitude of errors, lies, half-truths, and pseudepi-graphic utterances, for this is its first hammered smash into print plate, kept completely private and isolated from the eyes of you sundry members of the editorial trust. This was done on purpose, I assure you, since I have hardly the confidence that you will delight in my offerings, but have that heavy sludge of arrogance enough that bungs up the brain to keep proper judgement a stranger. Here you are holding, dearest swineherd and bric-a-brac salesclerk, the great chronicle of Dr. Catastrope & alia. Perhaps you will judge me harshly for not providing a proper pedigree, and so I indulge your request:

Dr. Catastrope's genealogical descent:
Soron, the goatswain who begat
Flattus the gaffesman who begat

The Vicious Circulation of Dr. Catastrope

Gaius Caligula, bootiekin to the rubberneck
        Romans, who begat (in secret)
Drusus the Ygdraasilian who begat
Commodus the flusher who begat
St. Jerome the form-fitted butterfly who begat
St. Saintus Santosanctus who begat
Cnut the clopstopper who begat
Augustine Hip-Hoppo who begat
Pseudo Albertus Magnus Minima Moralia who begat
Edvard the stench-mongering fuller who begat
Mandeville le Pamplemousse des Arbres who begat
Charles le Feu Pneu who begat
Francois Rabelais, esq. who begat
Francois Rabelais ex-esq. who begat
Francois Rabelais II, king of Nanterre, who begat
Sir Athanasius Preacherheavy Dogmaticon who
        begat
William "Pirate lingerie" Williams who begat
Charles the ever ready who begat
PseudoLouis XV who begat
Klaus von Wigglebottom who begat
Pierre Chiez the noble weftsman who begat
Jacques St. Putain the banterer who begat
Jean-Pierre-Marie Delacroix who begat
Napoleon of the fast donkey who begat
Napoleon of the faster donkey who begat
Louis-Charles le Bateau Lourde who begat
Bernard Moliere the nun-swiper who begat
Andre Dumas-Balzac of la rue Invalides who begat
Louis-Ferdinand Destouches who begat in himself
Louis-Ferdinand Céline who begat
Clovis-Freddy Dione of the rabble who begat
Randy Warhol, the steel wool sharper, who begat

Kane X Faucher

Jonkil Calembour, grand mufti, who begat
Dr. Lars-Frederik Catastrope.

As one may note, the history of Dr. Catastrope is a necessary one. Yes, it must be told! In detail! I have never written a fictitious word in my life, and I never tip my hat to those boorish practitioners of fictional writing... They are the bane of the true chronicler and biographer, mixing into their cups of alleged brilliance the alloyed ejaculant of imagination, which—as Spinoza the lens-grinder tells us— is precisely why we can never understand God, Kingdom or Country. Those scribblers of common deceits are the blatant sores upon the anus of culture, and should be routed out and singed with brands, or perhaps clustered together and tossed into the sea. It is hard enough to make an honest living doing honest writing when the field is so peopled with these hucksters, charlatans, brigands, rogues, petty-thieves, scarpers, card-sharpers, mealy-mouthed carpet-baggers, logophiles, word-whores, denizens of literary pimp-dom, prizemongers, common louts, assgrinders, shit-heels, line-coppers, vanitycroppers, slickers, weasels, flyspits, snotflingers, poxmakers, and even poetastors! Fiction is not even fit for the birds! Dump it in a pit and pour a generous helping of lime! Who do these "authors" think they are? The world is too serious and interesting to heap on the abortive fancies of creativity! I think you, my fair shallot-stuffer, will appreciate that I stick to the facts and alter, modify, and append not a jot more than the Truth—that Truth which God has in his Great Wisdom placed in the charge of Man between his legs that he may spread the word as a seed and watch how it blossoms forth as a tree quivering from the quim. O sturdy Tree of Truth that God allowed us to plant and to harvest! What insult to God when we jam a stick in the ground or in that fertile and amorous triangle of womanly flesh, to call that Truth! The imposture of it all...

The Vicious Circulation of Dr. Catastrope

It makes me sick! Sicker than this mixed concoction of whiskey and pills!

So, my dearest reader whom I purchased from the Gallow's Pole for thirty-odd silver pieces, lay back on your rented cardboard divans or wherever your ragabash and canting likes congregate in the close approximation of the salons, and enjoy the chronicle of our great Dr. Catastrope. If the tale sits wrongly with you, feel no imperative to continue reading or patronizing this humble biographer, but rather make your polite exit and drown.

Catastrope:

The people have discharged me... Good! A national disgrace... It is printed in all the newspapers, all awards denied me... even my peace! They come, they steal my books, my carpets! These little Gingpauper cowards, looking for remuneration for my alleged crimes... My acts of nefarious collusion! My sabotaging of the General Motors Line! I scan the obituaries... Another one drops! Another is hanged for the good of the country! What silly circuses... What the people want is a real circus... with much more gore! Super Spectacle, televised! And tits hanging over the heads of the butchers while they ply their ghoulish trade in service of the State – *chop chop!*... A thousand little Jesi marched through the arena, open the lions' cages! The people want to see a mauling... they'll get exactly what they deserve... Their dose of truth and the news! Let the cadgers of the new millennium gather round for a peek... see the new boss is foaled from the sour policies of the old! Nothing changes!... It's all repetitive injuries, ailments, cankers on existence that refuse to heal!... The disease has left us in a terminal state of near-death, but never with the balls to really kick us off!

I am wracked with fevers every day, and the noise in my head is unbearable... a great veteran of medicine... Now the new America spits on me... a liar! Thief! Your scribbling! A disaster! Of course... The people only have memory for the worst things, things they can pin on your ass... a few more surveillance reports, why not? Persistent cookies like Internet baking with men-in-blackguards tied with aprons! And while they're at it, come in and pillage my things! Sell the villain's modest worldly possessions... a few nice things in with the junk, previously owned by a turncoat! A buggering oaf! Oh, the people will clamber over one another to own a piece of this history... maybe even stroll in front of my place and flaunt their

The Vicious Circulation of Dr. Catastrope

auctioned booty! They will razz me, pester me with hard questions in order to expose me... On one side the new socialists
annexing my things, on the other my publisher fleecing me
blind... telling me I'm no good... A warehouse full of books
under a thick blanket of dust! "Catastrope, the people are not
interested in your stories anymore... they want light comedy,
some romance... " Oh, but sir, my stories are filled with that,
and more! One has only to read through them and see the state
of the human condition... We are all interested in the human
condition these days... and the workers, and our liberty! They
will find such messages in what I write... A veritable contribution to the canon of literature! In fifty years, my little tales will
be that other history of the land, the capsule version, the
underwritten truth of the human condition... it will make the
reading lists in the colleges, and young men will gain a fresh
picture of our cherished country a million thousand more times
accurate than watching the Wiki-mentaries and reading Poor
Dick's Almanac cover to cover! You'll see, sir! Door-to-door
salesmen will be hawking my books, not the Encyclopaedia
Metallica!

Where will they all be when the dead rise up and make the
place stink? The whole cabinets opened up to future inquiry,
how the Republicract lapsters bamboozled their way up by
slinking around like rats! And now the rats own the country, do
they not? Entire legions filled with the plague of revenge... a
desire to settle all accounts... payable to the republic! How
many more republics do we need? It is all fiction... or worse, the
entire history of the republic could be performed by harlots and
dancing girls at the cabaret, a million times more informative
than a hundred books by Patriot Pete... But this would be an
ignoble premise under which these dancers ply their craft. The
greatest literature and the greatest grace of dance are the same
things... And my style is such a grace that has won me very

little... In Bulgaria, maybe. I have no big ideas, neither about politics nor the state of the human condition... I'm just a story-teller... I just call it as I see it... in the trenches with my little notebook... I steer as far as possible from big ideas and those who purport to have them... They are sick and rife with disease, eating too much, inveterate dipsomaniacs! They are the ruin of the earth, and I am just a little doctor with his modest practice... haven't the heart to shill the pharamaceuticals grab-bags to make my own extra coin on the side! And yet all the Theresas and Private Miss Hero steal the hearts and minds of the people... All I get is a big bag of crumbs and a kick in the ass! You're no good, Catastrope! Bum! Filthy pig!

Anyhow... I feel that I've lost you? Where was it now?... Ah, yes, I had come back... Glorious return!... Trumpets! Medals! Fanfare! Ticker tape parades! One million citations from the governmental trust!... And my books—all superior best-sellers!... A thousand times more intricate and literary than the Da Vinci or Michelangelo or Basquiat codes!... But you should see the shit the people read today!... All drivel! Hype! Sea-sick bilge! Budgie cage droppings and glossy tit ads!... And they gather about like bourgeois hooligans... Oh, yes, spittle!... All together in their closet klatches sipping latte and Amaretto!... Talking about how the books make them *feel*... All gushy and mushy! Bah! Nothing a bomb can't fix... Now that's true feel-ing!... Right on one's bean!... Or maybe just a bagful of bricks... pow!... Fix you up really good... Now that is feeling! Good enough for the stage, and never mind the page!... Nothing more profound than a clobbering... the only way those snot-nosed brats will ever learn true literature... Oh, but not that I'm the litmus of such things... No! Far too modest... A humble man... I just put pen to paper, just killing time... It's Furlonghetti that snuffles it all up... Whoosh! Right up his pig nose!... Gonna

The Vicious Circulation of Dr. Catastrope

make you famous! Gonna bring you to the stars, kid, you'll see! A book of yours in every pot! Enough to make housewife Marthas blush!... Sure, sure, I tell Furlonghetti... just make sure I get my cut! My cut, Furlonghetti!... Oh, but the nerve of me! An affront to his character!... Dare I demand or even whisper about payment? Royalties?... Pfah! Out of the question! You get squat!... Work for free, scribbler! Just like the commies! Dragging your ass to all the book signings... Not a dime! Just the other day the bank ripped out the plaster from my walls... and the caulking! Sorry, Mistah Catastrope, but the bank has to get its cut... Yes, yes, of course! I'll steady myself with the pliers... take my fillings, too! Or maybe a kidney for the organ futures!... Take a pound from next to my heart... I'll convert, too! How about a new finger for the wife? Will that do? A cut, you say!... the bank is an expert at getting its cuts... Better than any *boulangerie*! Can't pay the bills because I can't get my cut!

I growl at Furlonghetti... Oh, but this just makes him angrier! More stubborn! He stomps and gnashes his teeth... tells me I'm being unreasonable! Imagine! I should consider myself lucky that he has deigned to put my little stories to work, the lazy things leaning in their sloppy metaphors on shabby grammar... I should see the backlog of manuscripts a million billion times better than mine... written by masters and sages!... Superior trendsetters of literary cuisine for the next thousand years... budding Shakespeares... prolific robo-Dumases... grittier Bukowskis by the barrel!... Dostoeyevskys falling out of airplanes and dotting the landscape with gobs of written brilliance!... And me over here, a putz! A schlep! A good-for-nothing troll he took pity on!... Ask for a cut? I'm not as shrewd as the banks... And, just you wait and see... One day this entire world will be a series of banks... floating even on the seas... bank barges! Flotillas of fiscal fortune! Islands of interest-mongering... the language of the world falling flat and subject to usury! Watch! Wait!... The world is a bank, and we will all soon march to the drum of debts unpayable! I can scream that I am judgement proof... no dice! Go fly a kite, Catastrope! We want our cut!... Furlonghetti is paying the bills... talk to him, that fat jackass with his wobble... his unsteady lurching, a belly full of stored shekels and krugerrands... like a gull's crop! Fuckers! Go soak your head, and while you're at it, go cut and tax Furlonghetti... He's been cheating you all for years! Mortgages and shady dealings up and down the coast!... Real estate frauds, dummy marketing companies really just shabby fronts for entire armies of illegal telemarketers and robocallers... and you, Mr Bank, the accomplice! You fronted him! You lent him all that filthy startup, that pelf! Oh, but that is not how real business is done!... The banks have no interest in pursuing Furlonghetti... He's an industrious saint of new capital! A hero! What they call an entrepreneur! Statues erected in his honour... a business genius! We like him!

It's true! Rats can always smell others of their kind... they congregate in the sewers of human reason to claw and nibble away at the foundations... our pockets full of holes... shoes busted! Houses carried away on their little flea-bitten backs! All of our property and possessions hauled back to where it really belongs... in the central abyss of the ultimate Arabian banking zero!... Back to Saudi Arabia to be pureed and distilled... fed to the crown princes... our lifeblood their champagne... in the canals! With the seals on tight on all those barrels of genie-bottle oil... Big fat riches! Solid gold toilets!... thousand dollar bill toilet paper to go with that!... And that other riches thief, the Sultan of Brunei... his billion dollar parties... every weekend! Every day!... Vast cargo holds of our pilfered wealth merrily poured into the sea!

As I'm thinking of this, I get jumpy... start making my demands again... Soon the banks will descend upon me again, this time to peck out my eyes, my liver... Plato — ignoramus when it came to medicine — at least got one thing right: the liver is prophetic! The banks want prophecy without paying for it... sell it to the stock traders!

"I need my money!... Royalties! The contract!"

"Catastrope, be reasonable... "

Yes, always be reasonable... His surefire way of dropping the topic!

"What I signed... in blood, yes!... I have stake! Claim!... Something is owed me... My last books... stellar successes!"

"Well, now, not as stellar as you may believe... "

Then he starts pulling out the charts and graphs... sales figures... a motley of them in a labyrinth of grids... Makes my head swim! My eyes all screwed up!... I have no idea if these represent sales or the mating record of donkeys in Istanbul!... Or the analysis of peony cultivation among lapsed Catholics! All of it gibberish! Graphese!... He's trying to throw me off his scent... that fucking jackrabbit! That mongoose around my owed monies!... I can't find which way is up!... It's most likely all lies!... just to pinch me out of my earnings... hidden fees! Screwy agendas! Plenty of smoke! Fictitious expenditures asso-ciated with the production and distribution of my little books!... Soaring into the millions!... By the end of it, I come to believe that I may actually owe him!... But that's exactly how he wants it... He wants me to be in his debt! That's why he crawls around here so much, demanding my next book... I should work for free, and faster at that!... I owe him a book, no questions! All proceeds to compensate the immense flop of all books pre-vious!... The more I write, the more I seem to owe him!... He doesn't look like a man who is hurting... Flab like his doesn't come from the scant fare of poverty!... He looks well! Healthy! Robust! A corpulent figure that gobbles entire troughs of truf-fles! Bathing in expensive perfumes with only the finest wines and scotches served!... Perhaps not so healthy... obese from lavish living... his guts overworking as much as his enslaved writers... Funny how the more my books cause him financial hardship, the more he wines and dines!... Fatter each time I see him... He begins to float... a blimp!... With his wiry scrub he fancies a beard... More like tumbleweed pasted to his face... says it makes him look more literary... Like Hemingway... But I fear that he'll get too fat to operate the gun with his toes... I tell him, my advice as a doctor, to eat less! Moderation! Give the guts a break! Working at all hours, a buzzing processing factory... I don't want to imagine the monumental shits he takes! Climbable structures!... toilet-busting monstrosities! The effects of "good living"... He sloughs it off... Good! Perhaps a stroke of luck will put him in the ground before I end up owing him a leg! Another book!

Again, I fear that I have lost my thread and abandoned you... Where did I drop you off last? The book signings... Forget that! All the piss and drizzle of semi-educated twats and dizzy deranged demimondaines with kiwi-scented bath soaps!... Not worth our time right now... Maybe later, once we get a handle... A grip! Get the engine running on my little tale... And perhaps I'll be induced to fall upon my sword, like Seneca... Who'll play Nero? Oh, that's no matter! Anyone can be Nero nowadays... just need bad poetry, a lyre, and a fat expense account! A penchant for flames... war-watching and assiduousness! Plenty of wild, vile swine to choose from, someone who can take issue with my scribbles... most of them with the clout to make life much more unbearable... if that's possible! Do I feel like Christ, a martyr to my cause? What cause?... Go sink yourself! At least Jesus got to keep the wood... the banks want all the timber back... they need it for the complimentary toothpicks for their rich mobster clients! The banks are very interested in my

The Vicious Circulation of Dr. Catastrope

books... they shake them in the hopes to hear the jingle of a few pennies falling out... they shake me harder!... When are you going to pay up, Catastrope?... Soon, soon! Promise! A guarantee from my publisher... a generous advance against sales!... Soon! In ducats! Doubloons shipped straight from the publisher's coffers!... No fairy money out of me!... The banks are wiser than the credit I borrow from them!... They don't believe a word!... They only hear money... words like soon or later don't have that make-rich sound... Sounds hollow! The faithless anthem of the deadbeat! Indentured slob!... Take possession of his liver as collateral!... Oh, that precious prophetic liver!

But all this is where I am now... mile end, high and dry, a deadbeat dud!... It doesn't take much you know... to balance my account... Fair payment from Furlonghetti is one way... a bullet between my eyes and a fat insurance policy is another!... Don't think I haven't thought of it already... Desperate times... I shouldn't care so much about debt... but I do! The whole system is built on phantom money, distended credit, credit cards wielded by the multitude that look at their balances and try to forget the minus sign... Doesn't exist! Call my lawyer (and put *that* on credit, too!)... Judgement proof! Banks won't chase me for this piddling amount!... Oh, but they will! When the banks get a whiff of money to be made, or that you are going to give them the old monkeyshine... *whoosh*! They send their knuckle-dusting cabal of collectors... hound you on the phone, by mail, staking out your shanty and performing a siege so that you can-not even go out to buy a roll of tissue to wipe your ass!... I've seen it! Fuck, I've been a victim of it... Still am!... And then it's 'we're sorry, Dr. Catastrope, but your credit has been retrofitted with lead ingots... sunk in the drink... suggest you follow it, after you pay up, you chintzer! Skinflint! No more credit! The house is ours, too!'... Oh, so true! Nothing more evil in this world in their eyes than to cheat them out of one dry cent!... Never mind the profit they rake in... like fat, shiny, smiling Vegas casino Buddhas!... Entire fortunes gobbled up, reinvested in arms sales... dog shows... silk brocade and velvet petticoats! Meanwhile the new Bhurgers are out in full style, so fat with wine and bags of money in their pockets... wagging their fat moralizing fingers at all of us indentured gentry... scum of the earth! The reason why taxes are so high! Your fault! Why it snows in the winter! And why little Persephone can't concentrate on her studies at the elite private boarding school! So much misery, all the fault of the debt-ridden with their lavish spending habits... You buy food with credit! Pure luxury! Another hole in your belt is much cheaper... Cheaper still, pawn the belt and find yourself a rope to tie up your potato sack pants! Save on rent: twenty-five of you in one bachelor closet apartment!... You have to be frugal! Table scraps and the leather of your soles for supper... spoil yourself with dessert by sucking on a few morsels of gravel, or chew the road tar... that's what it's there for! Public works! Everybody can eat on the cheap on the road maintenance budget!

The banks are the real captain of the thieves... But I have no more desire to talk about my debt woes... I promised a story, didn't I? You brought it on! All this talk of literature, which always has to fall back into negotiating the sticky money problem! Ok, ok, a story...

***

I should start during medical school... a good place to start, a good place to finish... It was very long ago, you must understand... during the time of nautiloids and pterodactyls, my Jurassic days... Might as well have been!... Back in the days when I actually believed people made the difference, that one could change the order of things for the better... What a crock!

The Vicious Circulation of Dr. Catastrope

A bold, shit-faced lie to keep you throwing a bruised shoulder to the mill wheel day after day... fairy tale hokum-pokum, the blahblahblah of youth... I was going to cure the sick... solve every epidemic... become decorated with Nobel prizes and Orders of highest Hippocratic honours!... A model doctor and philanthropist!... Such delusions guided my studies... chipping away at vast reading chunks of cardiology, obstetrics, practice corpses stuffed with livers and other organ treasures... Little did I know, until I began to intern, that medicine is a hopeless activity... making a twig dam against a tide of indolence, stupidity, and incorrigible fast living! You can tell your patients twelve thousand times, 'stop smoking! Quit drinking! Your kidney function is failing! Hallucinogens only expand your time on the ward! All that fat and salt is making your heart suffocate!'... And they nod stupidly, 'oh, yes, doctor, you are right... going to make changes in my life! Resolutions! Vows! Five year plans like the Soviets! Structure and order! Military precision! Frequent exercise and moderation at table! Ease up on the booze! Right away! *Sicher!*'... And then I find them back in my office, complaining and lamenting... more little pains... in the heart, the lungs, limbs that are embroidered with disease, sedentary asses!... Or I find them soon enough on the morgue slabs, ready to be fitted for an oversize coffin... Bad hearts! More strokes than Van Gogh!... Collapsed lungs, bad backs!... And the women are the worst with their aches and pains... 'ooh, doctor, it hurts when I press here and here... problems with my digestion, erratic menses, hot flashes, cellulite! Halitosis! Pernod Pecking at the liver! Spots and growths!'... Some want to get implants, like they were upgrading an automobile... Boombox breasts and Botox balloon lips... complete social lobotomy! All of that rough trade of the plastic surgeon who makes his killing catering to the Barbie doll instincts of people too lazy to diet and exercise... Stapling their stomachs to their spines... sucking out globs of fat through straws and suction hoses... always the quick fix! The Frankenstein urge! Patchwork cosmetistry! I counsel them against it... let them know where I stand... They never come back, unless something goes terribly awry... Their macromastic breasts, so freakishly enormous, perma-pert, while the rest of their body-fortress is sagging into ruin... And then we have to fish behind all that silicone for the cancer... A bad scene! Or the bags burst and they are dripping it like a wax candle on the inside... silicone in the body cavity, in the blood, pure poison for nothing!... It can be said that I prefer my women natural, healthy, fit... Oh, I'm nothing if not a connoisseur of bodies... I inspect them thoroughly before jumping in... age them mentally, look where the trouble spots will be... in the hands, the feet, the propensity for obesity... Like scrutinizing a sow... Not so flattering, I know, but I keep my reflections to myself... The men? The men are awful, too, but for different reasons!... They puff up tough, never see you! Maybe once a decade! Too macho to admit that they are mortal!... Worst hearts of both genders... Heaps more self-abuse! And everything you say, your medical recommendations, all wrong!... What? They glanced at the anatomical instruction manual and have it all figured out? Fat and booze! Hypertension! The way they moan about their flagging manhood, perhaps it is a stroke of mercy to all concerned that they generally pop off earlier than the women!... Ah, but this, too... my reflections on gender... women especially since my story would be nothing without the presence of woman... Why not go by negative confession?

I absolutely cannot stand that type of woman who is frou-frou about everything... the ones who primp and preen, acting as though shit never falls out of their asses but rather bath oil bombs and aromatic pastries!... I appreciate a woman who can take a shit in your house... fearlessly! Not distressing the colon by keeping everything corseted in by a silly waste of

The Vicious Circulation of Dr. Catastrope

willpower!... A mean shit, since there is nothing at all supposed to be pleasant about it... just the relief! Plop! There it goes! And another one! Down the hole! Untroubled innards, huzzah!... No, don't try to mask it with a can of aerosol freshener, or by blaming the maid! Own up to it! Say, 'yes, sir, that is *my* shit! It oozed out of *my* ass, and, yes, I am a *healthy* person for it!'... We all stink, in our own way... no sense hiding it! Idiocy! I get sore at coquetry and the dandy refusal of all bodily functions... rococo denial!... except when the fecomancers are reading Louis' royal stool!... Sure, whatever launches your rockets!... But what I mean to say is this: if your shit doesn't stink, chances are you're unwell! A stinking copra is a sure sign that you are healthy, all organs on deck and functioning at good capacity!... but there are limits, like my fat Furlonghetti whose chamber-pot perfume has the smell of a rendering plant... Not the usual healthy stinking shit, but something off, wrong with it... like burnt chemicals mixed with something unholy... Anyhow, the women! Don't let me leave you stranded in the water closets!

A fine woman, as I was saying, for me, is tall and of athletic build... not too bony, not too muscular, but enough on both ends to delineate form and health... You see, more than just the ability to shit... that's something more for psychological investigation, for plumbers and sewage experts and the diviners of Louis XIV!... I'm talking just looks, now, and one can hope that mind follows body... I hate bodies that follow minds... what a perverted and hopeless genealogy... our minds are generally sour hash, and in no way could produce a fine body... operas! Cures! Literature! Symphonies! Entire stacked warehouses of philosophical speculation on the highest matters... sure, fine! Minds can produce those just as it can produce atomic bombs, fuel inefficient cars, environmental catastrophes, disco music, shopping networks, whorehouse liquor bashes in front of monotonous television screens... we can create those, too...

and more! But never bodies... Bodies, I maintain, are too rarefied, refined, exquisite engines and complicated machines that no mind is powerful enough to produce... Only with other bodies... Sure, make them in labs, but what a waste of cash!... Bulgakov was right! Why produce a thousand Einsteins in a lab at such a high expense and over such a long period of time when any whore along the strip can produce one any other day of the week? But, bodies, women's bodies... the kind I like... strong! Dynamic! My fetish!... good ankles! You can tell right away when you look there... fat ankles? Stay away! She'll be carting a double tire in ten years... or else she'll be playing the finicky accountant at every meal, anxious over such things as calories... Oh, I despise the calorie counters! What hatred of life! Eat moderately... no need to bring a diet chart to the table, recording everything you eat like some officious taxman! Consulting the astrology columns for menu choices... Booze, too, will kill the figure... bad for every organ, especially the brain... where it counts, or the liver and kidneys... once they blow out like over-pumped tires, it drags the rest of the body down the drain with it!... Women with strong features, not the little porcelain fragility of dolls... Why men enjoy such frail things, I will never know... too much care involved... too much coddling and doting!... and they become infirm grandmothers by the time they hit 40!... with their aches and pains and varicose veins!... Break a nail? Catastrophe! Call the fire brigade! Emergency! The seventh sign!... and to become amorous with these types? So frigid... irregular... lifeless automatons who need to be trained to behave in the simplest form of human decency, and not without long hours of trying to overcome so much ethical doubt... like sleeping with an overly polite and emotionally reticent pocket watch! What's the point?... Give me women with fire, who know what they want, not those complicit types who just lie on their backs and think of England or just how much longer this should take... I want strong women only! Aggressive! Feisty! Demanding! 'No, you klutz! Not there... to the left... faster! Slower! Not so rough with those fingers, that tongue, that *implement*... Get it right or I'll do it myself!'... like they're conducting a precise procedure. I am a doctor... I know the importance of precision... life or death! Orgasm or zilch! No fictional frictions here... Never a waste of time... and their appetites... healthier in bed than mine, at times! As voracious as the beastly nature of the activity, the carnal intention... Think of it... Why one requires a woman with an athletic build, a good heart, a horse's stamina... but one who communicates, not just some pile of pink steak and blobby flesh that stays mute and suffers! Martyrs always take the shape of miserably thin old men or pudgy insecure doll-faced women! Up on their pillars, their crosses, tied to the stake, or corpses in the event of *amour*... same thing! Like they're waiting to have their files processed or for the grocery clerk to ring up their items... they just lie there waiting, perhaps making rehearsed sounds they caught in earshot of actual living people making love... Oh, how many of them making identical sounds as I see in Hollywood movies... same pitch and timbre! The rise and fall the same... one can even detect the actress' voice they impersonate... maybe even name the movie! What happens between the sheets should not resemble an opportunity for mundane entertainment trivia!

Oh, but I'm being puerile and prurient with you... a preachy, lascivious satyr... A how-to man of sexuality... Not my intention. Just making a note of my preferences... Of course, this is making a mockery of me... This has no place in writing, my little preferences... Publicity like this is disgraceful... Feminists will be lining up around the block to pelt me with bricks and hard words... the only affirmative action being the one where they say yes to my crucifixion... up on the phallic cross of hatred, revenge... Feminazis! Hideous misandry! How I despise their ilk... as bad as the chauvinists, maybe worse!... I can't tolerate them any more than I can tolerate college-kid communists... ultrafeminists and faux-communists... they usually attend the same dumpster-diving potluck dinners... or are one and the same person! Marxist Feminist Eco-pontiffs! Let them go out and work in the factory for a few rubles an hour, or cleaning the oily shit off a duck on the shoreline... will they be preaching then, in their exhaustion? I tell you, it's a lack of execution, pure airy speculative theory completely divorced from the reality of practice! Sure, it's all fine to declare oneself a Marxist when you're happily snurfling from the capitalist feedbags of mom, dad, state, and fast food joint!... Hypocrites! And some scream themselves hoarse about equality... Pfah! Bullshit! Nettles in my underpants! Equality isn't even fit for kindergarten children... teach them the value that some people just get more because they're better, faster, greedier, or more evil than everyone else... that's life! Look at me... shit all! They plumb me dry!... Auction off my things... because I wasn't evil enough... too good a citizen, and for that you pay! Equality? Go soak your head... Go become a mathematician and balance an equation, that's your lot in life! Otherwise, if you expect equality, you'll get trampled... no matter if you're rich or poor, man or woman, Marxist or capitalist, leper or schizo! Maybe equality seems like a fine conversation topic while drunk in the philosopher's pink, fuzzy dream salon... throwing around utopian feces like wine-skins at symposium, minds of gurgling sewers, rivers of well-intentioned bullshit purling over the drains of dignity's final farewell... And once something like equality gets into your blood, like cancer, you're finished! Fucked! No use to anyone but as a campaign speechwriter for a lying old wretch trying to pimp out your labour to get votes... Equality is a disease, cura-ble by massive and frequent doses of *reality*. Anyhow... how did we get on this issue? I wanted to get on with it, so let's do that! But, wait! A critic nipping at my heel!

"Absolutely abominable, this seesawing polemic of yours!"

Okay, okay, I admit it... not exactly a tolerant exercise in this age of exercising tolerance! You don't need to tell me twice!... I keep my mouth sealed shut! Not even the sesame command will make it pop open so that the miasma of my political convictions will spoil your posh dinner party!... Let me just get this straight with you... I'm ten times more an animal and environment lover than these self-professed demagogues of poor fortune!... I don't even drive a car!... I recycle like I've got a compulsive disorder!... Half my pay goes to the poor in the street, not to the smiling gimcrack oily guy in the suit who says he operates a charity... My whole ass is on the line everyday!... My problem is that I love the earth and all its animals, but I hate human beings... Is that a crime? In some places it is... I'm not so keen on religion either... You can have all the clerics, priests, ayatollahs, rabbis, and yogic flyers bop me over the head with their scripturalala, but I'm not buying!... You put Christ or Buddha or Mohammed or Vishnu or Zeus before my eyes and you'll give me cramps!... Religion is organized boredom, and you can cut and print that!

"But your comments on women—despicable!"

Who is that?... I can't have a preference? Not allowed! *Verboten!*... Misogynist! I'm not shopping for an oppressed dairymaid! Someone to clean my soiled bibs! Not at all!... I want an equal!... O but I've given up that chase!... Best that I be left to die alone! Just what the people want, if they could just leave me alone for once!... They scream that I deserve exile, to die in cold isolation... and yet there they are, always at my door, keeping me company with their abuses... To think I did them the biggest favour by voluntarily extricating myself! Auto-exile!... Not good enough by them! Hell, no! They want the *privilege* to drive me out, by their hand!... it can't look like a personal *choice*...

***

Medical school was indeed a toilsome chore... but it was some innate love of medicine that pushed me through... Doctors had always seemed sagacious to me... miracle men, or at least the good ones. When I was a child, they would come and go... a sense of class, good manner, but no beating around the bush. 'Madame, you need to be more diligent in taking your medication... the osteoporosis has advanced to a critical state... take better care or I don't predict good times ahead.' Just like that... pure honesty... a Spartan sensibility tempered with an innate sense of good social adjustment... They seemed to read their patients so quickly, could tell in an instant what their insecurities and prejudices were... But unlike the salesman who will manipulate this information to make the sale, the doctors I remember didn't play up to those failings and foibles of human character... it just made them more nimble-footed... step around some of that psychological garbage, the land-mines, the shit-holes... Back to the business of the body, to the relevance of health... Figuring out exactly how to talk to the most obstinate patients with a heavy dose of telling it like it is... no fooling around! Most people back then treated their doctors with a kind of reverence I don't see today... No, today everyone thinks they know more than their doctors... Harbouring such a deep mistrust of the medical industry... People falling into homeopathic and herbal fads left and right... self-diagnosing themselves from Internet summaries, and then making the move to self-medication... They always get it wrong... They read it like they read astrology columns. 'I have a few of those symptoms... That's me! I must have smallpox and rubella and polio and

The Vicious Circulation of Dr. Catastrope

jitterbug fever and town crier syndrome!' Pure idiocy! And they become disgruntled that they can't write their own prescriptions... a matter of right to them!... The entitlement of hasty self-education!... Armed to the teeth with a million billion printouts from dubious websites detailing this and that about their alleged illness... And they begin to argue with me!

"Your weak spells are a result of hypertension. You need to cut down on salt and booze."

"Well, doctor, I read this article online, and I think I have chronic fatigue syndrome and carpal tunnel and post-traumatic disorder, and I found this site that says that if I eat more salt and gulp down twelve beers a day, it will cure me completely!"

—Just like that! You can find any remedy you like for any ailment! Don't want to take antibiotics for an infection? Fuck it! This website advises that you smear your body in pureed dead otters! Have a failing liver from drinking? Not a chance! This website says you ought to switch to drinking pure ethanol by the washtubful! Drink more, not less! Panacea! Just pick your symptom, pick your remedy!... And this is what I have to deal with... these snotty sub-literates who think that they know their medical condition better than I do... Don't mind me over here with my medical school degree! Why did you come here if you already figured it all out? Why are you wasting my time? Did you want to rub my nose in your precious dial-up-purchased knowledge?... Your *modem vita*?... The shit these people think they have... it's like reincarnation theories... everyone is descended from Julius Caesar and Albert Schweitzer!... Every patient thinking he or she is something fucking special!... It doesn't help that there are charlatans in my industry, too... discredited or non-practicing doctors who write these colourful, fluffy, overly-simplified books... claiming their miracle cures, how their unorthodox methods were frowned upon by the medical community as though we were afraid of letting out a secret... Oh, of course!... that's the entire purpose of medicine... to keep the cures from all of you!... We have the cure for every disease and ailment, but it is out of our atavistic and misanthropic nature that we are trying to withhold it from you!... Because who has ever heard of a doctor that wanted to *help* people? Isn't medicine about keeping people sick, trying to kill them off as quickly as possible?... Government-hired executioners in white!... Of course! We just can't wait to palp you with brass knuckles! Maybe stick our scalpels in you and twist! Pump your veins with floor cleaner and stuff rat poison pills down your whimpering craw!... We're a mean and hateful bunch, us doctors! Population control! We get a thrill from repeating ourselves retarded that you eat too much, drink too much, and don't exercise! We love giving you the horrible news that you have cancer and have three months to live... or to share the news of a lost childbirth... Happy day! All through the ward, huzzahs! Party hats! Kazoos! Break out the champagne... we just had to cart someone out whose kidneys failed!... Heart attacks gives us boners! Strokes and paralysis really make our day! The more pain and death washes through here, the bigger our smiles!... Is that what these moronic sub-doctors think when they write that awful drivel for the uninformed public?... Worse than that, the public are constantly misinformed... they have the false arrogance to believe that everything is in their hands, that they can know everything!... If I need a serious plumbing procedure done in my home, I don't rush to the Internet to do it myself... No, I call a professional!... I can't know everything... don't want to!... The Internet is a problem! Everyone going to it like some sacred oracle!... super encyclopaedia!... Wiki-prophets!... Online Gods!... Why don't you go look up how not to be so suppurating! So asinine and stupid!... Do they have a cure for sheepish idiocy? The Internet has as its contributors people like you and you and you... people who know shit about

The Vicious Circulation of Dr. Catastrope

shit!... Fuck credentials! Schooling, too!... Go and become a brain surgeon online, like a video game!... three hour course... just a questionnaire and they'll mail you your license to practice... While you're at it, why not get a mail-order badge and gun for junior so that he can enforce the law?... You look at me as if I'm an unenlightened schmuck. 'It took you four years to become a doctor? You're pretty dumb! I did it online in a day! Now I can do quintuple-bypass surgery and deliver babies painlessly through the arsehole! I have it here on paper... licensed medical doctor! I can suture the femoral artery in the sphincter! I can repair broken spleens! I can make the toe bones pump blood again! I'm a bloody genius!'... Oh, yes, yes you are! How stupid of me to actually undergo years of study!... Learning the specifics of my trade? What's the point, right? All you need is a good Internet connection and a hacksaw!... Fuckers!

I was fresh out of medical school at this time... working the clinics and the hospital graveyard shifts... rough work, even for a young man... The hospital shifts were indeed the worst for pure sensationalism, barbarism, tribalism!... Cops would be bringing in their shootout quarries, handcuffing them to the beds, all the while, these bullet-ridden gangstas were screaming about the pain... Not so tough these types when weighted down by the lead of law!... It was always tricky business to tend to them, what with the cops standing right there in their thick Kevlar vests... smug smiles, hatred in their eyes... If I hadn't been there, who knows what would have happened... Cops would have finished the job... execution style right there in the bed with the IV unit dripping... I would ask these burly creatures to leave... The stress of their presence was putting my patients in shock... "can't do that, have to remain present, make sure he doesn't escape." Sure! But I sincerely doubt that a guy with a bullet in his kidneys is going very far!... If so, just follow the slow blood trail... I tell the cop, a real big fellow who passed from rookie to maniac... bitter in three months on the beat... bad neighbourhood... I try to reason with him, tell him that his presence may induce shock... all the while, my patient is howling... the nurse is applying the dressing to the less serious wounds, and another is making sure the IV is hooked up all right... I tell the cop that no rational being in a state of distress is going to feel comfortable lying in the same room with the guy who plugged him... basic human nature!... Oh, but this cop is thick, a block of wood... won't budge... Orders! Procedure! Protocol! Potential escapee... I ignore him, but he's getting in my way... The cop keeps trying to interrogate the guy who can only answer now in soft *wahowoo*... The pain is making the crook delirious... The cop is taunting him... I blow up, in a restrained way... don't want to add to the patient's shock... He's really touch and go at this point! We need to perform immediate surgery... stop the bleeding... Did this cop really need to put that heavy calibre into this guy? Guns scare me... Human beings have invented the one tool that makes my job that much harder... I can't seem to reason with the cop... I tell the nurse to stabilize the patient while I seek out some semblance of a superior, an *oberkop* of some kind... My patient is being processed as all this is going on... I hear a loud commotion in the waiting room... A very corpulent woman is yelling... claims to be the patient's mother... Demands to see him right away... Three cops are blocking the way, telling her that she can't... Oh, but she isn't the frail type... Must have given birth to about twenty bull-sized sons... fists like Christmas hams... big fat arms that can smother with love or deliver a mighty wallop!... Noting the size of my patient, about 260 pounds, 6'5" clean and easy, she would've had to be strong enough to discipline her kids... No white-racist big cheese cop is going to tell her otherwise, that she can't see her "little baby"... I get there in time for the real fireworks... She

The Vicious Circulation of Dr. Catastrope

lets out this stifled yowl and knocks one of the cops flat on his ass!... All 220 pounds of her behind that blow!... The other two cops are stunned before they spring upon her... trying to restrain her... She's yelling blue murder!... She wants to see her son, and no fooling!... I have to agree, she has a right!... Hoodlum son or not!... I try to play peacemaker... nothing doing!... *thwack!* her ham-fist right in one of the cop's kissers!... She's a feral beast... ready to charge again!... The flattened cop is calling for backup... My Rambo in the patient's room has come to assist... A good time for me to attend my guy without Super Fuzz getting in my way...

He's having difficulty breathing... worse than just a shot in the kidneys... another bullet pierced the lung... It seems the longer we work on him, the more bullets we find... By the end, I'm surprised this guy's still alive!... An immortal ox!... but hurting something bad... extreme pain management doesn't seem to cut more than the edge... can't give him any more without the dose becoming fatal, even for a guy who seems to have taken entire clips of ammo in every major organ!... He'd have made an excellent war weapon... This is emergency surgery, for sure, with the orchestra of hysterical mother in the waiting room for accompaniment... He keeps moaning for mama... Some weird connection only mothers and sons can have... Every time he mumbles for her, so softly, she picks up speed and determination... she gets louder, calls out to him: "Tyrone! Tyrone, mama's coming... mama's coming for her little boy!"... The cops are having a helluva time trying to pin her back... The line between mother and son is a traversable distance no force in the universe can block... an inevitable magnetism... She's going to bowl them all over, maul them... Walls will crumble if they get in the way of her stampede... I'm getting nervous... She can't be in here, not at this stage... She'll start bellowing tears and crying to god almighty at what's happened to her little

Tyrone... he's in bad shape, and no mother ought to see this... we're covered in his blood... It's a race against time... Mama's presence will just complicate matters...

"Doctor, you're needed in delivery," a nurse calls to me, entirely oblivious to the fact that I'm already in the midst of emergency.

"Impossible! Too busy trying to keep one life from slipping to slip a new one out!... another doc on the ward... not me! Up to my elbows, here!"— in what, I'd rather not say... bedside manner, and all... can't alarm the patient... I'm doing all I can to prevent shock... the real teetering edge... The pain is something fierce... the handcuffs are digging into his wrist, bleeding... This can't be his first gunshot wound... still painful, nonetheless... We dope him up more... he's more lucid at this point... pain dulled, or he's resigned to it!... he asks me if he will live... I tell him to hold on... tricky business!... I've requisitioned as much equipment as possible... his breathing stops... Just then, the cop has returned, my burly fanatic!... He wants this guy to croak... mama must be in restraints... the cop tells me... They have her out in the van, cooling off... says that they won't press charges for assault... a mother's duress... How gracious of them!... But I'm not at all interested in the update!... I've got an urgent and critical situation right here!... I don't care about the bear-trapping prowess of these cops, or mama's determination... not now!... later!... when we have this guy stabilized... The cop is going on, telling me what a rotten fink this patient of mine really is... a list of horrible crimes... drug peddling, gang wars, major theft... I've had it with this trigger-baron of the law!... I begin barking at him over my shoulder... telling him to get out! It's his fault... him and his happy gun... He's not used to being spoken to this way from a citizen... but this is my domain!... It may be the wild frontier in the streets, but this is my place of business!... I'm the boss!... I tell him that it may be his job to

The Vicious Circulation of Dr. Catastrope

pump the baddies full of bullets, but in here it is my job to patch them up... no matter what foul atrocities they may have committed... Hippocratic oath!... I will not stand for a continuation of cops and robbers inside these walls!... This place is an asylum... free of guilt and innocence... Injury is the great equalizer! The cop has no business here... This is my arena, my rules!

No thanks to the cop's presence or mama's fury, I did manage to stabilize Tyrone... A job well done, if not under rotten conditions... The cop was sore at me for telling him off... Big deal!... He was interfering with my job!... How would he like it if, during a delicate sting operation, I came up to him and counseled against his eating habits in a loud voice?... He posted himself outside the door, and I posted a nurse to check on the patient... but more to keep the eager cop from unplugging machines or suffocating Tyrone with a pillow... Soon enough, the detectives show up... Took their time! They pull me aside.

"How is he, doctor?"

How nice of them to inquire! Was I dealing with the first rational being of the night?

"He is stable, but has been shot up pretty bad. It's half and half odds on him to pull through tonight."

The other detective, a guy named Mulligan with a permanently etched mien of sneering disgust, informs me about this Tyrone character:

"We've been after him for about a year. We've built a considerable case file on his activities... He heads up a notorious gang on the north side. With him down, we expect gang activity to weaken considerably. Very considerably. We consider Tyrone to be the most dangerous felon in town."

Mulligan sure enjoyed considering things in a considerable fashion!

"That's none of my business. I patch and mend... that's my job."

The other detective pipes up:

"We understand that you were a bit brusque with one of the officers."

"Yes, I was, and justifiably so. He was stepping all over my toes, getting in the way. I was in a very delicate situation, and his presence was impeding my efforts, endangering the patient."

"You may want to apologize to him. I understand that it must have been stressful, but we need to keep an air of tact and respect."

"He sure does! I am not in an apologetic mood... I was doing my job."

"So was he."

"I had no idea that harassing my patients was part of the job description. Those conditions are unacceptable."

Seeing that I was not amenable to their request, they stalked off. No sentimental goodbyes or sincere concern for the patient or acknowledgement of my role...

My first practice flopped, and then the next one, too!... I was sabotaged! I could have stayed in the city... the waiting list for a GP is no longer expressed in years, but in generations... You have to book a prostate exam for your future great-great-grandson right away!... I decided to go where I would be needed more... the sticks! Rural regions need doctors... the cities need them, too, but it's truly bad out there... At least in the cities you can be seen by someone, at least in emergency... In the rural zones, forget it! Not enough perks! The doctors all want to stay in the cities!... The government can give them all the incentives they could ever want... free mansion! No taxes! Private masseur and a gaggle of personal servants! Limo rides everywhere! Solid gold sedan chairs!... 'No, thanks! I want to stay in the city.' I should have held out... but, no... I volunteered

The Vicious Circulation of Dr. Catastrope

to go out there to the farms... so I got squat! And I had an on-going war with the local doctor already stationed there... in league with the only pharmacist within 200 miles of there... They had bible study together, ate dinner together... Everyone knows everyone... a truly potentially explosive situation... The locals know everything about you, and should they decide to spread a rumour about you, you're sunk! Becomes gospel truth! No way of shaking it! The only thing more consistent than their dipsomania and machine-related accidents is their memory... like a Mosaic tablet! Anyhow, like most small towns built on hope and kept stitched together with fear, it was a deeply religious town... There is a correlation between poor health and Jesus, I'm convinced... an ignorance that proliferates more effectively than the plague...

You see, a young girl of about thirteen came to see me... just the fact that she consulted someone about this was an amazing show of strength in this tight-lipped god fearing com-munity... She had been raped by a relative, not so uncommon an event in these parts... it was truly a despairing and de-spicable place... completely forgotten, out of sight and mind of the cities... She was perhaps expecting me to chastise her, to beat her black and blue with a bible... I could tell that I was her last hope, I was not from here, and maybe I could help... I calmly gave her a thorough checkup... pregnancy test, the works... I checked for permanent damage... She was resilient, given the circumstances of her violent rape... I sympathized, but kept focused on the task at hand... priority number one: ensure that she is in good health. When traumatic things like this happen, someone has to take charge and discuss options objectively, concretely... they need someone with answers, someone who can take action, settle the necessary affairs immediately... the mind can wait... It does the mind much bet-ter to recuperate if the body is handled decisively... She didn't need someone sobbing all over her any more than she needed to be beaten and called a scolopendra... We discussed her options... I told her about the dangers of going through with the pregnancy... her small frame... the genetic complications of inbreeding... Although her moral conditioning was against it, she was the one who desired an abortion... I didn't force her at all. She was the one who asked. I did my duty by laying out all the options... she was wise, operating on that motor-mechanical level... the most prudent option. It didn't have to be as invasive as that, I said... the event had happened only a recently... she still could get a morning after pill... I prescribed it, willingly. What I didn't factor on was the pigheaded buffoonery of the pharmacist, himself a friend of the other doctor, the pastor, and the religious freakdom that presided over this town... He refused to fill the script... I was livid! Who was he to second-guess my prescription? Who gave him the right to trump my medical expertise with moral dogma?... Pharmacists and doctors alike should relax their religious principles... no place when you deal with bodies... Unless Buddha is doing your blood-work and Christ is personally attending to your chemo, keep your principles in your Sunday pants...

She came back to me in tears... explained the whole thing... He really did a number on her, a lecture, humiliating her in front of everyone. I fell into a quiet rage... I told her to wait in the office while I made a call... That pharmacist wasn't just going to get a piece of my mind, but the whole hemisphere! And I have a double-barrel tongue! I know how to bark when I have to!

"Sam's Pharmacy, Glen speaking."

"George, I have a young upset woman at my office... She shouldn't be here... Someone didn't follow the script. Maybe you know something about this... Some preachy asshole that looks and sounds just like you had given her a working over... withheld medicine I prescribed. Maybe you could look into

The Vicious Circulation of Dr. Catastrope

this... some soft prick who assumes his judgement is more viable than mine... An outrage! The calls I will make! The pharmacy association! Do you know about this, George?"

"Dr. Catastrope, I presume, heh... Perhaps you don't know how it works here yet. I cannot in good conscience fill this prescription. Another pharmacist would have to do it."

"Then let's get one!"

"None around. I'm it. Tough tittie. It's wrong to prescribe this to a woman, just wrong. You should be ashamed. Maybe you need Jesus in your life."

"Listen, George, the last thing I need from the blithering likes of you is a theology lesson!... I see enough of this garbage in the streets... All those sandwich men for Jesus cruxing the roads, clogging my ears with their threats of hellfire and damnation and stale cupcakes!... You have no right to refuse!—"

"Correction, I can use my discretion at any time if I feel something is awry. Go ahead and lodge your complaint... I'll just maintain that I couldn't make out your signature, that I thought it was a forgery."

"You sodden ass! Discretion? What discretion? Shits like you pour everything through that wide-assed threadbare diaper of Christian stupidity! She is the one with rights, not some 2000-year-old mummy or his blithering chronicler from Tarsus with all his epistles! What does the bible know about women? Shit all!... or medicine? Less than zip!... All it knows how to do is lobotomize its followers and force them to be galloping cannibalizing gourmands on Sundays!... and wage wars! And make life fucking unbearable for themselves and those around them!... She isn't having a Christ child! She isn't Mary!... She wants and needs that pill!... What would you do if Jesus came lumbering into your confessional pharmacy with the rood stapled to his back?... You'd write the prescriptions yourself!... all the ointment and painkillers he wants! For his wounds!... You already hand out the Viagra like candy... Does God smile on that? I doubt it's all just for 'procreation'! If I were there, I'd be dishing out the saltpeter by the bag!... The last thing this town needs is more breeding!... It already has an unbearably high oversaturation point of Jesusism and preachy nihilism!... It's places and times like this that make me sentimental for eugenicists!... Maybe the saltpeter would calm your religious fevers... keep that religion rod soft!... Religious mania should be treated with heavy doses of Thorazine! Valium! Diazepam! Toxic doses of Lithium! Maybe electroconvulsive sessions!... You repulsive Christian pharmanazi!... They should drag you out to be raped by the bulls and stuck up on a big Golgotha pogo stick!... I'll have you booted out! A disgrace! A moral zealot! The world is really turning to shit when we're letting the lazy monks dole out medicines again!... A fucking herbarium of biblical proportions!... A goddamn theocracy! Next time your prostate acts up, let me prescribe that you stick that big iron rosary of yours up your ass and twist hard! You'll feel your Jesus!... your convictions!... your 'good conscience!' This type of dented copper-bottomed clang-speech really makes me want to let go of all my stomach accounts... You gelding in mid-castration! You lowly clothier and boastful coward with all your ten thumbs wrapped around the drinking glasses, so drunk on Jesus-liquor your back teeth are floating! It's all fine to take a quick excursion to see the abbess of the brothel, to make communion with underage slatterns, but your one night of jiggy is at least eighteen years of crushing inconvenience for her, all because of moral oppression! Because you can't keep Jesus in your pants and out of plain sight! Indecent! If it were scandalous for you or your bible cronies, you'd be right there with the coat hanger! Don't act outraged! I know the score, what's up!"

"Doctor, I think you are being horribly unreasonable. You better mind your words."

The Vicious Circulation of Dr. Catastrope

"Oh, I'm a very meticulous goatherd over my words!... Every one of them aimed straight and true. No doubt about it! Of course!... I'm not about to join in and turn pirate along with your despicable kind, you Christian cutlets! This is wartime, and I ration my best words for the best moments!... Letters sent! Demonstrations in the streets! A counter-moral whiplash! I know the game you're playing... Just like foreign policy... carrots and sticks! If the flaccid carrot o' Christ doesn't entice the population, you reach for the big stick of moral tyranny!"

And that was when he banded together with his bible study doctor friend, Dr. Max Wells, and actively siphoned off all my patients... the horrible stories! Molesting the patients!... Misdiagnoses!... surgical blunders!... drunk on the job!... Overcharging!... malpractice suits a mile high! There was no stopping their little muckraking! Their slander campaigns! Their shit-slinging! But that was not important... A month or so later, I had to leave... The girl who had been denied the best remedy was in such a bad way that she threw herself into the river... suicided by those who marched the cross so far into modern medicine that real health was drowned in its shadow... After that, I couldn't stick around... It was too hard. The whole town started using me as a scapegoat... that it was my fault, that I confused her with my 'big city' solutions!... They were out to lynch me, no bones about it... I had to make it out fast, find safe refuge. I was the devil incarnate, preaching the sinful abortion! Crime against God! Fetucidal maniac! How dare I protect a woman's freedom in the scowling face of a disapproving Jesus!

Just when I thought the whole town was against me, I received a peace offering from Max, the other doctor who had helped snowball this whole debacle... He wanted to meet me at his house... bury the old hatchet. Like the unwary idiot I used to be, I went... still then thinking that the world was pieced together with good intentions instead of invidious scraps of unrequited hate. That's the real quilt of human history!

His house was enormous... truly an opulent country-style home with all the architectural flourishes and curlicues... immaculately detailed fascia boards and only the finest wooden wraparound porch... French doors... crown moulding... the whole house sturdy in that rural way, but elegant... Not too elegant or frou-frou like the aristocratic mansions, but walking that line between form and function. The only part that turned me off was that the family bible—a hulking mass of a book the size of a gravestone with all the appendices and maps—was in full view, given privileged position... opened at Leviticus, frighteningly enough!... Perhaps the whole town took Leviticus literally... I'd be the last person to be surprised to find that out!... He led me in, asked me if I wanted a scotch... Naturally, I said no, not a drinker. He helped himself. The Lord likes people who do that!... Real do-it-yourself men who can be bibulous now, repent with the bible later! Moral financing at 33 and a third percent!

"You know, Dr. Catastrope, people in small towns are more set in their ways... Easier to find oneself, to set oneself. Only natural."

"Oh, yes, of course, only natural!... Yes, yes."

I had to play nice... He had seniority over me I'd rather not relate... People in the know, people with the power to grant or withhold my opportunities.

"So, you see, Dr. Catastrope, it isn't our place to trouble the waters, if you know what I mean... That incident with that poor girl... tragic, yes. Avoidable? I suppose these things are always avoidable... but that isn't the matter. No sense trotting out who is to blame, what could have been done differently... the time has passed."

"Agreed, Dr. Wells, agreed!"

The Vicious Circulation of Dr. Catastrope

I totally disagreed! This left-handed slap... this attribution of blame farcically withheld!

"And what with your patients disappearing... That is just the moral tide of the times... just the natural migratory patterns of taste and preference."

"Understandable! Completely! Our profession is a business, too, Dr. Wells, I know! Competition is the lifeblood of economic free market activity!"

"Even your harsh words with George will pass... I'm sure he will find it in himself to forgive you out of Christian mercy. Until then, have you considered your options... elsewhere, perhaps?"

"One doctor per town is enough, right? Well, yes, I consider my options thrice daily... more even! Before I got here... Only natural! And with George blocking my prescription, and then him selling Ritalin to the kids on the side, well... Not exactly my dream place to set up practice."

"Ritalin?... Now, now, doctor," he said, in that mollifying voice one uses with flustered children and oppressed women to whom one administers laudanum. "There is no need to cast aspersions and pile on allegations on poor George... Surely, there have been several people who have already done that to you... and surely you know the sting. As it says in the Good Book, he without sin cast the first stone... "

"I sure do know the sting, the whole rock-storm!... But more importantly, I know whose barbed stingers are in my flesh. One does not walk through a hive every day without knowing who the troublesome bees are... Those pesky bees, like in *Paradise Lost*... Just need netting and a swatter... or to avoid them entirely."

"What are you talking about? I think I lost you."

"I am getting the sense that this is a farewell... that I'm being pushed out with kindness... the mock variety... We don't have to like each other. Nothing in our mutual profession states in letter and law that we have to be eternal pals... I'll walk away before I get chased off... a common cur! A monster in the village!"

He stiffened with authority. I had gone right for the throat of the issue. He said: "I think it would be best."
So I gathered myself up and took off... in the night, like a thief! So what! I found another place to practice, a bit bigger... more elbow room... perhaps more despicable. It would be a second try... Let's see what happens! Follow along now!

**

Ok, so I didn't go too far... a few hundred miles south and east... It called itself a city, but that's all *als ob*... more like a rural hub, an agglomerate of farms that traded in its pastures for insurance towers and dilapidated housing... at least on the east side where I held office... The downtown was deserted, all the businesses folding up like umbrellas, either permanently defunct or making tracks for those uber-malls and box-stores out in the burgeoning suburbs... Nothing left downtown but strip clubs and pawn shops and used car dealerships... Undesirable elements that make the bourgeois stew taste awful... And in the north all the mansions... The streets were all broken cookie crumbs, and the buses were rickety jalopies one would find in Ethiopia with a thousand people with pigs hanging from the sides like living tresses... The mayor a bible zealot, a corrupt city council that sponsored neo-nazi gay bashing "family values" festivals in the vast public park. In my end of town, everyone looking like a Dickensian character, a Tom Waits song... so many abnormalities, deformities, displaced aboriginals, dipsos and schizos, crack junkies and battered women... I worked twice a week at the methadone clinic, and once a month at the recovery house... real down-and-outers... I worked at the

The Vicious Circulation of Dr. Catastrope

emergency emotional disturbance ward, too... On top of my already fat list of patients, most of them needing the same care I was providing at those shelters, wards, houses... Circumstances had beaten them all to a pulp... Middle-aged people looking 85... No longer the joking drink binges of college kids, but real serial alcoholics, a career in crack and everything else... It begins to weigh down on you after a while. No way of airing out one's conscience to get the stink of misery out...

Since I lived on the east side, I'd run into my patients all over... Always trying to bum a cigarette, forgetting that I don't smoke... or a few dollars to buy booze... Maybe stopping me at the corner store to roll up a shirt and show me a lump... Not here, in my office, I'd say... I'm not working right now... They didn't listen, and so I was always working, in or out of the office. If Jesus got tired with the mob of the sick and infirm, think what an overdrawn and tired little mortal like me must have felt... Absolutely exhausting! Wretchedly hot summers, so I had to keep the windows open... the stench of failure, vomit, the sounds of the lumpens from the decrepit pubs where it was "cash-only"... Missions and cheque-cashing joints and Salvation Armies dotting the landscape, the whole of it a gurgling sewer of devastation and hopeless despair... Like a Russian ghetto!... The pharmacies shuttered and locked tight every night... gangland graffiti tags here and there, a passed out cluster of bodies sleeping in a bank vestibule... The vortex of human misery. I cannot understand how so many people do not realize that places like this exist in their own cities, or it must be complete indifference... Forget the have-nots, don't exist... I have my car and my job and I can't save the world... How many complicit with it all, disgusting! And no money in treating them... always voluntary... I barely made enough to keep my broken apartment where the toilet and sinks rarely worked the way they ought to... a landlady expropriating rent monies... fixing nothing, doing nothing, but sitting on her fat ass, smoking cigarettes and counting her crowns! Some of the junkies had more cash on hand than I ever did! How does that work?...

Well, junkies have the best work ethic on earth... they can pull in thousands of dollars a week if need be to support their habits... If they were to channel that energy into the stock market or entrepreneurial ventures, they'd be billionaire barons in no time! I met quite a few in treatment... Wearing stitched-together rags, yet finagling from every conceivable corner enough money to purchase a fleet of BMWs, but squandered on powders and crumbs!... scams more effective than Am-way and the Roman Catholic Church... It wasn't encouraging, but it demonstrated the zeal of human endeavour, the will to survive at all costs... Things were hard at the clinics, we had to put up signs asking the patients to not bring weapons on the premises... Imagine a sign like that! Here, in a city less than 500 000! In Los Angeles or New York, for sure... wouldn't blink an eye to see that... Expected! But here?

I have to say, this city was a crumbling southeastern ruin... a rotten cavity lodged sorely along the dentition of the highway map. Who would even bother to extract it when it was just so much easier to ignore it... like how my patients constantly ignore my advice that they quit smoking, drink and eat less... Kind of like that! But even though this place was a world unto itself of dilapidation, failure, and ruin, like some spin-off Baudelaire poem rewritten by a clinical depressive, I still managed to find love here... How, you may ask... Philosophers of the French persuasion call it a fortuitous encounter, a kind of scene straight from *Nighthawks*, or perhaps just all the rotten luck in the world compressed so tightly as to implode and convert to its opposite... You have to understand that this place did have some winsome traits... A university, for one, even if it was mostly populated by robe-Barbie sluts and frat-boys in the

The Vicious Circulation of Dr. Catastrope

belfries! An opulent university, founded by dementedly rich protestants... Buildings raised on cheap labour and the finest masonry, sky pinchers! Bell towers everywhere, and ornate doorjambs... porticoes, marble lintels, roughly hewn sandstone facades, well-behaved ivory creeping carefully around instead of over the most attractive architectural features—the genuine article through and through! Like Cambridge or Oxford or Trinity!... Very well-funded, replete with corporate sponsorship... Buildings named after every conceivable business pontiff... a building named after the local-global brewery... In fact, if you were not in university, chances were that you either worked for one of the insurance conglomerates in what was left of downtown or at the brewery... All other industries died long ago, but still the rails criss-crossed through the whole city... the neighbourhoods growing all around them... Murder during rush hour when a five kilometer train is slowly inching across all the major traffic arteries... Never occurred to the city planners to build overpasses, bridges, underpasses... Perhaps no one meant for this place to grow. Anyway, the woman...

By this time, I had had my fill of crummy relationships that always ended up in sour regret, lack of sex, or psychoanalysis... All one and the same! Younger women by the barrelful... so tiresome! One has to wait patiently for them to come around, to figure and find themselves out... I was already pretty much finished forming by this point... I had dibs on a future and was moving toward it. The flaky years were well behind me... Medical school really cleared that up that ego acne, and the practice, and responsibility and the terrifyingly necessary realization that no one really gives a shit about anyone else... Nothing and no one to fall back on... You fuck up, too bad! Next in line, please! You don't get a second shot! Poverty? Bankruptcy? Unexpected pregnancy from too long a stay at the bar? Again, too bad! Drinking and driving make you lose a leg, a life? Shucks! Flunked out of school, evicted, and developed a dependency on narcotics? Sucks to be you, but the crowd moves on! It's like the Exodus... You don't find the manna, you lag behind, you're left to rot in the sun and sand!... Here comes the pharaoh to put you back to work after a long and solid beating! Moses waits for no one! Hup-two! Get in step with the others or be vulture-kibble! Many of those other women hadn't figured out that hard iron lesson of life... Because they were younger, and their experiences never seemed to wander past the cattle gate! So I fell for someone ten years my senior, which was fine!... Experienced in matters of existence and sex... No fooling, no coquetry or whimsical little emotional dances... no games! Right to the point! Time is short!... You get to know someone pretty quick when you know how to inspect the other... And when you know what you want... or, better yet, what you don't want!

She was a tall, thin Nordic woman... timeless features. You couldn't place her age so well because people from the north have their own biorhythms... their own way of aging so unlike the those that landed here centuries ago from England-France... The northerners never seem to age as fast... or they age differently, always much more interesting... Never looking dowdy! More ravishing over time! A grace! And they know the meaning of keeping fit, eating well, not letting go of the body like so many of the clumsy oafs here: "Whoops! There go my thighs! Plop goes my ass! My implant-tits are swinging like dandy sacks of potatoes! My neck is fusing its fat with my collarbones! What a klutz I am! Hand me that crate of bonbons!" So many of the women here get ugly and fat so quickly... By the time they hit mid-twenties, their flub is showing, the accumulated reserves of sophomore late night pizza binges after a heavy night of daiquirizing... by their thirties, the hands and face start getting that melted candle look... and by the forties it's all downhill... It's because they look so "pretty" so soon... By fourteen or eighteen

The Vicious Circulation of Dr. Catastrope

they hit their beauty peak, like recently manufactured dolls with their tits like a solid shelf sticking out so proudly... Whereas the northerners of Europe, they ease into their beauty, take their time... No rush! And they keep it up... The woman's name was Ritva, as stolid as all that, I suppose... long blonde hair, grey eyes accentuated with a blue ring... high cheekbones, long athletic legs... not too muscular nor frail. You could tell that she was strong in her way... She looked like she could hold her own against an aggressor, that wiry scrapper look... Doesn't take shit from anyone. Stark features like hers, any half-intelligent attacker would just walk away... If need be, she could make her countenance look cold and murderous... This was important to me because I hated worrying about those times when my girlfriend was alone... I wanted to know that she could take care of herself when I wasn't around... Perhaps even better! Weak little girls exasperated and disgusted me... frail little dolls that want to be pampered and carried, who whine a hair is out of place, a broken nail... who take to shopping for shoes like therapy... who do girly things like do each other's hair or have girl's nights out where they gossip about boys... Who expects chocolates and flowers and all the pointless things... Who want to be treated like princesses and have everything bought for them, who use pouting as a way of getting what they want... I truly detest that sort of woman, if one could call that a woman! I despise equally across genders: those who spend an inordinate amount of time negotiating the right colour of blush and those who glue their minds to televised sports... fuck it all! Mundane rubbish! Mind-pap! Turns one's brain to sour pulp... I like a woman who doesn't fret over the pointless details... I like someone who looks fit and healthy, not one who tries to combat aging with an alchemist's pharmacopoeia of ointments, powders and paints! I can see right through that lacquer job! It's body-hatred and insecurity, and I despise above all those anxiety-ridden insecurity cases who always need constant confirmation that they are beautiful... Insecurity is what makes ugly, and self-hatred just crowns the whole thing! I don't mind jealousy... within limits. When it becomes borderline psychotic, then it needs to be rectified with therapy or pills... A small, cute kind of jealousy is okay, nothing too serious... We are, after all, wild beasts in civil clothing, and it is healthy to be wary of the other... Self-preservation, the way I see it. When someone is jealous with me, I take it as a form of flattery... as long as it is partially rooted in jest.

So Ritva and I had met at the university. I was giving a guest lecture on my specialty, epidemiological techniques in the hospital... I had written a thesis on the subject and a few articles. We bumped into each other when the department took me out for something to eat... She was mid-career in the department... Everyone was introduced... As the drinks flowed, people got chummier, as is the case. She and I were sitting side by side at the restaurant, a real crowded situation. I was getting visibly cold and she let me rub up a little on her arm, a fine big-knit sweater that seemed to be as long as a dress. Seeing her in profile, I couldn't pin her age. As the night wore on and people slowly faded away, it was just her and I having found some conversational common ground... Actually, it was much more than just a ground, but was like an entire planet. We were completely at ease in conversation, enjoying ourselves. That she and I went somewhere else after that, and somewhere else even after that, is none the matter... details like that I leave to the satyrs and pornographers and romance novelists... She and I were a great match in many ways, in mind and body... That suited me fine... It suited her fine, too. We weren't much for the games, and so we just spoke openly on that impromptu first date what we expected, what we were willing to do and not do... We found that our demands were in accord, and so began

The Vicious Circulation of Dr. Catastrope

those first two weeks where lovers are extremely selfish in wanting to be just with one another, never mind everyone else... And entire days were spent lounging around in bed, talking, etc... Things were like a dream... and every once in a while, I let down my guard and believe the whole shebang!... Like an idiot! I cannot help it... Hopeless romantic, hoping for the best... If it's too good to be true, chances are it wants your wallet or has plans to decapitate you, stick the shnozz of a big rifle in your back! Big, damn heavy heart! I'm not like that anymore for good reason!... Had my heart tinkered with by the pros!... the real parasites of the age!... master manipulators that would make Stalin smile beneath that communist cookie duster! Every "lover"—just a scummy insurance sales agent in disguise! A crook with a smile! Ratbags! Deyes! Finks! Dolts of the Liliput Order! Claqueurs and jongleurs at all the new guignols! Idolaters of the pyrite calf and the presidential chimpanzee! Brutish louts on a stroll through sludge!... Romance? Romance is for the doped and numbed!... Romance is synonymous with suffering... with suckerism! Fraught with dissembling and dementia start to finish!... I no longer have time to chase the targets of the heart... You just end up growing old and bitter, getting angry at your heart and your dick for wasting your time!

Things took a turn for the worse... She was moody, which is okay since I'm a moody guy, too... At first, the mood switches were not so rapid, and were rarely directed at me... but as that comfort level sets in and you start getting used to that bicycle built for two, the careful observance of one's own actions starts to fall away, the niceties fade... The deeper the claws have sunk, the more one can feel one can thrash about like a lunatic... I guess... She became openly hostile to me, wanting her space but not leaving my apartment... She began to resent even the most basic courtesies I extended... And then she would switch back and become amorous again... A basket-case! Her mood rhythms threw mine off, and I'm always trying to keep some firm grip on the harness of personal temperament... lest I bark at the wrong person at the wrong time — fireworks!... She would alternate between treating me like shit and being pleasant, in rapid cycles, but it seemed that the psycho-factor was starting to increase while the good times were being truncated... And I was beginning to become concerned with her drinking... For sure, she could gulp down a sea without much worry, but it was the long-term and cumulative effects that concerned me... I have to worry about these things, as a doctor... She even called that into question, making all sorts of illogical claims, not capable of arguing a point, but meandering about until she could find a table upon which winning was conceivable... And she had the nasty habit of telling me what I was thinking, but always getting it wrong and never admitting to it... pure arrogance! Without genius, arrogance is a hard sell... Sometimes she would use her age as a means of winning arguments "by experience"... bullshit! She was more a princess than I thought... despite her fallen-on-hard-times experiences, which she had many... but always landed back on her feet... The drinking made her nasty, too. Always telling me how this relationship can't work, only to reverse her verdict the next day, pulling me along like an ox! That lousy femme fatale!... Why didn't I see it before? I have had only one experience with someone like that, a decade prior... Had I forgotten everything? Back to boot camp! Rub my nose in that shit once again!

I had had about enough of the roller-coaster... Drunk on wine, and after a long bout of hostility, she fell asleep on my carpet... I told her that I was setting the alarm for 8 am, that she would have fifteen minutes to shower, pack her things, and get the fuck out... I suppose the effect of the wine had thrown her into a different world... beer and spirits just made her nasty, but wine completely rearranged the connections in her brain... She

The Vicious Circulation of Dr. Catastrope

didn't register my command, and so when the next morning came she was completely confused as I started barking my orders... She didn't remember a thing from my little speech the night before! Looking at me like I was a madman!... I was pacing about like an SS officer, "*Aus! Los! Schnell!* Up! Up! Up! Fifteen minutes! *Nun!* Pack up, let's go!" She was groggy and dis-oriented... Who was this crazy man yelling at her?... She was lucky I didn't throw her through a wall... And I'm not the violent type! Suffice it to say, we talked it over and she warmed me back up... sucking me back in... These blowups would happen once a week, and then we would get back together stronger than ever... I tried to fool myself, that it was the true spirit of romance whose ticket price is bought with intense strife... One can feel these things like nerve endings through a telephone call, or some such!... Well, goodbye to it all, for even semi-regular sex is no reason to hold fast, though for some this is a convincing reason, which explains why her past lovers could ride this bull for much longer than I could... Years of her... I can just imagine it, the torment, the madness.

It was only when she was booted that mysterious emails started to make their way to me... people from her past warning me about her, all too late!... Where were they when the shit-storm was raging? No doubt still licking wounds... Well! And another ex-lover being much more charitable, calling her "an eternal woman"... Eternal? Torment! Just confirms my view that eternity seems to house all the cretins and shit-ass properties of the universe, that the truth of this world is precisely the misery it conditions!... But I am not one to have big ideas... Those I leave for the philosophers who are all idolaters at the collected altars of Reasonable Concepts Completely Divorced From the Real... The rational is the real? Go soak your head! I've seen the so-called Real jabbering at the bus stop and beaten half to death by a roving band of drunks! I've seen the real as a fourteen-year-old girl selling her mother's paralyzed body for crack! I've seen the Real take half my possessions and nail an AUDIT to my forehead... for laughs! If this Real is the Rational, then I'll take my chances in the abyss, thank you kindly!... Ritva was once a philosophy major of a kind before getting her stride in the biological sciences, which seems to explain everything... A failed pragmatist or an idealist who soils herself at the very mention of experience... Fuckers and tarts the whole brigade of them!... Philosophers can indeed form a long conga line and fly off a bridge!... I'll lead them there like a carnival barker!... Philosophers on this side of the bridge and publishers on the other!... Maybe we could drug them up and have them go at each other's throats... That would be entertainment and ontology wrapped together!... The Truth is always at the circus because all we have left of the gods of old are the cheap supplements, copies, shreds, and torn prayer guides no one knows how to read anymore... Now, it's ingredient labels, cinders, chaff, and trans-fat warnings! Let it all go up in smoke!... I've got myself a box of matches and a large portion of bitter outrage! Let the witticists and playwrights be biting about the modern age... I'll take bitter and forget the whole blood-dripping mess... The empirical is a messy thing, and I'd just as soon deport it along with all our "big ideas" and "cultural products" and "literary classics"... all flummery! Produced and cared for by the shit-for-brains trust, potty-machine Inc. Think I'm way off base on this one? I've got your first class deportation ticket right here in my hand... Off to Darfur with you, non-stop non-connector flight on Lufthansa!... Would you rather stand here and give me your earful? Your opinions are worth as much as mine, and that isn't saying much... But if you think this is a democracy, then you have your thumb up your ass!... Your touchy-feely utopias are just part and parcel of those Big-Idea pontiffs, so keep on buying! Your call is important to us, and so stay on the line... a

The Vicious Circulation of Dr. Catastrope

surly representative will be with you shortly to settle your hash good and proper! You sofa-bed loafer! You addlepated city pimp! You urine-swilling degenerate of yesterday's hippie falsity! No time for you! I have to move on...

I thought I was devastated by this dissolution with Ritva the Emo-Golem, but it turned out to be just indigestion... of that mental kind that rises up like gas and just sticks there... Obsession, perhaps? Lust? Who cares! Moving right along to more important things!... The shabby props and sets of a life started being torn down, almost all at once! A meaningless inferno made quick work of my apartment, and still I had to honour the lease... I ended up paying every month for a luxurious spot in the sky!... A loophole, should have read the small print!... The building was just ash and rubble, and I could point a few levels up to that abstract box in space that was once my apartment, still real since I was paying for it for another six months!... Oh, I fought it in the courts, but lost... Seemed like everything went up in the fire except the landlord's contract... printed on Kevlar fire-resistant fibres and with a thick gloss of derived asbestos!... Wouldn't be surprised if the landlord didn't set the fire herself, to collect the insurance... maybe to purchase another little slum villa and start the process over again... meanwhile collecting all our rents on phantom residences! Shrewd, but sloppy!... I had to start over again, all my things, my clothes... 'Oh, but you are a doctor and so wealthy! No hardship could befall you and your fat coffers of gold!' How wrong you are!... I was working mostly gratuit... And I was living on the credit the banks were floating me... back in those days when the banks liked me because of those two little letters in front of my name, the *D* and *r* and the *punkt*. It was just a matter of course to extend all the credit I desired... A medical doctor is good for it! Well...

I found a new apartment which was shabbier than the last... Best I could do on short notice. It was a tiny walk-up squeezed on both sides by noisy student bars and tattoo parlours... Always with the booming bass, the thumping and bumping below, the ambulances taking the kids away who had succumbed to alcohol poisoning... Or always the fights... Every night! Always the same monotonous dialogue, the long stream of *fuck yous* that really stretched their capacities in vocabulary... I may have taken an oath instead of these kids who merely swore them, but I knew not to enter that little war zone of protracted adolescent idiocy... Let them drink and pummel themselves to death, into a gooey paste the street cleaners can spatulate in the morning... But this meant I hardly got any sleep... All red-eyed and dark-ringed, laggardly and nodding off on the bus... The bus was the only place I could catch a few winks. My lunch hour, too... I had to adapt to the situation, so I planned naps before the ruckus at the bars began in earnest, but I couldn't on the nights I was volunteering at this and that place... which was often!... It was worse than Parsifal... All those tarts swooning and whoring and drinking themselves to oblivion and back to shriek about it! And the brutes and bulls competing over these deplorable prizes of the flesh... All for a night's quick fuck or the opportunity to puke in a stranger's sink... And it was replayed ad nauseam every weekend, every day... Always new participants, but imbued with the same dialogue... I was at wit's end, and no fooling! Tuesday night was the only slow night, but as though to compensate for the omnipresent noise, I had an asinine neighbour with a loud electric guitar... a crack addict, too, which meant I could hear people clopping up and down the stairs at all hours of the night, talking loud... I was sick of it all... But I settled his hash. I decided to get a small firewood axe at the local hardware store, and when the next Tuesday rolled by and he was busy filling the immense abysmal void in his life with noise, I knocked on his door with the axe in my hand... Not so meek this doctor!... I asked politely if he would turn down his music while I

The Vicious Circulation of Dr. Catastrope

was sharpening my axe... in full view, and no amount of crack could offset the blind fear a man at the door with an axe produces... It was like a Kantian ethical problem... 'Should I tell the axeman where my friend is or will lying function as a categorical everything?'... No, not like that... But he was never a problem again... The tribal law was in effect here, and so I had no choice but to rewrite the laws tribally... You would do something similar in my situation! Especially after weeks of insufficiently short excursions to Nod! It drives you batty... can't think or see straight... Sleeplessness makes barbarians of us all!

Still, it was perhaps worse to be sitting on top of Babylon than to be out in the middle of the cold night in stocking-feet while the firemen were spurting impotently at a blaze that was consuming all your things... Better than the ambulances shrieking off to put another kid in the emerg for me to tend to... I should have been more preventive, to go down below to that third ring riding Geryon... to snatch the drinks away, or have the fucking place shut down... Underage drinkers, blowjobs and cocaine and rape in the bathrooms, the dance floor slicked with their greasy and grimy lust... Having the time of their lives, unwittingly at my expense! I decided to go to war with this dance club...

The place was called, simply and mono-syllabically enough, Bob's. It was quite popular among those who would end up as the gurgling dishwater of the social drainage system in five ten years... Jiggling and thrusting their STD groins at one another with an alcohol level well beyond the possibility of rational judgement... And the servers continued serving these wild beasts, making them wilder, more savage... What did the bar care? It was busy in the back counting stacks of doubloons! Hordes and herds of young fools paying for the privilege of being stupid and doing harm to themselves... Disgusting. I decided one night to investigate the source of all my sleepless pains, to glean if there was any purpose that may have been beneficial to the world at large... I watched as the bouncers let in a woman so drunk she couldn't stand, buttressed by two horny men that had no doubt found their quarry... It was ladies' night, a more wretched and misogynist idea than anti-abortion laws... For what does it entail? What does it mean? It means simply this: you men are just far too ugly for any woman to faun over when sober, so liquor them up... eviscerate them from their capacity to think... All of which, I think, is tantamount to a kind of rape, given sanction by the club owners who know nights like this are a cheap draw... Some people are just plain stupid, and they will drink themselves in a state even worse than stupid. Although these little tarts bring it upon themselves, they don't deserve the outcome... Ladies' nights need to be categorically banned! The purpose is so obvious and transparent that it sickens me... Where are the legislators? No doubt lurking in the dark crevices of places like this and hunting for "fair game"... Assholes and lechers, the lot of them! Who was feeding alcohol to these beasts?... It was a frenzied riot of flesh gone sour and silly... all tarted up and down... in skimpy clothing, getting less graceful as the night wears on... The trolley of doom that leads to last call when there is that rushing mob of desperate alcoholics plunking down their tuition money on another stale beer or a fruity cocktail filled with rufies!... Make it a concentration camp, and still they wouldn't be able to tell the difference!... Spoiled denizens of a despicable republic of failure listing treacherously on the seas toward doom!... I like dancers, but what I was seeing on the dance floor was not what one could call dancing... more the disco gyrations of an enormous squid of scantily clad nobodies stuffed into tube tops and spilling flab everywhere, while the beer-bellied boys with their chin-strap beards sidled up to them making obscene movements with their hips, rubbing up to the tarts... trying to seduce

The Vicious Circulation of Dr. Catastrope

them with ungraceful alcohol-logged bodies... Complete and utter failure! I looked around and tried to find an ounce of sense to it all... finding nothing, I was about to go, but then a kerfuffle on the floor... a fight was breaking out! I couldn't tell over the seething swarm of heads and bodies how many were involved... The bouncers pounced like panthers upon the scene, trying to suppress it, locate the cancer and remove it... but the violence was spreading... Proof of life that mob rule exists... All those within viewing distance of the altercation suddenly succumbed to a radical polarity shift, something switching on in their brains... all that misspent lust turning to a desire for violence... Fists and feet randomly pummeling anything in sight... A carnival of fun! A complete lapse into frenzied sava-gery... I had to negotiate a quick exit, but the exits were choked with bodies straining to either see the fight or to start another one... Like little vortices and whorls, the fights were beginning to pop up everywhere... I heard the sound of a bottle having been hurtled at the bar, smashing more bottles... The music had stopped, and I was waiting for the bouncers to turn the lights on and off... There must have been over two hundred patrons... well over capacity! How would the police round them all up? Would they take me in as well... But, of course! I just had to play Pliny as the volcano of rotten and condemnable doom was erupting... I felt a bottle whiz past my ear and clock someone right in the forehead... I felt hands pushing and pounding me from all sides... I toppled! A pile-on of bodies biting, hitting and kicking in the throes of hysteria had fallen on top of me... I was trapped! I tried crawling out, but there were far too many oafs stepping on my hands... The heel of a woman's boot had connected with my eye... giving me quite a shiner!... I felt the mass on top of me begin to wane or shift its weight... I took the small window and squeezed myself out... Oh, yes, I felt like toothpaste!... Everyone was smashing one another... We were all lucky that the stools were bolted to the floor, but there was a pool table... Out came the sticks and balls! This was a Neander-thal rage!... The windows were being smashed... Shrieks and screams and yelling... Someone drove their fist but missed his mark, deafening me in one ear... I could hardly breathe... It was so hot and fetid, this stale air, the sweat... I had no idea whose blood was running down my cheek... I was wet and sticky... I was pinballed between several bodies, and then finally pinned to a wall while not two inches from my nose two brutes were trading drunken punches... Alcohol and pugilism seem to be a toxic mix... My shins were being stepped on... Thwok! Another punch to the side of my head! Foomf! A kick in the gut... I was down! No, I was not down yet... I was being propped up by the clog of bodies playing tug of war... One solid mass of bodies heedless to everything but striking whatever was closest... Even friends were beating each other... All bets were off! I was in a bad way... I do remember hearing the police sirens, and this was the cold hose on all these rabid dogs... Just as quickly as they had fallen into this rampage, another instinct kicked in: the need to flee!... The crowd dispersed and scattered, the rats! Those of us too weary or unconscious or injured to move remained... Easy pickings for the police... A mere thirty people to transport to the station... I remember asking a gruff officer what took him so long... He just gazed at me with disdain, as though I was a willing participant in this vile circus! How dare I criticize his tardiness!

My wounds were tended and I was processed at the station. I gave my full account of what I could remember... I told them how I had been suffering the racket for weeks... that I was a tenant above the club... I implored the officers to shut the place down. Once they realized that I was legitimate in my claims, they drove me home... On that next horrible day of pain, I filed a formal complaint with the city, and the club was fined and

The Vicious Circulation of Dr. Catastrope

shut down... but only for a few days. I complained to the land-lord, but I had no idea that he owned the club... Once he found out that I was responsible for his precious club being shut down temporarily, things were very strained until the final release: an eviction notice scrawled in pencil and taped to my door. I didn't even have a chance to pack!... When I came back from the office, the fucker had changed the locks and dumped all my shit in the street, no doubt pawning what was valuable – which wasn't too much after most of it had gone up in smoke and flames!—and discarding all the rest amidst the usual stacks of garbage on the curb. Not even twelve hours notice to vacate... the goon jumped the gun! Leaving me homeless again!... But I got my revenge... I contacted the health department and tipped them off... rats and cockroaches... a building far below code... a firetrap! I brought out all the big guns!... The place was subse-quently condemned and the club, too... The last I heard of that landlord, he had tried opening up another club a few streets over but was denied a liquor license... Good! The only real justice in the world is pitting one corruption against another!

***

Goddamn the ululating and yodeling Matildas strolling down my boulevards, pelting me with fruit for what they call my "misogynist literature"... they are all ganging up on me these days, calling me everything short of a leper... A disgrace!... Lock him up! Throw the fucker into the sea, toss his carcass to the wolves! To the lions' jaws with him!... They would fire up the effigies on my lawn if it were politically apropos to do so nowa-days... What am I saying? Anything goes today... All these post-modernists running about with their heads up their asses, claiming that they can remake the context any they choose... That's the fashion today: You can march up and down the runways of Paris with a big black swastika tattooed on your face and call it "art", or "wry satire"... No sense of history, these doofs! And yet they come to me with all their bundled up insults, their repressed hatred!... Go pester Freud with your miseries! He'll pop out his false jaw and weep all over your mummies and daddies! He'll strap you to the couch and take you around for a drive, maybe offer you a cigar for being such a good little failed lumpen-whelp of this civilization of fizzy contents under pressure!... Everywhere I look, I see real misogyny! Not in my little books... But that's what you get for calling it as you see it. No one has the time for reports on How Things Actually Are... No, sir! No, madam! You get your balls cut off in a flash if you speak the truth... worse than the Soviet Union! Max Stirner was only half right... It's a Stalin in every breast nowadays! The people want the fluffy pink fabulations, the romances, the reality TV schlock! No room for truth!... You offer real social critique? God help you! Not even a banquet hall of apostles will keep the new Romans from putting you up on the prime time stick of national enmity!... They'll round up your apostolic supporters, too, so no one is left to write their accounts, the apologies... What am I saying? Why would I need someone to write an apology? Apologies are for the guilty, or for those who have any sense and energy to defend themselves... Myself, I just don't have the time or the health!... Trot me off, you won't hear a peep of apology from me! And meanwhile, Furlonghetti will continue lining his pockets! That's the real farce—a public that despises me so much that it buys all my books! Why? Don't they have enough rigged evidence against me? Do they want to convince the scholarly critics to find fault, too?... Maybe they want to come and bury me under excess copies of my rantings! Must I waste my time defending my little stories against whatever fashionable and topical crusade of the day? How about I beat them all to the punch and

The Vicious Circulation of Dr. Catastrope

publicly declare myself an enemy of Indonesian coffee-growers... cripples with chronic flatulence... amnesiac Laplanders... Old Prussian nobility advocates of physiognomy... Bible manufacturers in Surinam!... I am the enemy of labour, of women, of three-legged donkeys and ethnicity puree operators everywhere... Sure, why not? What a stinker this Catastrope is!

Ah, I will declare myself peerless! That riles them!... Peerless like the Chandala! I have to drink from puddles made by filthy oxen and postal carriers! I have to clothe myself with rags from the dead!... Even my books are made entirely 100% out of recycled panty liners and diapers!... We all get what we deserve, right?... Look at you with your flatheaded democracy! It's making you an anonymous schlep! Democracy is bad for the health of the mind... it poisons culture! Don't come exporting it on my doorstep! I'll only come to the ballot box to cast my vote for its abolition! Leave me alone! Anyway: we have to move on from here, don't we?

***

Well, even a doctor needs to see a doctor every once in a while... We can't just be the gong-bangers and pedagogues of health!

—Dr. Catastrope, your heart rate is, I would say, almost dangerously low, especially for a man of your age!

—Of course, of course... A marathon runner's heart! I owe it all to a steady diet of raw vegetables and avoiding irritation at all costs... Meanwhile, the rest of you are not in the best of shape... downloading scat porn and tentacle sex... double-stocking the liquor cabinet, and that almost obscene chest freezer full of pig fat bacon!

—But your blood pressure is higher than I like to see it. Are you under any stress?

—Why, always! Everything gets under my skin! People, events, the whole shebang! It's why I ought to give up reading the news... Better to scan the obits! All the newsworthy people and their exasperating events come to an end there! Or maybe I could just read the paper differently—read a few lines, turn to one side and vomit! Every few lines! Maddening, nauseating world! And all of it tracked via satellite for full 24 hour coverage of our failure and misery... No end to that! More of it! More out in the open, more dirty laundry airing from the clothesline of news network scandal! More political skullduggery, gerrymandering, double-talk! Everywhere, all the time! No escape! I'm surprised we all haven't had strokes... Oh, but I should cultivate a sense of resolute indifference... My mistake!

—You don't smoke or drink at all?

—Not a drop, doc! Not a puff, either! Raw veggies and the occasional serving of unbuttered bread... No wimpy food pyramid for me, but an immense Spartan ziggurat of healthy fare!

—I'm sure, as a medical doctor as well, that you are concerned about your blood pressure...

—Oh, of course! My heart beats hard! I'm suffering a temporary bout of hypertension... But you knew that I knew that!

—Are you taking steps to reducing your stress?

—Not steps, but leaps!

And it was true! Maybe he'd turn around and let me palp him, for a comparison... Once I'm done writing these little books of mine for Furlonghetti, my debt finally clean, I can die in peace and with normal pressure! Not likely to happen! I'll be working for Furlonghetti from the grave... I'll have to work off the chintzy headstone, too! My royalties increasing in the negatives... The more I sell, the more I owe!... Life is cheap, but labour's cheaper: that is the motto of our new social republic

The Vicious Circulation of Dr. Catastrope

of finance! The accountants have finally managed to secure a means by which to scalp absolutely everyone in every way!

The doctor prescribed me some medicine that he thought might work... A second opinion doesn't hurt, especially when all opinions are equally daft and pointless! Opinions are like the Medusa's head, each one a nasty biting serpent full of pre-judicial venom and two fangs in stereotype... It takes a mighty mirror indeed to turn all those opinions to stone, and I think Socrates is out to lunch... Why round up all the wackos and ostentatious professional snobs just to tell them something the rest of us already know: everyone is an idiot, myself included... Some are just better at hiding it. I am much more at ease with my situation, my idiocy, and so don't take on any foolish notions that I would have only later to sit and bale! Thinking that one is not an idiot is a sure way of sinking really fast!...

Back to the story...

The end... if only! No, it only slides from here, the great tobogganing descent into the freezing lake...

$$***$$

So! I was alive and doctoring in this, our collective age of hyster-ical terrorism and hysterical terrorist-hunting... open season! Soon on my doorstep, too... a HUD trained on my sorry carcass, mistaken no doubt for a dissident... an unpatriotic so-and-so with a closet full of Ayatollah and Red Army paraphernalia... Sure! It is a wonder what they can do with Photoshop these days!... They can print out all sorts of altered pictures and feed them to the blind press that will gobble it up whole, indubitable truth, splattered on every front page!... Maybe they'd like to print out a version of me on a playing card... I'd love that!... I'll be the six of bad policy initiatives... or maybe the Jack of

Asses!... A bounty on my ass worth a whopping ten dollar off coupon at Chucky Cheesewagon! Why not?... And the irony is that Google's satellite imaging will find bin Laden before any of the soldier boys do!... Ah, the soldiers... Soldiers raised on video games need targets and hi-scores!... Join the army, get a 1-up! Complete the levels and fight the big boss... Since when do I have time to wear my thumbs raw on video games?... Hours and months sunk into it... What are these kids doing? Adults, too! Accounting for bewildering obesity rates! Do they perceive their environment in this way?... I'd say more, but I'd deviate and stray too far from my story... Besides, my opinion on the matter—and yours, too—stink accordingly!

This is where my tale gets a bit depressing... Maybe not for you!... Maybe you'll find it hilarious! My imprisonment... and torture... barrels of laughs!... There's nothing funnier than concentration gulag for goons and other rabble, right?... Once we round up the pariahs and lock them up tight in cells for a beating, everyone sleeps easy at night... It is the scene of the specious triumph: Step 1: population of 6 207 813 433. Step 2: we have killed the idiot-tyrant. Step 3: 6 207 813 432—success! Victory! Parades on every street and little lasses throwing themselves into the arms of uniformed boys and kissing on Union Square!...

How was I to know that my colleague had an inveterate and sick appetite for child porn? How was I to know?... I'm too trusting, especially with my computer... I should have been tipped off when he spoke on certain subjects... his longwinded episodes of reflecting on the relation between cock and cunt...

When I set up my practice, the overhead was killing me... I needed to invite another doctor to share the cost... A snug roommate situation... There was barely enough space for the two of us, let alone one!... We fought over supplies, tripped over one another, stuck in the supply closet, mixed up our

The Vicious Circulation of Dr. Catastrope

filing... My administrative assistant was powerless... The other doctor insisted on doing his own filing... a point of pride! Little did I know that he was keeping another file... a complete gallery of printed pics of little girls and boys... Disgusting! At my place of work! And when the raid happened, guess who went down with the ship? One guess!...

Doctor George Cummings was his name, a reader of Catty Hacker poems and a bit of an oddball... That was fine at the time, sure! Oddball, ok!... He paid his half of the rent, and that was all I needed!... I didn't need to inquire into his medical ethics or step on his toes to offer my second opinions... His patients were his patients, and mine were mine... A good arrangement... But he insisted on lunching with me everyday!

—Dr. Catastrope, have you ever considered the mouth of the lover who has given you a blowjob? To watch her as she is clothed, in public, speaking to you or others... to the bank teller or the bus driver? How different the mouth looks then, and it takes an effort to remember how that mouth munched on your nether region... Perhaps the head, at its oblique angle, as you stare at it bobbing below, takes on a different aesthetic.

—I know nothing about blowjobs or aesthetics.

—But, I need to press this idea further... Why can I not see her mouth differently, as not the public mouth, but the completely private one... Why do I construct these divisions almost automatically?

—It sounds like a philosophical question to me, and I plead ignorance of the whole thing. I have no idea... Not my specialty! I don't trouble my mind-water with the particulars of existence. That is a luxury for people who don't have to worry about eating tomorrow... I try not to complicate myself that way. I do my job, end of story!

—Are you saying that you have never had this thought of a lover's mouth sucking cock *and* holding converse with others?

Kane X Faucher

Have you ever wondered if she only has one technique that she has used with past lovers?

Just like that! Every day at lunch... monotonous! Puerile! Prurient!... A pointless discourse... He couldn't take a hint unless it was lobbed like a hand grenade upon his precious lap... I wanted nothing to do with the topic... it was juvenile! Ridiculous! Grotesque!... Why did he feel at ease with me enough to share such intimate details of his sex life, his private thoughts? I surely don't inspire or encourage that behaviour in anyone!... Your thoughts are your own, and I'm no nosy busybody... I'm not a therapist or a tabloid journalist who wants all the sick details, how you tick... Not interested!... People are generally the same: idiotic, desperate, arrogant, and completely clueless... I count myself among that camp, but I'm not about to disgorge myself upon anyone I see!... I have cultivated a certain thing called *tact*... a rare and underrated skill these days!... We're all overburdened enough already! Perhaps George's reflections would have been a la mode for decadent French poetry that autofellates its own ego and considers these morbidly sexual points of view, fucking under obscenely enlarged Bosch paintings... Who cares! I'm too much of a committed realist!... I've no time for poetry or navel gazing... Such pursuits are found in those whose minds have gone slack and idle... No longer a cracking whip, but rather a kind of... dulled edge in relation to the most key element and function these days: survival!... Those who are trying to survive have no time to wax poetic on disembodied mouths giving blowjobs! I can think just far enough to get my table scraps and run... No sense lingering about waiting for the shadowy figures to emerge and give you a sound beating!... Staying idle only invites the barbarians!... Stay and philosophize all you like, but I'm living the life of cut and run!... A rat's life, I admit, sure... But a long life!... Not like those simultaneous suicides of *to art* or *not to art*! If you

62

The Vicious Circulation of Dr. Catastrope

want to play Hamlet, I've already got the answer for you!... Fuck your existential crises... You exist by chance, life is misery, suck it up or go sink yourself in the sea... There's no time for moaning! No time for writing sentimental poetry about your banal confusion... your value upon the earth—which is absolutely nil! They study reams of this shit in the universities... crippling young minds with a load of garbage that will only make them unbearable citizens!... Make them seem self-important, fooled that they have even the slightest clue... What a shame and waste!... I say, skip the contemplative aerobics and struggle with the rest of us!... Don't call your pretension to 'higher knowledge' a noble pursuit... I can chase phantoms all day, too!... I've got a big one that I focus on: my survival! My continuance!... Should I sit and question my existence? Should I stop and consider my metaphysical status in a world of shit? No! All of it flummery and word-hoaxes!... It's just more talk to pass the time... What people without televisions do with their time!... Knowledge is nothing but a hobby, and some people just don't have the instinct to set it aside and do something else!... Or to shut up!... And, George... what kind of doctor has the time to consider these alleged 'deep thoughts'?... I barely have time between avoiding one catastrophe after another to remember where I am... my coordinates on this shifting map of disease and failure!

This is not to say that I reject reading wholesale... Not at all! I do have my preferred authors, those I can stomach!... For instance, I do like Michel de Montaigne... No pretension to him! He freely admits his foibles, that he is an idiot, fat, flatulent, useless... and, unlike Rousseau, he isn't posturing as a miserable cretin in order to place his genius into higher relief... Rousseau's confessions stink! They are about as genuine and sincere as Socrates in the Agora!... Ugly, too!... Montaigne is a great essayist... Yes, he can lapse into these periods of introspective whining, but we can pardon that!... I appreciate his honesty, a trait so few authors have... I think only five authors in all of history have it!... Who else?... Ah, I do like Nietzsche... No bullshit to him!... He tells it like it is... He knows his German culture stinks, and that he is a product of that stink... He can barely scrub it from his skin, which is why he's such a Francophile... Although, that is arguably to make a move from shit to vomit... The French are terrible, too!... They like to cultivate that 'philosophical mood' and talk for years about everything... Princes of indecisive politics... How many republics and empires have they cycled through? I've lost count!... There are also parts of Hobbes I like, too... I agree that people are generally cretinous and nasty... They need to be controlled! Given absolute free reign, our species would auto-terminate itself in four years—tops!...

—What was the best blowjob you received, and what made it the best?

—I don't feel comfortable talking about this subject. It is neither interesting nor productive.

—Oh, don't be such a prude. We're men speaking on manly matters.

—Gender division gives me heartburn. I don't believe in the postmodern afternoon talk show need to disclose everything, to share our intimate feelings. I appreciate the ability to clam up. Sharing only leads to hugging, hand-holding, and asinine weepiness. If not that, it becomes the seeds of contempt, suspicion, and violence. We're all alone, so let's just jive to that. Sharing thoughts and feelings has not advanced our lives one iota! Made things all the worse if you ask me!

—Well, since you're not offering, I'll tell you my best...

Of course he would! The whole conversation was tipping in his direction... Every request for information in the spirit of

The Vicious Circulation of Dr. Catastrope

'sharing' is merely a veil for one's opportunity for a confession! I'm no priest! Leave me be!

I could barely tolerate George's infamous "lunch talks", and it was hell to get him on the subject of our operations... the nuts and bolts of managing the space... He always seemed to turn the topic over to some ridiculous matter... to sex... I just tuned him out... I shouldn't have! It was probably best for me to have paid attention... I would have spotted the symptoms of what was to follow... His carnal desire for committing pederasty!... I was working with Jerry Lee Lewis! Socrates!... a buggering doctor!

It always seemed that his computer was per-petually "in the shop", so I was courteous enough to allow him to use mine... for billing purposes only!... He convinced me to get cable Internet for it... saying that we could keep current with various medical journals online... I foolishly assented. Since he was using the computer more often than I was—myself being an archaic man of pen and paper—I let him keep it in his office... Oh, I should have known something was amiss when he would cancel appointments with patients and lock himself up in that office... for hours!... With a DO NOT DISTURB sign on the door!... I wasn't about to inquire... His business! And then the lunches dlsappeared... George now preferred to lunch in his office... said he had a mountain of work to do, articles and the like...

One frosty November morning, I found my computer back in my office and George gone... He had cleared out overnight! A midnight move... the bandit! Rogue! At least he left the computer, but little did I know that it was the one thing I wish he had taken with him!... He raided the supplies closet and took a lion's share of syringes, gauze packets, spare sphygnano-meters... That afternoon, the office was raided... A full swat team in full imposing regalia... an SS battalion of helmeted fig-ures barking sharp orders... I was immediately thrown to the floor with a knee in my back and later handcuffed... They seized all the files... and the computer! You know where this is going, right? George must have been tipped off... decided to make tracks, lickety-split!... And, meanwhile, I was left holding the big bag of collected child porn... What a swell guy I am! Just give me a mop and I'll clean out the stables, too!... Hell, do you want me to be the fall guy for murdering infants?... add it to the list of things to do!

The special task force made a point of having contacted the media well in advance of the raid... To save her ass, my assistant spouted a whole slurry of incredulous claims... that I was a weirdo... kept to myself... that she suspected all along... What is coming to this world when one cannot get any decent help? What happened to loyalty? Ah, such utopic thinking... I need to give my head a shake!... People betray each other every chance they get... You can barely trust yourself these days—or any days! History is built on treason and disloyalty! It's the only way it can move! Otherwise, history gets obese, flatulent, dies of boredom!

As I was escorted out, the papers and the TV crews were already fanned out on the steps, taking their pictures, filming every moment... getting witness accounts from random people in the street. "Yep, he looks like a pedophile"... Bastardly circus!... And me the fucking dancing bear to be shot through with electric tongs!... A slave to be cut down by the gladiators of Law and Decency!... Within the hour, my mug was gracing the front pages of every daily in the country... on every 24 hour news channel... With gross appellations: "Nefarious Evil GP Has Storehouse of Child Pornography"... "Child Porn Ring Busted—Doctor at Head of File Swapping"... "Sick Doctor Wants to Molest Your Children: Immense Accumulation of Porn Seized"... "Amassing Indecency: Doctor Charged for Child Porn Possession"... "Largest Child Porn Seizure to Date: GP Faces Stern

The Vicious Circulation of Dr. Catastrope

Charges."... And so forth! You get the picture!... Me, a pariah! A fall guy! A scapegoat! The accused and accursed! This is the circus the people want... a bloody one! A sensationalist blood-letting!... String him up! Capital punishment!... Protect our children from this Monster!... Should have his balls cut off, kept in a jar, and prominently displayed for the satisfaction of the mob!... It never fails: if they can't get the guy they're after, they'll just go for a substitute... A cry for blood must be ans-wered!... Who cares who it is... Justice must be served!... A pound of flesh!... Come get it!... We can't just draw a blank... Someone has to stand tall before the broken wagon of Law! This is the real lesson of "justice", and if you think all is fair, then you're of a juvenile proto-simian type who has orgasm at the very mention of liberal idealism... This is nothing more than tri-bal justice, wagon law, frontier ethics! You can bet almost every judge wanted this case... slavering and climbing all over one another... dumping their current cases to push this one up to first on the docket! All so they could get their faces in the papers, show their spouses and friends!... Have to respond to the public outcry for what they dimly perceive as "justice", right? And all my claims to innocence were dismissed, made me look twice as guilty!... Like I should be ashamed for declaring my Innocence... Bad faith!... Just shut up and hang!

Well, the call is out... and I'm sunk! Lock up your children because the punctilious gorilla-handed will of the Law has de-clared me the uber-monster!... An *unmensch*! You can imagine what kind of deplorable types came to my aid... No help at all!... Belching this and that about the rights of men to enjoy child porn... What a turnout!... Not exactly the type of crowd I want snuggling in my corner, defending me...

If the public wants to have done with child porn, they are stringing up all the wrong schmucks!... There wouldn't be child porn if it weren't for post-Camus youth cults... The source of all child porn taboo is our idiotic obsession with cosmetic surgery and youth uber alles!... Don't think my connection is firm enough, not filled to bursting with convincing argumentation?... I could lay it all out for you, A to Z! What difference does that make?... Nada! You'll still be locking up all the wrong doofs!... And I'm not just talking about the sick 'connoisseurs', but honest Joes like me... In the clink on suspicions and dubious evidence... Or, shall I say, a dubious connection to the evidence. But that doesn't wash with the courts!... I was left holding that bag, and there is a rally for my neck outside the courthouse. Lock up the cosmetic surgeon! The television execs who cast underage starlets to play adults in adult situations! Hell, why not ban diaper commercials, too!... Anyway... I meet with my lawyer...

—Dr. Catastrope, I may be able to enter a plea of guilty and aim for lenience...

—Aren't you a prodigy! I'll take my share of the guilt, but only for being so gullible! I've given you the name of my office-mate, the rat!

—Yeah, about that... The case cannot wait, and the guy you mentioned is nowhere to be found... No one by that name in this area, really. The prosecution thinks you're just biding for time.

—I'm already up to lose my license to practice... My whole life's work ruined over pictures of naked children I never even knew existed on my computer! Is this justice? If they can't get their man, any man will do?

—It's not that simple...

—Of course, of course, I know... I understand you are doing all you can. Let's take a day and rethink the strategy. I'm not about to pitch it all away on a bad plea.

The Vicious Circulation of Dr. Catastrope

I couldn't be too hard on my attorney... He was young and fresh from school... and perhaps the only decent representative on my case, the last man who would take my case fairly. Even if he lost, he would climb up that legal anthill... make partner... Oh, I'm all about helping out the professionals... Give them a leg up, even if it's my sawed leg that gets them up there... Maybe his future newfound fortune would be so nice to send me a box of gourmet chocolates at Christmas in the Clink... Lord only knows I was sinking vast fortunes of my own into hiring his services... Of course I was infuriated, too... All that money to have this guy tell me to plead guilty!... A chimp could have done that... Hell, I could have done that without representation! It's the path of least resistance... The most convenient use of my money... Efficient, even if it inconveniences my livelihood!

He had it bad, too, I must admit... The community fire-bombed his car, left hate messages on the doorstep, sent knife-wielding stripograms, bouquets full of killer bees, snubbed him in high society as an accomplice of child molestation... That works!... Whenever a community forms, gathers in packs and gaggles and squishy masses of hate, they return to the level of apes... Their rule is violence and snarls! I hate **it** whenever people band together for anything—they relinquish their individual judgement and share one rotten brain. It's the shortest path to mere action and no thinking... A kind of communism for chimps! But resourceful enough to find out where you live, what your schedule is like, what you buy at the grocer's... Like the Nazis and the Stalinists—always knowing all about you before even you do. Nothing makes people more resourceful than collective hatred... Like these volk are idling about in listlessness and non-direction, waiting to be triggered by some common foe... And then it's all men to their battle stations... Get off the office computer, drop the spatula, leave the kids with grandma, and pile out into the street to join the throbbing mass of idiocy!... Everyone is just waiting around for a circus to join, to run away with...

On the other side, a small contingent of child porn advocates, making it much harder for me to announce my credibility in this too high stakes game... The press skips me, goes right for these yahoos... Having the audacity to speak on my behalf, trumping me up as a hero... Fabulous! Why not invite all the wackos, degenerates, and hatemongers to give their endorsement of me as well? Hell, let's make this a real circus! Send in the KKKlowns and the neo-nazis and anti-abortionists!... Maybe some flat earth society members for good measure, and the Pimp Collective... They can chant their slogans about my inalienable rights as the law tightens my manacles!...

No wonder my books are a hard sell these days!... People only seem to have memories for the bad... The only anecdotes we seem to retain are the ones that paint each other as embarrassments, monsters, goons, drunks, stains of sin upon the vestments of humanity... Never mind that I worked mostly for free... leaving religion in the dust to consider the real needs of people... I don't mind saying it, the immodesty of it: I am a good doctor! Too kindhearted, perhaps... can't help it! It comes with the job description! People's health and well-being! This claim of child porn really cuts to the bone, a point of ethical honour!... I demand recompense, a public apology! I want honour restored? Now who's dreaming!... I can go soak my head... Even if the state would begrudgingly grant me a million pardons and apologies, no one would come... People would rather retain that other more fortified image of me, the monster who preyed on children! The surveyor of smut! And you can bet that the bulk of my sales come from that reactionary bunch who scan every word I write for even the most remote mention of my alleged carnal preferences... You can't imagine the stretches of

The Vicious Circulation of Dr. Catastrope

interpretation they have utilized against my work... Shabby arguments by the ton!... My use of the definite article must be a sign of pedophilia... Of course! They'll grasp for anything!... I have to be extra careful in these things I write... It's like having KGB goons with guns jabbed in my back, just waiting for a censorious word... Do you think the situation I'm under is *cute*? Too cute for words?... Well, if only I were cuter, maybe I wouldn't have need of words!... No, like the harlots of the celebrity industry... I can break with a few tears, all scandals forgotten! Oh, poor madam! Here's an award! A mansion! Little servant boys to bring you boxes of silken tissue!... You're not cute? Off to the slaughterhouse with you and the rest of the ugly cattle!... In the stocks so we can pelt you with rotten fruit and bent horseshoes!... Cute people have no need for words, for grand apologies... Their lives are a living encomium to how Beauty trumps accountability... and how! What do the rest of us get? Warmed-over kibble and a kick in the ass! I've told you... It just gets worse from here! The ugly gets uglier, and the fat fatter!... Write to save your thinning soul, your threadbare honour, redeeming your sense of self-respect... Bullshit! They'll hunt you down yet, and they'll throw you and all your well-meaning scribbling into a ditch on fire!... Forget all about you!... Haven't I warned you a thousand million times yet? Writing won't save anyone... No matter how eloquent your defense... Your side of the story holds no muster unless you're cute or have a fat wallet... That's just the way it goes! And when you lay it all out like I do, you get to thinking... You get the big picture... I'm a slow learner, but I catch on! I have a catch-fire brain... It learns its lessons fast once it gets going... A puff of air and *whoosh*! Inferno! I cut and run! I have every right to be paranoid! I'm not about to set out a timetable for those goons in hot pursuit of my gangly frame... No, sir!... I withdraw immediately... hills, valleys, dens, bogs, shacks, swamps, who cares! Away! Fly!... I must think I'm important... Only paranoiacs get this feeling intensely... bred in the bone! Megalomaniacs just sit and wait, listen to the birds, and get cut up in the end!... To shreds!... Arrogance is no way to live... I'd rather have the shits!... Splits-ville, and no fooling! Go ahead and sit, drool your defense to the mob coming with pitchforks and torches!... You'll be swing-ing by next Wednesday to cheers!... Once the people converge on your sorry ass, it's *finito*!

Luckily, I know no one's interested or patient enough to hear my side of the story... I don't host any illusions like that!... The goose is cooked, might as well roll over and get roasted on the other side, too!... Wait for it... They'll dig you up every year, exhume you for another crucifixion, burn your books, but keep the printing plates so that the festival can go on in perpetuity!... Your estate ransacked by Visigoths and critics... tax collectors... Even in death there is no peace!... You're hounded even after the worms are done with you!... Install an answering machine in my grave... leave nasty hate messages!... Kick my tombstone over! Drag your dick over my plot and give it a piss!... What do I care? I haven't long to go, never fear! I won't disappoint! May-be pleurisy! Maybe some painful cancer of the intestines! May-be a gunshot wound in the gut!... You never know! The way things are going these days, it would take a thousand returns of Christ for me to raise an eyebrow...

I've left you in the lurch again, haven't I? Back to brass tacks! Away with this bitter reportage of how things are... Back to how unbearable things were!

I was herded off to court... Indictments read, poor defenses deployed, prosecution's triumph... I think the public garlanded him as a hero championing human decency... Right wins the day!... Rejoice! The fucker's in the tank, maybe he'll be eaten by rats or gang-raped by the other penitents and their own code of justice... Who cares!... Behind thick bars! Let's all forget about it

The Vicious Circulation of Dr. Catastrope

and go back to waking up every day and inspecting in the mirror how boring and banal we are becoming... How devoid of life, independent thought, purpose... Go to work, maybe a chit-chat around the water cooler... Maybe a raise! Whatever! This doctor's in pinstripes now!... Numbered and ready for the box! Why go into the details of how I was found guilty... I must have been wearing my patented unlucky guilty pants... Maybe a bad tie... I was sentenced on flimsy evidence... Case closed! Next on the docket!

***

A request for solitary denied... They'd send me there soon enough... No fooling!... Just a matter of time... some misbehaviour... Oh, not mine, but others... death threats... fellow inmates who are as bad as the public and the court officials combined... Never ceases to amaze me how those who claim the "system" has given them the crummy turn can be such hypocrites!... "I'm innocent!" they yell at all hours of the day and night, but when it comes to your claim, you were put away on only the best pretext... Everyone is guilty but you!... That's how it works!... Share your grievance with a fellow bunkmate, and he'll give you that indulgent unbelieving smile... "sure, sure, you're innocent. As innocent as the devil just slithering up to say hello."... There are degrees, a whole hierarchy... Surely you must know about it, from all those hours of popping candies and salted crusts in front of the television... prison life, a big rage for television!... Don't look too hard to find the irony in that! But, surely, you must know... the divisions of respect... Murderers are left alone, petty thieves and vandals the middling aristocracy, and the sex perverts way down at the bottom... worse than the Chandala!... Most hated of the bunch by guards and inmates alike! Guess which "class" I fell under... Solitary was not only a matter of time, but a matter of urgent preservation... Everyone knew why I was there even before they assigned my numbered pajamas! That's the thing about rotten news... the more despicable it is, the faster it travels... The sicker it is, the more grease it has! Look to your own headlines for proof of that statement!... Move over charity bazaar for the orphans, we need the million point headline for suicide bombers at the cancer ward!... With footlights and commentary!... Round the clock coverage! Analysts endlessly prattling nothingness, mulling over speculations, speculations about those speculations... every notable face gets their chance to weigh in with their asinine opinion, qualified or not! That's what makes news... keeps the 24 hour channel moving... Updates as they consult everyone on the contact Rolodex! Dr. Catastrope in prison after being charged with child porn? Let's gather the commentary... See if the Sultan of Brunei is available! The out of work sitcom stars of the 1970s! We have the Prince of Wales on live video link right now! Stay tuned for the analysis of this scandal... we're pitting Janet Reno against Gary Coleman! MC Hammer versus Boutros Boutros-Ghali in the studio just waiting to get into an opinionated tear!

The guard walking this end of the corridor on most days had a lisp... it was comedic. Oh, but wait for the real comedy... the way he compensated for his lisp... with discipline!... The walls are thick for a reason! You want access to a lawyer, to make an appeal? Go rot yourself, you bum! Dreck! Scum!... Insistent? If the beatings don't wear out your morale and your convictions of innocence, they'll send for the doctor who will force laxatives down your throat... I'm convinced that this prison was partially funded by that laxative corporation since it was the prison's panacea... Cold? Headache? Broken bones? Syphilis? Gangrene? Have some laxatives... do the trick just fine! You're not diseased or in need of mending... you're just constipated... that's right! It

The Vicious Circulation of Dr. Catastrope

was their fiendish trick because there's no time for complaining and howling when your ass is cemented to the toilet letting out streams of "cure"... Hilarious! Effective! Why bother trying to curtail any possibility of an uprising with frontal assault violence when you can just incapacitate everyone with diarrhea?... as if the prison food was not enough to inspire your intestines to do that already!... And that food... so starchy... I'd have preferred the North Korean 21 ounce diet a day over this... I'm built for it... Not this tasteless starch in everything... They probably ground up laxatives in the food, too... I'd have to endure this for five years, two on good behaviour... not likely! Good behaviour is at the discretion of the punishers in uniform... and if anyone picks a fight with you, bully and victim are both to blame!... Goes in the report... "Instigator"... I was bullied in elementary school and middle school... I know the tricks of the administration in evading the problem of bullies!... Now the trend is to show bullies compassion... they come from broken homes... their brand of terrorizing the weaker children is just their call for help... Balls! Why not shift all personal accountability to broken homes?... Our prisons would be less crowded... We could just set up large therapy gulags... armies of shrinks trying to brand Oedipus complex on you... I say let the bullies roast!... They're savages! Animals! Unsocialized!... The principal in my school, soft-hearted and soft-headed!... I got followed home, beaten up, every day!... I complained, got stamped an instigator! Expedites the whole matter to settled oblivion... Why, of course it's my fault that I run off in terror and get beaten to a bloody pulp!... Maybe he was right... Maybe this is why some kids who are at the end of their rope raid daddy's shotgun cabinet and decide to dispense their own kind of justice – a few *there-theres* from the guidance counsellor isn't going to help!... In schools, in prisons, they need to have a kind of witness relocation program... An amnesty needs to be declared, or the appointment of a personal bodyguard, like in Sri Lanka for all the posh and rich whites!... I should have turned this all around, claim that institutions are only good at breeding bullies!... Ah, but that kind of truth is unwelcome, cuts too close to the bone... Assholes!

When news spread that I was in for child porn, life went from bad to shit... I already sleep in fits and starts anyway, but now it was one eye open... this Argus wasn't about to lulled to sleep with the Hermetic flute... only to wake up with a pilfered dining hall fork in my balls! A shank lodged in my arsehole!... with the guards watching on in stitches... Great amusement! It gets boring in here... Especially if you're illiterate... Blood really brings the colour to the drab grey everything... Maybe that is why the communists like torture and shooting each other in the head... They suffer from a dearth of colour... Their ideology would be much more pleasurable if they put a fern or a flower-pot somewhere... Not too bourgeois! State-issued vases, maybe, with colourful peasant scenes... Oh, but the old soviets had their kitsch... the million billion porcelain ballerinas... the ugliest sweaters... Moscow style!

I'm taking you for a ride... It's a sign of my age, I'm afraid... I get distracted easily... the horse blinders are a bit worn through, and my words quite shopworn, cliché... Not that I want to call attention to my foibles... Back to the story!

I cultivated a kind of survival trip... I did my best to warm up to the guard... the one with the lisp... I knew a few things about human nature... not enough to get me out, but enough to be affable... It only takes a slightly more intelligent perception to detect what makes people tic, their psychological garbage... I had to play it slow and carefully... win his trust... get him to open up, always sitting tight and never looking bored when he wanted to lay out his entire life like a stinking buffet... Look interested, ask questions that show you're listening... that's the key! People love to talk about themselves... give them the inch,

The Vicious Circulation of Dr. Catastrope

let them take their yard, their mile... You're not going any-where, anyway!... The more they talk to you, the more they feel that they can talk to you without being snubbed or you looking bored, the more they like you... Iron law of human nature! We're all egotistical!... One has to play it to one's advan-tage... The beatings from him stopped... Of course, he would occasionally take the distance, remember what I was in for... Couldn't compromise his position... I was, after all, linked to a sex-related crime... His name was Benson... it said so on his uni-form... Didn't know if that was his first or last name... Wasn't about to inquire! I only wanted to appear friendly... I wasn't going to be pen pals with him on my release! We talked about all sorts of things... Or, rather, he talked about himself... But the subject got around to me, once the steam ran out off his story-telling... his banal life... But amazing just how long he could stretch out his life story... weeks! I sat there all that time, strain-ing to feign interest... He asked me about my profession in the outside... I told him about my medical practice, and just the important details!... Skimpy, but simple, direct... just the high-lights! In terms he could understand... A few jokes thrown in for good measure... Oh, I always keep my ear trained for good raunchy jokes... Jokes have gotten me out of many tight squeezes, endeared me to princes and paupers alike!... Always have a repertoire of dirty jokes at your command, learn the art of deploying them in the right circumstances... a matter of appropriate space and time! Dirty jokes are not so much the rage at posh dinner functions or to share with the bank teller... Dirty jokes are the common currency of miserable men... It equalizes all social classes... Know some good ones, fresh ones... Keep them laughing! That's my motto! It keeps the bludgeon at bay! Jokes and stories – just ask Schehezerade! She knew to keep the king occupied, keep him from executing her!... Jokes function even better than stories, though... It's what passes for wit among the failed... I rolled out some of my best, the ones I overheard in my time... Easy to conjure up all sorts of memories long forgotten when you spend all your days in a grey cell... It all comes back to you in big waves!... Torrents of memories, most of which are not so great... But you start recalling all the dirty jokes... You get to brandish them... Benson was in stitches... But I had to ration them! I wasn't one to be able to create them... My mind just isn't geared that way... Some people had the gift... I had a finite supply of these jokes... Good ones, that is... and I had to release them one a day... If you run out, God help you!... Once the punisher stops laughing, you're cooked!... It's like *A Thousand and One Nights*... the imprisoned need to keep the people amused or it's curtains for you!

So, Benson and I were bonding... Good!... It had its perks... He would share some candy or a sandwich he brought from home... He offered cigarettes, and although I didn't smoke, I pretended to in order to seem gracious... All sorts of non-smokers come out of here pack-a-day smokers... I can see why! Nothing else to do! It's the chief currency in a prison economy... On holidays, Benson would give me a bit to drink always with the tacit promise that I wouldn't snitch... against prison policy!... What I valued most was the information exchange... He would tell me to skip the option for the exercise yard on given days when the other inmates were planning something horrible for me... He had his ears on everything... Of course our little sessions were not very long... I did have another inmate in the cell, so Benson and I could only conduct our little chats when the other guy was out in the yard or mopping the head... I was excused from any of that labour on account of my fragile state... More on that later...

Oh, prison life is great... You'll see soon enough, and I don't mean through this secondhand reporting!... Just wait!... You'll be pacing the box very soon once the world falls off its beams

The Vicious Circulation of Dr. Catastrope

again... gets its bearing for the cruel and indifferent incarcerating mood... just stuffing you in its pockets, afterwards stitched shut!... You'll be like a mummy in history!... Prison is just like camp... never mind the rape!... the abuses!... The cell is just waiting for you... You think too much? *Pfft-clank*!... quick like a breeze to the inside with you!... Think too little? Maybe there's a job for you... prison guard or acrobat or office worker... Can't keep your mouth shut at the right time?... I hope you're famous, for your sake!... If you don't realize your real destiny as heading toward the shit-pile of grey-bricked up future, you're definitely an idiot!... Once they have you in shackles, you might as well have already evaporated and mingled your soul with all the other forgotten ghosts!...

Ok, this is not healthy!... Furlonghetti says I'm a bit too harsh with you... That my "give and take" with the reader is not a kindly affair... that I berate you, insult you, get smug... A misunderstanding!... I'm not smug... I'm infuriated and aged... I know much better on some points, but obviously the proof of my failed wisdom is in the sour pudding in which I live!... Wisdom can go to the dogs!... Same with simpering!... I'm not berating you... No, it's nothing like that... I'm riling you a bit, horsing around, provoking you a little... I'm seeing if you still have a pulse... or if television and modern cinema has completely lobotomized you... I'm angry, sure, every right to be... decades to reflect on it all, to mull and ruminate over the details... It's all I've got left... after they took the rugs, the chairs, the walls... A man with nothing is everybody's favourite target... They whittled my dignity down to the quick, if there is anything left at all!... My humanity? What sore, suppurating wishbone fantasy are you belching and farting about now?... They took that away, too... My "humanity" is stowed away in some bank, carried against my debts!... "Oh, such a sourpuss! Be more optimistic!" Pardon me?... stick hot bamboo splinters up your urethra and crack a smile!... Between the crud and the cloaca, that's where I'm living!... Indistinguishable! Put that on the Internet where it will stick, like all the other shit you fling at it... stuck to the walls, hardening, a crust of your efforts...

Furlonghetti has come to see me again... Surprised he can find the time to waddle out of his counting safe... A regular series of visits... leaning on me to finish. "Page six-thousand, almost there... almost! Patience!"... What does he care about patience? It doesn't increase my debt load, that tidy sum, the tune I sing into his burgeoning wallet... Why not push me harder, Furlonghetti? I haven't dashed my bones on the stairs!... Maybe I ought to have been a word-jerker for one of those news combines... I've got the rhythm down!... and much more!... Enormous blasts!... Bouts of writing, hard to tell fever from labour... especially at this point... busting my balls... declining health... Just shut up and produce!... Of course, I get weary of it all... My dream: to ditch all my pens into the trash... take off somewhere private where no one knows me, where I don't ever have to speak a word... Forget my name... Die in the sea or the desert... Who cares! Forget all about it!... I deserve a retirement as much as anyone... maybe more!... My publisher is the Minister of Torture... Production will make free!... I'm marching to that beat... Can't be helped... Yes, I do scribble to get it all out... A long vomit!... Some of it gets stuck in the teeth, in the nostrils... the force of it... I'm not exaggerating one word... Sure, I horse around with you, get sidetracked... but I'm losing my bearings... These conditions!... The workers are all about conditions, and security!... My conditions are rotten, and security is a laugh shared in the offices above me... "That Catastrope? Har-har, and har-har! Let's work him harder than the mules! Make his teeth rattle with the effort! Cut his heat, too... make him work faster!" But of course... I will die of

The Vicious Circulation of Dr. Catastrope

acceleration at this rate!... Sweatshops in China don't have it this bad... I'm sure of it!...

Why not quit? Ah, the easy solution!... Nice of you to conjure up these on my behalf... Always you simpering and doddering buffoons with your 'simple solutions'... I've got bags of them! Why not croak? That's an option, too... untried, but I'm considering it!... At this rate Furlonghetti will drive me to it... Doing a fabulous job as it is!... My bones are creaking louder with the effort... Unbearable!... But the show must go on! The pages must be written... settle all accounts! The debts...

"I quit, Furlonghetti."

"But, Catastrope, you owe me so much money... the trust I put in you, the chance I took, the risks I took... All because I thought you had potential... "

"But, this is ridiculous! If I'm such a failure, why not drop me? A stone! Into the pool and forget about it!"

"I can't do that. You owe me money. You work gratis until the debt is paid... "

"But my debts only mount! The more I write! More risky ventures... More publishing!"

"You sell a bit. Print runs can stay small. Not too risky then. You're a niche-builder... You have your fans. Must capitalize on it while the fashion is still in season."

"My fans? What fans, Furlonghetti? I get hate mail by the bag-load! Everyday! You make a point of showing me all those nasty letters, underlining the most biting and vicious comments... You read them all! You cackle yourself to sleep under them, and on your pile of pilfered gold!... Why not just publish the letters? Loads of literary excrement in those!... Enough for a thousand polemical critical editions... "

Furlonghetti's not into it... Doesn't realize a moneymaker when he sees it... What could sell better than hatred? Hatred in a series of books... like most of postwar French literature!...

Kane X Faucher

Maybe he hasn't the stomach for it... would rather keep hate-writing a private enjoyment. No doubt he gets a kick out of those mean epistles... those little threats on my life in the post... the moral outrage, that I have set back the clock on literature back to the time of Hammurabi, and beyond!... He knows it's better to goad them on, to get their crotches in a tight knot by releasing another book by me... He wants to paint the whole literary market into a red rage... He's a sensationalist!... An instigator!... A provocateur! No other explanation for it!... He engineers this whole disaster... The only thing keeping me from the firing squad are these writings... the people don't want to give up a new excuse to despise me... to exchange mean gossip... to lose their number one object of enmity! Who will they hate with so much passion and zeal once I'm dead?... Oh, I'm not worried... The people will graze to another pasture, find another scarecrow to munch on... The capacity for hatred is endless, a universal human trait!... Without hatred, there'd be no community! No history! No cruel and vindictive laws! No garden parties or salon luncheons or shopping networks!... All human progress is traceable to a preternatural instinct for hatred... Hippies, take note!... Love is no glue that binds!... That was your failed interpretation on How Things Actually Are... It's hate that brings more people together every time!... You want proof? A foundation for this claim? An argument from authority? I can think of several... Christianity has fared pretty well... two millennia strong and as hateful as ever!... Churches and bibles and sermons... in every way appealing to the hatred in all of us... Maybe you didn't understand Christ's joke... love thy neighbour as thyself... You hate yourselves, too! Not hard to share that cup around!... Take a big gulp!... When there's no one in the immediate vicinity, you turn hatred on yourselves... fad diets, cosmetic surgery, indolence, stupidity... With such a boundless resource, it has to go somewhere!

The Vicious Circulation of Dr. Catastrope

You are as much a creature of hate, if not more so, Cata-strope!... Ok, I admit it!... I'm not about to flaunt myself other-wise, to posture as a creature of love!... "hate breeds fear"... Sure! I agree, hundred percent!... I'm afraid all the time... Will I eat tomorrow? Will the guard descend and put me in a de-tention camp? Will the mob devour me whole?... My hate comes from fear as much as it produces fear!... "fear engenders violence"... Me, violent? In word alone!... I'm too ineffective to put it into deed! If I could, well, empowerment on that order is a strange thing... We call those people monsters because they have the power to act on their hatred... The rest of us are flail-ing about in our powerlessness... Our blows land on nothing consequential... Impotent gestures!... Futile wrath!... Craters of nothingness!... I'd just as soon withdraw from the world than to go to war against it... What's the point? An act like that presup-poses I have *hope*... Hope is for the spastic, the fake madmen begging for alms, children, lollygaggers, campaign trail party-boosters, sorority slumber parties, traveling salesmen, heavily medicated tram operators, sports announcers, dizzy rich philan-thropists, members of the UN... I'd have to dissolve all my memory to even consider hope as an option!... Hope comes in only one package: death!... That's the only thing you can look forward to, the one thing that matters!... So, why not commit suicide? That's an option, too!... I'm too ridiculous, too stupid to go through with it... It's my curiousity, this inveterate need to know what happens next... I was born with a bad case of it!... Always afraid I'm going to miss something, and then disap-pointed that it's all the same garbage, the same old repeti-tions... Maybe that's my last sliver of hope!... I can't seem to shake it!

Furlonghetti is still talking about niche-building... his new publisherspeak... and bench-marking... another empty concept! He must attend those godawful suppurating seminars for emergent professionals... Maybe he organizes them... trawls the dictionary for those words impressive-sounding and vacuously ambiguous enough to give the audience boners... inflame their petty dreams... puffs of hot air!... Business needs a constant refreshing of its lingo... It needs to travel from one hot fad to the next, can't let anything cool on the sill for too long!... Yesterday's lingo? No one remembers! Instant amnesia! Selective forgetting!... How I wish I could have mastered that skill!

"You see, Catastrope, our publishing model needs to become one of integration and dispersion."

More hot air words! Integration? Dispersion?... It sounds like a zoology class gone all screwy!...

"Of course!... It's all clear!... Crystal!... You are a prognosticator of fortune... a business magnate... a mogul!... the sibyl of the slick-a-dee... "

"Why aren't you writing?"

Oh, that's rich!... He comes over, three-four times a week, never when I want him... always *disparu* whenever I do need to see him... always here when the larder's empty... when I've had enough of his ilk, his plethoric face all stuffed with fine dining!... Still see the foie gras on his chin!... Fresh from luncheon!

"Oh, just killing time... Being a good host! To you, of course, playing host... Working my fingers down to nubs to meet your deadlines... No other task or purpose interfering... completely devoted to the deadlines... Nothing else! Live and breathe it!"

"But your production... less than last week... A sliding in quantity and a denouement of quality. Of course we can't have that!"

"No, never!... I have to edit more ferociously... I'm being too soft on myself... Getting slack and cross-eyed!... I'll brew more coffee... You'll see, Furlonghetti... I'll make the monks in the manuscript cloisters toiling by drafty windows and candlelight look like laggards and slackers!... I'm just building up

The Vicious Circulation of Dr. Catastrope

momentum... Page six thousand and counting! Another couple of thousand dished up by month's end! All good unbroken promises!... Won't find me leaving the writing for anything at all... not for wars, cholera outbreaks, raging infernos, somersaulting clowns in the street... I'll handle all my business from the chamber-pot... installed right under my writer's chair... shackle myself to the writing desk... Breaks and interruptions are for tired old mummies and welfare pensioners... Yes! Double-time! Watch my dust!... *Arbeit macht frei* and the whole bit! My philosophy!... From Auschwitz to the household... "

"Watch what you say. Your words, they grate something awful! Not so politically correct... A bit abrasive, offensive... Perhaps you should cultivate higher offenses, bigger insults... Take aim at the charities and philanthropists and all that people hold dear!"

His idea!... He wants me to dig myself deeper, to make myself an uber-pariah!... I need to outdo myself, knock myself out with more invective, more reasons why I should be put in front of the moral firing squad!... And whatever isn't damning and polemical enough, Furlonghetti's team of crack editors will fix!... Exquisite corpse the text, a fine substitution of adjectives, nouns... Those beady-eyed rats at Furlonghetti's publishing house know exactly what they're doing!... Bringing me to critical mass!... Adding to my infamy by the barrel! Pour sourer sauce over my words... make them real stinkers! Resonating with hatred! Blood!... Hyperbolize everything, even the most modest copula!... New, more offensive connections... a sensationalist super-event!... A literature of excess and excrement!

"I will endeavour to put more puissance into the text, for sure, Furlonghetti!... I never forget my spices!... I'm cooking up the most inflammatory verbs!... pointed adjectives!... barbed and poisonous comparatives... superlatives by the ton, imported from the most hateful regions in the world!... It will be a book that makes the former Eastern Bloc invective look like a bunch of whining dopes!... Real clinchers!... Ad hominem a-plenty! Puns, thrown in as well, for the ad homonym!... A text that cascades like a drunken waterfall, a waterfall of bile and acid!... A text so hot with polemic it burns the fingers like phosphorous!... Yes, a book like a phosphorous bomb barrage!... "

"I look forward to this, but work faster... and better!"

Furlonghetti's edict!... Have to fall in step! *Nun, punkt!* No lollygagging... I can't put it off like the eternal Romanian tomorrow!... No money for an editor of my own... have to rely on his team of character butchers... instigators and verbiage assassins!... I have to act as my own Pound to my Eliot! Boss myself around... cut and burn!... Raze entire passages before the logovores get at it!... They want their meat and their blood and their hacked up big tits!... Details, Catastrope!... I'm not about to spare on those... But they'll add them for me... And what's a little exaggeration among editors?...

Of course I have my sympathizers... the ones who turn away from all the ideology-triggers in the text, the grievous personal politics of the author... the types who don't make that ethical turn or who blush when anyone mentions Heidegger's Nazism, etc. They point to the stylistics of the author... not his or her politics, her bad choices, his unforgivable racism... and so forth... Turn a blind eye, focus on the text as text... Salt of the earth that salts the earth... Don't drag his prior pamphlets into this!... Style, style, nothing but style... setting a precedent for future, safer authors who don't shoot their mouths off like creased cannons!... Look to the text as a work of maturation... didn't he recant his involvement with that heinous green supremacist group? That scientology-cross burning cult?... Forgive, forget, focus on style... I can't pardon their lot, either, these apologists... Like I need apologists!... I stay firm to my convictions without any change in course!... If I believed that

The Vicious Circulation of Dr. Catastrope

there was a man-eating unicorn behind my closet door when I was five, I am committed to still believing it!... I don't develop!... I am not in transition, not a mutable agent, a work in progress... I plopped from the womb fully formed with all my stupid opinions in tow!... Tethered to them still!... A life sentence!... Bah! To listen to all my tweed-decked apologists... the presumptuousness of it all!... You'd think that all my shit was merely a fruity-fragrant production from my glorious anus tree... Can't do wrong by these yokels!... Sure, they're right about my being unfairly persecuted into my golden years, but their touch is soft!... Cutesy-poo with fluffy mittens!... The polite society of textual redemption... salvage machines!... They're the types who trawl the garbage heaps looking for treasures to prevent the majority from burying the whole mess under sand and gravel, forgetting, oblivion... Still a solid and glistening crystal over here! Don't just chuck the baby out with the dirty bath water! Bah!... All their efforts are for naught... I'll still be made to take a beating, to get stuck with the blades of popular opinion... Nothing to prevent that!... The people have spoken, never mind the fetching bow-tie that was planted on me!... They'll see me hang, and that's an order!... Augustine was right on that score... you can't put the ocean in a small hole any more than you can change the tides with a few well-meaning exhalations... Exhilarations win the day, and if all writing is but a minor exhalation against a hurricane, my advice is you better save it!... Never mind me!... My die is cast!... Their blustery assessments, no matter how poorly drawn and bankrupt and ignorant, cannot be matched by a few soldiers in arms... Not a chance!... You'll get blown over, too! The steamroller of public opinion trumps all!... Want to get flattened on my account? Be my guest, but never say I asked for you to stand in the way!... I'm hardly a cause worthy of comparison to Tiananmen Square!... I'm just a lout, a mote, a dry tumbleweed... so will you be if you take up my case!

Well, whatever!... I promised some exhilaration of my own... instead, I'm exasperating you! Your patience!... You've got a million billion better things to do than hear me bemoan the present... A thousand little luncheons and emails and track meets and database gulags and milky soap operas to record... On with it!

***

Early release? Amounts to a hill of beans, if you ask me!... I'm marked, making Cain's tattoo look like a small birth blotch by comparison!... I watched as the most inveterate types... the murderers, sharpshooters in primary school cafeterias, hunch-backed Judases, tit-collectors, serial kidnappers, and baby milk-poisoners... all let loose into the streets before I was even considered for early parole... Three years solid! Even on my best behaviour!... They had a real hard-on for me at the top!... "what's that, Doc Catastrope? You want out *early*? Ho ho ho! You must think we're stumbling idiots! Ho ho ho!"... Well, that goes without saying!... especially these days... with television and circuses... instant messaging and bad jokes that disguise a need to be loved!... Perhaps, or just to get by... There's a hole in this leather suit of self, everyone get patching...

Okay, let's drop this prison cell philosophizing... Get back on our rails... Where'd I leave you last? In the hole!... My prison guard, the maniac prisoners who wanted to settle my hash quick!... You don't doze off for long in an environment like this... Might as well tear off your eyelids... Not a chance of using them here!... And our doctor with his big bag of laxatives... No need for riot gear in this joint!... Army generals should take note!... A war wouldn't last a week with everyone shitting their guts out...

The Vicious Circulation of Dr. Catastrope

dehydration... Hard to get the morale up and over the trenches when your bottom feels like it's going to blow any second... No one's so courageous with a pants-load of brown goo in tow!... Hard to get taken seriously when you smell of having soiled yourself... In war and in prisons, smell still matters... You don't lose your nose on the battlefield or in the holding pen... Isolation and fear make you notice all sorts of things in much more acute detail than ever before.

I had a new cellmate... A big bruiser by the name of Greg... a biker in for multiple homicides and other barroom-related mishaps... Beat up a few cops, too... drunken rages, coke peddling, you name it... To top off his fetching aesthetic, he had a big black swastika tattooed on his hand... No second guessing what kind of stable guy he was!... He immediately disliked me... I'm sure guys like him just hate everyone for the most banal or arbitrary of reasons... But I was a frail and lanky guy, looking a tad educated... In here, looking or sounding remotely educated makes you a target... Play it dumb... Laugh at the most ridiculous jokes... say little, but don't say nothing... Quiet people are suspicious... makes one look as though morally superior... Can't have that!...

Greg immediately made the political reorientation known... He told me on which bunk I was sleeping... claimed his space... A dictator and a neo-nazi... He snored loud enough to rattle my fillings!... If I wasn't sleeping much before, forget about it now!... When he was feeling particularly nasty and mean at nothing in particular, guess who doubled as his punching bag? His walking stress-release ball!... With bruises and cuts, the doctor made frequent visits, administering his miracle laxatives... Just made Greg madder to smell my feces in the cell... increased the beatings... and the time I had to spend glued to the john... unacceptable!... The beatings became routine, and the doctor made scheduled visits... It was like they had an arrangement!... At least the laxatives kept this beast from considering me his buggery-buddy!... Diarrhea spoils the mood, and thank god for that!... Thankfully, after two months, Greg had himself put in solitary after an incident in the dining hall involving a tray and a fractured skull... Back to my lonesome!... Finally!

My friendly guard had been reassigned to another wing of the prison... We had a women's wing kept entirely separate, and another for minor offenders... This wing was designated for the real hard-timers and the sex offenders... I spent about two years plus in here before my attorney was able to appeal my case... Turns out that I was innocent, surprise, surprise!... They finally tracked down my old officemate pulling the same deal in another town, this time being sloppy and the lawyers actually in accord with facts. What good was it?... The state paid a pittance in restitution for time lost, a career sabotaged by their bungling!... I ought to have sued!... No precedent!... No case! The state covers its ass, and all it has to do is shrug its shoulders in weak apology with a stupid look on its face... all forgiven!... Now that my name was clear, where was the press? Oh, they were legion when I was being hauled out as a monster, as public enemy number one, but not even a phantom whisper of their presence upon my absolution!... I told you already: people only have memory for the bad... don't pester them with the facts, that someone made a mistake... it's easier to believe unto eternal perpetuity that someone's a sicko!... The public isn't built for taking blame for being wrong... Boring! It didn't matter that my name had been cleared... my practice and any chance at opening a new one was shattered... a name besmirched for even having been under suspicion!... Appeal to get my license to practice reinstated? You must be an idiot!... I could be rubber-stamped by a thousand court officials as to my innocence, but the board would always find a way of delaying

The Vicious Circulation of Dr. Catastrope

the reinstatement. "It's in process"... Sure! It's still "in process" and has been for going on twenty years!... I've gotten passports faster! Tax returns! Reimbursements from shady service companies!... Once you're dishonoured in this industry, you're sunk... Go pick fruit on a migrant labour farm!... An official pardon doesn't mean shit!

***

What to do with all this newfound freedom?... Jobless and with no other skills than medical, what could I do?... Once you're on an infamy trip, nothing left to do but push it to the limit... It came to me in a state of delirium and starvation... Sick of the world as I was, the only place left to turn was to run for public office... character dents and all!... I fixed my sights on the mayoral office... A good place to start!... I wouldn't be the first shuffled doctor to make tracks for politics... I had to decide on a campaign platform... I had to organize. I've always been an organized and strategic man... I just fall into hopeless states of confusion. I already knew what was wrong in politics... that's a good start!... The incumbent was a corrupt money-guzzling buffoon who played reverse Robin Hood with all the infrastructure and social programs... Inviting the bigger cities to dump their trash here to taint the water supply and contribute further to the wretched genetic retardation of the citizenry... to manufacture more clueless corporate helots like him!... A city of chimps!... A hoodwinking boozer who made no clear separation between church and state... funding white supremacist groups to hold "family values" festivals in the public park to discriminate against homosexuals and immigrants... Shades of Le Pen and Hitler!... In this white bread town, this type of shit really flew!... I would take on city hall with a thundering roar from the dispossessed... the debilitated and discriminated... Champion of the oppressed, the hated... I was already a pariah myself... Might as well be their representative!

***

The whole lot of them were completely unbearable... Why couldn't they talk about something else? My head was with the fishes at this point... I was staring off, trying to dissolve that disgusted look on my face... We must be sociable! Approachable! Democratic! The tolerant society in the age of attention span zero! Avis Perry was not bothering to conceal that he was staring at Uma Drab's cleavage... She was a doctor now, no longer a ditzy object-harlot—so she thought! Not in Avis Perry's eyes! But he was always sinking himself into pointless troubles... I wouldn't be surprised if she slapped him before the night was through, or even enjoyed it! Full in the puss, one great movie starlet backhand... Great for the doctor's tennis match! Oh, she was fit, and very pretty, and Avis just couldn't keep his eyes from straying... He was very drunk, his head swimming with the fishes, too... but nowhere near as disgusted as I was.

"Yes, yes, absolutely!" I said, dragged back into conversation.

"You think so? You really think so?" she asked. Avis was interested in what I had to say on the matter, too. This bar stank something fierce... Too many old and young people, and too many in the between ages, too!

"It doesn't matter, really it doesn't," I said. "Elect who you will... Same shit in a different body bag... The campaign trail asslugging, the lies... The lies are what keep politics alive in every country! From Napoleon right down to Pinochet! No wonder the popes blessed them... twice over, even! What a farce! Listen, you really want to make a difference in politics... You eat your vote! With a fine sauce! Stick that ballot in your craw and chew! Jawbone it into mush! Stick it in a bottle and hurl it out at sea! Maybe some enterprising revolutionazis with no country to disturb will find it... Send their rogues over for a few laughs! Trash a few storefronts and burn a few government land-marks!... Democracy is passé! The Playwright was right: the masses are asses!"

"Oh, come now, Catastrope... It's the patriotic thing to do... a right! Imagine if they took that away!"

She was getting on my nerves... She and that lusty satyr, Avis.

"No," I dismissed, "being patriotic is shopping... Your presi-dent said as much. He is an idiot, but he's right about that! You do more honour to the flag by opening up your wallet and charging it than to cast a ballot like some lone, pathetic line in a swamp of pundits! People shouldn't have as much say as they do... It's all an illusion! People are stupid and idiotic at their very core, even and especially in their patriotic core! Rotten, stinking chimpanzees!

The only highlight of the night was in batting a few words with a geezer named Francois... He was as irate as me... perhaps more so... I'm sure he had every right to be. Misery loves com-pany, and we sure were in a state of commiseration with these two other jerks... Why didn't they get a room?... I hate sexual politics... It gives me a rash!... Any time sex becomes a political event, it makes me want to hurl... It's the games that disgust me, the Rococo dandyism, the protracted Victorian social tennis match of the repressed and desperate genital will!... The rest of us, hopeless captives, onlookers... Didn't they know that every-one else knew exactly how this was going to turn out?... As plain as day! As a gorilla molesting you!... Francois was sick of it, too... motioning with every polite gesture he had left that this evening had to be put to death... I understand all too well being old myself... we get tired... It's not because we are feeble... We get exasperated easily by repetition!... We've had it up to our necks in this shit, with all our experience, the same old garbage recycled over and over again... We're impatient for something new, and forever disappointed!... Politics, sex, war, ignorance, poverty... all of it left unchanged for millennia... You start feeling the weight of all these millennia of repetition when you hit a certain age... Call it what you will: surliness, bitterness, irateness, crotchety senilitude... You just can't understand for as long as you continue to look at the world with green eyes!... Everything seems so flashy-new!... People like you don't need to read history, you need to be pulverized, crushed, and pulped by it... like we have!

And what of my dim political aspirations, you ask? Into the drink with the rest of it... tied to that heavy stone of failed hope. It's golden years and curtains for me!

The Vicious Circulation of Dr. Catastrope

Incipit Dedicatio

Constructed, created, and haughtily crafted by the tender yokes of the broken eggfaced trust, the presiding Monkane the Greek, a bounding tale sprinkled with oriental peppers, and other spices filled with the verjuice of colonial acquisition. This is a chronicle of epic and urgent importance, sung as an eternal hymn to the stars that shine over our posteriors and posterity, making our rumps shine with the assiduousness of ass-molded chairs, these chairs a delightful *objet du contemplation* for philosophers of the flat-foot and the high-crowned and the furrowed burrow-brows and the sardonic grin. This tale, shewing in absolute lurid detail the panlit grotesque in which our tragic hero of heroes, most tragic of the tragic, Francois fights against the furies, muses, and dipsomaniac nymphs of the modern era.

Printed this day, July 27th, or 24/7, the year of the three-legged wombat, at Belcher's Wharf near Boston's only location where one can have a slattern shod.

Kane X Faucher

Book 2

Author's Prologue

It was by the King's decree that I continue this tale, and indeed it was he who detained me with his crackling whine and tearful lamentation that the story not be at its conclusion. It was quite embarrassing, actually, and an unkingly attitude to strike this wee and whelpish commoner born of a whore and a carnival barker (whom the Bible commands me to honour, as I do in my own way best befitting God's humour rather than his spiteful wrath). If it were not for my good spirit and duty to my Country and Crown, I may have faced the gallows had I not complied— so amiss was the King's state, his noble comportment and great carriage that succors us all brought down to a kind of crestfallen and browbeaten tit-saggery. You may thank the King and his weepy insistence for the continuance of my tale. But I should explain why I was initially intending to break with the chronicle at this point:

It was my intention to end the tale abruptly, just as I must do at the tavern when the little harpy I betrothed so long ago screeches from outside the public house doors loud enough for the whole town to hear, a sonorous voice that can etch glass and cause a man to rip off his ears because of its pure vertiginous Beauty. When my darling Scylla—whom I love with unsinful, devoted reverence, and with whom I conjugate in copulation only for reproduction purposes—sends me out on an errand to fetch a few yards of sausage and a flagon of C-grade bovine fat to fill the larder and the figure of her womanly corpulence, I usually set a spell in the olde tavern, making a kind of segue from the quotidian labours to wag tongues with the lads. It is here we mix tales of courage, bravery, and Man's eternally invanquishable Spirit in the face of all tribulations – including

The Vicious Circulation of Dr. Catastrope

that fine institution of marriage (God granting, and with a pure faithful heart). When the round is passed a few times, I am called upon to offer up a tale that will give these men hope and further reasons to rejoice in the spirit of Fraternity. Alas, the exquisite spawning-mother of all my precious pupae does usually beckon me from my tale in mid-stride, she being lovingly persistent as only the most glorious of goats one sees in the garden of the Hesperides, or with the constancy of a Homeric potato in the pocket.

Dr. Catastrope is not here resurrected in his due honour, and I recommence the tale I so fiendishly left off with another like soul named Francois. But amidst words of lofty praise and the call for my deification within the canon of Letters, there come the sour note of those gimcrack lollygagging critics whose only gift—as it is granted from the boweline depths of most vicious Hades—is to publicly ex-coriate me with their idle slanders and barbaric invectives. O the heaped insults against such a fine person that I am! How may I endure their pickled talk, born as it is from the lowest of the barrel-houses in West Manchester or perhaps the unkempt brothels of Upper Brunswick? Of the things that have been imputed to my person, I find these items in the worst of taste:

That I am:

A bagharper

A clodsniffler

A colonoscopic burst

A pus-filled tumorous excrescence

An execrable word flaunter

A verbletter

A loose spigot

A corrupt wine-barrel sheriff

A shiller of hard pitch

A wharfsman of mean disposition

A miser of description
A toilsome narrative voice
An inveterate listmaker
A hackish dwarf
A purveyor of literary emesis
A broken gangplank of Reason
A toppled tower of turpitude
A rainfeverish troll
A snapped wet twig in the kindling
A one-ended bridge
A fimbriated mannerist
A rugmerchant of lies
A mercenary of bad fortune
A diviner of phlegmatic spittoons
A plodding mendicant friar
A crass flytrap hanging from the rafters of alehouses
A double-dealing madcap
A shellfish of human misery
A chamberpot poet
A scat-meter of Man's lowest watermark
A fabulist
A cinder in the wine
A frog-eyed belly-padder
A mattress-bound dilettante
A sinus-blocked cracker
A sawduster of sausage filling
An all-beef patty
A solicitor of a drain of pale
A cloudy fuller
A woadmaking lettersmith
A walking pox
&c.,

The Vicious Circulation of Dr. Catastrope

Am I to endure such things? I think not! My chronicle is surely immune to such vicious criticisms by these lean snarling curs. Anyhow...

Is this a disastrous turn I see before me? Methinks I spy... a metaphor! Turn your better cheek before me lest my elegant club find your conceptual backside! Little did you know, you speakers of twin-tongues that Dr. Catastrope is also a verb formation that one can no longer ignore. Bring out your slate boards and copy this out for memory:

Catastrope (ka-ta-strohp):

1. Proper noun of Dr. Catastrope
2. A noun that signifies a disastrous turn, composed of the Greek *katastrophein* and *trope* (a turn).
3. Catastropic: Adjective meaning that which pertains to the fricative and post-labial sound that is emitted in a time of distress. Ex.: This musical noise brings me to the point of utter distress, it is so catastropic!
4. To catastrope: infinitive of the verb, catastrope, meaning a desire to strangle people who think they can write tales about children committing suicide. Ex.: If you publish that tasteless shit-for-shit text, I will personally catastrope you! To Catastrope you would be a necessary function of my being!
    Verb usage of *to catastrope*
    I catastrope
    You catastrope
    He / she / it catastropes
    We / they catastrope
    You (plural-formal) cataspin

Kane X Faucher

Present perfect continuous: catastroping (we were catastroping all weekend until our ears fell off from imagined leprosy).

Past: catastroped. Johnny catastroped his way to ruin.

Adverbial form: How catastropely our lives go, leading forever to that Great Toilet.

Comparative: John is almost as catastropish as Mary.

Implied Superlative: John is the catastropiarch of the group. He is more catastropely catastropish than anyone he knows.

Ebonic form: katasdope, cat-stroke, catapa-tatapope, schizosoap, k-tope, k-topaz bling dang bin phat dawg.

Addendum note: The rumoured second usage of the word as a proper noun denoting an island in the Atlantic measuring three metres square is unsubstantiated, for it would make the *man* an *island.* The other use, in biology, is a recent addition. A catastropod is a type of mollusk that dies of ennui due to a porous shell and an internal intolerance to salty water that negatively affects its psyche. It usually reproduces grudgingly.

Now that we have cleared up these nasty grammatical matters, I owe you the continuance of my chronicle in this second book. Anyhow, let us get to it since I must get back to my long neglected beverage to which I must pay flapping lip service rather than to the dry non-distilled likes of you.

> Catastropely,
> Your Fabulous Narrator.

The Vicious Circulation of Dr. Catastrope

Francois:

The people of New Orleans have all come to mock my accent, my Parisian manner. They have no soul. They are a constellation of stupid, unblinking eyes made so by too many cheap espressos bought at the pointless combine. They are fools. They make me sick. I begin to fear for my patience.

Like Orestes, I have flies all over me. Today maybe I should brush my teeth... but why bother? It is all failure. Let them all fall out! Let a long trail of broken old, stinking teeth follow me everywhere I go, I do not care! I am not vain! Other people can fret stupidly like little cats about how they look, but not me! Just give me more wine! The brushing of my teeth can wait another day. If they wait this long, they can wait forever.

All around me, people with shit for brains... No, instead, it is like they shit in their brains and speak as though it is all coming from their assholes. I do not like this. People say that I shout too much, that I argue pointlessly about pointless things. But these people they talk and talk, fart and fart out of their pretty polished anus face teeth. Oh, sure, they have the time to take such good care of their teeth while they fart to one another... But this is only because they are pointless cattle. I am asked for my email. I do not have an email. What is this email? Another excuse for people to harass one another... I hit little buttons and this is supposed to mean that we are talking. People talk too much already. I wish everyone would stay silent for but a minute, stop farting and shitting their stupid, asinine opinions everywhere they go, talking and talking between their pretty polished teeth! They do not certainly understand just how stupid and pointless it all is, how much a failure their lives really are, how all life is failure! But all of them want to keep shitting in their brains, farting out opinions, polishing their pretty teeth, and to hit little buttons to talk to one another. I hate them.

I hate this. What is the point? I pick up a book where the author is saying things like the way I am saying this, or how I would like to say them... but, still, what is the point? I close it again. I just want to be left alone, to drink my wine. We have spent too much time already pretending that we are somehow very special, flashing our polished teeth like pretty harlots on magazine covers. Away with it all!

I receive a phone call. It is from some advertising place. A little girl who has been hired to harass people is asking me if I am receiving my flyers. I tell her that I throw them all away, I don't read them, and I don't care for what they are trying to sell me with all their pretty glossy pictures of dead animals and little baubles. She persists. I do not know if it is because she is actually stupid or paid to be stupid. I would not pay her a centime. I tell her that I demand my name be stricken from all their lists. I start demanding that all my personal information not be sold unless by me, and at one thousand Francs a piece. She doesn't understand. She gets her supervisor. The supervisor is as stupid as she is. He doesn't understand. He keeps reading off the same sheet no matter what I say. I tell him to go fuck his mother and leave me alone. He continues reading to me about how their flyers are good for me. I ask, "What they are good for? Can I eat them? Will they get me more wine? What good are they?" He tells me about a range of products that I do not need, and never will. I tell him that I am not interested. He persists. I tell him to keep all his flyers and stuff them very far and deep up his ass. He apologizes for disturbing me, and would I please reconsider their offer. I tell him, no, I will not reconsider. I tell him how cross I will be if my home is invaded by any more of his stupid, pointless flyers. I tell him if he wants to send me anything, to send wine, in cases. That is what I need. I do not need more of other people's greed and failure. I ask him where he is from. He says Greece originally. I tell him that Greek

The Vicious Circulation of Dr. Catastrope

people shout too much and own too many automobiles. I tell him that I have the combed forward hairstyle of a Roman statesman. He does not see the relevance... He is probably polishing his pretty teeth. He probably has a date with a pair of fake lesbians later tonight. He is not a very good Greek. I let him know of this. He chokes back this insult, tries again. I let him know that he is going nowhere, that his trying to get me to take his flyers will be as successful and meaningful as his entire life. He still does not seem to understand. I am getting tired of arguing. I need an answering machine or to pull the plug from the wall. I tell him that the ancient Romans were better than the Greeks because the Romans knew how to die. He wants me to elaborate... he is getting interested. I tell him that in imperial Rome, there was no shame in taking one's life, especially when one's life was useless or without honour. We only continue living because we somehow feel guilty and obligated to do so. After a while, when life itself has ceased to have any intrinsic value, we enter into an endurance race to see how far we can go. I find this disgusting. There is no dignity in the life of marathon. Life is no gift. Let it go! Finish already! Get it over with! He asks me one more time. I am getting very angry. I tell him to die and I hang up the telephone. I tear it out of the wall and throw it in the toilet. I piss on it, spit on it, yell at it. Stupid, stupid telephone. It is just as bad as the television... every time I turn it on, there are always more clowns and tits, clowns and tits. This bores me. I have only kept it in case one day something of value plays. But so far I have been disappointed. Books are beginning to disappoint me, too. Why, why, why must they publish all the same things? Today's writers are failures, and should be hung. I would hang them all myself. I would march them along Rue Montmartre and hang them all together with one big noose. I would first make them eat all their books, one page at a time, every copy. I write to Gallimard and Puf. I tell them to stop producing so much garbage. They do not reply. They have pretty teeth, all of them. They like the shit-for-brains farters who write stupid books for stupid people. They like to sit down, all day, just sit. They like to make deals, many deals. I need a tumbrel. Our writers have forgotten how to write. All they do is stick out their hands for the Palme D'or, or to be buried in the Pantheon. France gives out décorations like pamphlets to everyone, like flyers. One day every citizen in France will be buried in the Pantheon, each one of them with the citation of Louis XXIII or the 17th Republic. I do not care. I do not find politics interesting either. All I care about is to get more wine.

I would like to tell a small story. It is about an American friend I had made years ago. He did not have pretty polished teeth. He did not drink wine; he drank whiskey and rum. He had vitality, or what is missing in everyone else around me. He was loud and smelly. He hated many things. He did not like people very much. He hated America. I hate America, too. He had style, puissance. We met in New Orleans. There are no French people in New Orleans, which is both good and disappointing. We did not go to Mardi Gras like so many horny little boys who throw beads and seashells at little girls trying to get attention. Instead, we stayed indoors and drank, looking out the windows occasionally and spitting. He lived in an old colonial house. There was Spanish tree moss hanging everywhere outside on his estate. The house looked abandoned, dilapidated. He drank too much to keep it up. We both had a similar history. I was coming into my own during the revolution of May 1968, or what it could have been. He had seen the LSD explosion and the anti-war movement of his time. He was not one of the hippy flower children that just sat around smoking plants and screwing each other out of having nothing left to say. The hippies were failures... they were just daft children who spoke in empty slogans. They did not oppose the war: they were the war. I

The Vicious Circulation of Dr. Catastrope

have similar opinions about the alleged revolutionaries on the left in Paris... people running around with Guy Debord, situationists and leftist Marxists and all sorts of confused political nonsense. They did not have a clue. They read themselves stupid. Once summer vacation came, they all went home, back to reading Marx in the cafes. Foucault was running around fucking little boys like an old Socrates, and the workers and students were fucking one another because now it was okay for the academics and the labourers to be together. All class division was being dissolved. Centuries of keeping them apart had built up an incredible momentum of desire. So they became politically sexual... every protest just another veiled sexual act. Celine and Bataille were dead seven years, and for my friend many notables were dead, too. I do not believe that France produces more great men than America, but instead that France talks and brags too much. If our nation is to be believed, we produce one great Frenchman every four and a half minutes. In America, the great men are not recognized until they are dead, and even then it is not all that big of a deal. Except when presidents are shot. But I like it when politicians are shot. It demonstrates to me that the system is still working. I do not read Hegel or Sartre anymore, so I do not know.

I would like to tell you about my friend. His name was Leon, pronounced in the English way. Good. He and I were once artists, which meant nothing, absolutely nothing. Perhaps it was that we lived our lives with too much style. But Leon is dead now, and I hope to Jesus and all the other motherless cretin angels in the sky that I will not be long in going into the black sleep, too. I taunt God. I yell at him every day, shaking my fists and drinking more wine. I dare him to kill me, I invite it. But I believe if there is a god, he is a Frenchman... which is to say that he is both a terrible coward and an asshole.

Kane X Faucher

I had a dream. A woman I had known in the old days was in it. I hate dreams because they remind me that I am not yet dead, that I maybe still want things. But she was still her age as I knew her and I was how I am now... I remember the flat plateau of her lower back, how we would make love and drink wine and make more love. She liked Brahms and petticoats and old books that smelled like dead men's caskets. She was turning to me and telling me that I needed to be more open. "You are incredibly difficult. If you would just let a woman into your heart..." "She will rob it blind. I know this already. I do not see the world through my Cyclops cock... I see much more than a pretty bloom between a woman's legs." "Let me love you, for your own good." "Pfah! My own good? What good will any of this bring me? Love is failure. We all read Marx now. The revolution has no time for love. Love is not in the agenda even if our leaders are yelling it from the rooftops, saying that it is love that powers this revolution." "Then love me, now." "I cannot love anyone! I am just an old Frenchman dying in New Orleans!" This is what I yelled in my mind, and then I woke up. It was all so very true: I am just an old man now. Perhaps I always was, spilt from my mother's loins with a taste for drink and a withered old face. I am nothing now. No one can love me, I am too old for that. But I do not want it either.

Today two men with silly short sleeve shirts came to my door. I told them to go away... I was not in the mood for visitors.

"We want to talk to you about your Salvation."

"I do not want to talk about my salvation, your salvation, anyone's salvation. Go away! Don't come back! I spit on God and shit in the baby Jesus' crib!"

"Have you heard the word of Jehovah?"

"Who is this Jehovah? Do I know him? If this Jehovah has said only one word, he has said one word too many. I want to be alone. Go away."

The Vicious Circulation of Dr. Catastrope

But they would not! They were very stupid! Like the girl on the phone! In France, we did not have people in silly shirts going door-to-door pestering everyone about Jehovah and his stupid word. But it has been a while... Maybe all of France was now just populated with these people who wear funny shirts and speak of this Jehovah.

"Jehovah has opened his heart to you, and we are his messengers—"

"Then you should find another job! I do not need people with funny names to open up their hearts or their livers or kidneys to me! I do not request any of these things! I need wine! I ask nothing of this Jehovah! You are the messengers of his word, no? If there is only one word to deliver, why are there two of you?"

"It's a pretty big word," the other one said.

"Oh, you talk, too?"

"Only the word of Jehovah and his infinite love and mercy."

"You, you are an imbecile. I do not want to hear you speak anymore. I liked it better when you just stood there silent. I already do not like you."

"But we like you, and so does Jehovah," said the first one.

"I do not care if you, Jehovah and the little boy at the supermarket who picks his nose like me. I am beginning to think you are an imbecile, too."

"May we come in and speak to you about your Salvation?"

"Have I not made myself clear? Is my English not good? I am not interested in salvation. I do not need to be saved! Money and cheese is for saving! People are for tossing away when they are done!"

"But your soul is in jeopardy. You must pledge your love in Jehovah in order to realize his kingdom—"

"Good! I spit on my soul! It is worse than the shit at the bottom of my shoes! I do not want to love this Jehovah! I do not care about his kingdom! Let him rot there! What is someone with a kingdom want with me? I have nothing! I sell my soul for a moment's peace!"

"I can tell you are plagued by demons."

"No! I am plagued by people like you... you who never leave me ALONE! Always people like you call me, knock on my door, telling me what I want. I want NOTHING! Life is nothing! Go save someone else! I'm finished... *fee-neesh*! You hear me? I yell at you people and still you come! What is wrong with you? Are you all bred this way? Get off my property! Go away! I talk to no one today, about Jehovah or salvation or people who carry a word! I carry more than just one word! I tell you to fuck off! Now! Away! I want to be alone! If you want to save me, you'll go away!"

And then I slammed the door. I did not need their noise today. But just when I thought I would be left in peace, my irritating neighbour came to my door.

"Hiya, Francois!"—he always pronounced it "Fran-swarh" like an idiot. He was a bumbling fool like the rest.

"How many times must I tell you? It is 'Francois'! *Fran* as in *frog* and *cois* as in *swamp*. What do you want?"

"A couple of things, really, Fran-swarh... First, I wondered if ya'd do something about your lawn... I am having some people from outta town and—"

"No, no, categorically no! I tell you once, I tell you a million times: the lawn is not to be cut! It reflects my tragedy in the world! It is the beard of my house! I have no time to go out and clip, clip, clip like a peasant! Why must we fuss over these stupid little things! Leave the grass alone! It wants to grow. Let it grow."

"Heh, heh, yeah, I'm sure it do, Fran-swarh, but let's be reasonable. I mean if you need some help or—"

The Vicious Circulation of Dr. Catastrope

"No, no help! I am through with being reasonable, too! All my life, always being reasonable! Being reasonable has put me in this black pit, made a big joke of my life! Reasonable is for rich liberals who can afford it! You are a rich liberal, so you go away and be reasonable... just leave me alone! The grass stays long! As long as my misery!"

"Well, okay, Fran-swarh, but there are *rules* around here, y'know. Mebbe in France ya don' haveta cut yer lawn, but here in America you gotta. If you don't, well, there'll be *repercussions* and *consequences*."

"You fat fool! You come here speaking to me of repercussions and consequences! You issue hollow threats over stupid little things like how long I grow my grass! Do I go to your house and tell you how long your toenails should be? Hm? Well?"

"Yer grass is going ta lower my property value."

"Oh, is that so? What does how long my grass is have anything to do with your stupid property value? If you are so concerned about your property value, then move! You are so very fat! Does this not lower your property value? If I wanted to buy a home around here and saw what a fat pig you are, I would let the crocodiles in those swamps tear me into pieces before living near you! Fat people are what really lower property values! Especially fat rich liberals who tell other people what to do with their grass!"

"Well, now, really, I'm only bein' neighbourly, asking ya nicely... It is a bit of an embarrassment... "

"If grass embarrasses you, then you need to see a psychologist. How can grass embarrass anyone? It just sits there and grows! It says nothing! I like grass because it doesn't speak, it isn't a fat rich liberal who bothers people who want to be left alone! And you say you are asking me nicely! You are nice like a whore who doesn't get paid! You threaten me with rules and then you tell me that you are being nice! You are very confused!

I know this because you are a fat person worried about his property values, embarrassed by grass! You are an imbecile, too! First I am visited by someone with a word, and now I am being visited by someone who is embarrassed by grass who wants to hit me over the head with rules that are stupid! Made by stupid people for stupid people!"

"What I'm really getting' at, Fran-swarh, is that if ya don' cut your lawn, the city'll do it and charge ya money."

"Is the city embarrassed by my grass, too? This place has many problems! It is too full of fat rich liberals! This is the problem, no? Why not go to Italy where they pour concrete over all the embarrassing grass? You would love it there! It is full of fat rich liberals who won't go away when you tell them to! Who makes these stupid rules? Let the city come! Let them all come and blush at my grass! Goodbye!"

"Hold on, Fran-swarh! I'm just askin' ya to cut your lawn is all. Leon did it without me havin' to come over here."

"Leon is dead. Maybe you could dig him up and ask him to cut it, no? Maybe he would oblige! Why don't you go try! He's in the cemetery up the road! And don't come back until he pops out of the ground and follows you here! I am not Leon! Leon might have been embarrassed by the grass, too, but I am not. I like it. Why do you come here like I am Leon? Are you stupid naturally, or is it because the rules tell you to be? I will never understand this country."

"Well, you can't say I didn't warn ya."

He got off my porch finally. I yelled out after him, "Yes, you have warned me that you are a very disturbed man! The grass frightens you! You think I am Leon! Your fatness is lowering your property value! You threaten your neighbours! You are an idiot! Idiot! Go see a psychologist and leave me alone!"

And so I slammed the door and went into the kitchen to make up a sign: GO AWAY! IF YOU DO NOT GO AWAY, I WILL

The Vicious Circulation of Dr. Catastrope

STAB YOU! MY DOGS WILL EAT YOUR FACE! I then hung this sign outside my door. But I knew that this country could not read, even their own language, especially their own language.

Back in Paris, December 1967... I was a very young man with many dreams. Only now I know the truth that all dreams are stupid. They are always crushed by reality and mashed between the perfect pretty teeth of cretins. It was during those days when I painted and wrote many beautiful things. At night we would gather, the many of our artistic kind, and read what we had written, show around our sketches, and talk openly about new theories. Many of the students—myself included—were not happy with the way that the university was being run. There were many bright, new and daring professors who wanted to go beyond the traditional curriculum, but their hands were slapped. Also, the workers were not being treated fairly, and many of them were denied access to the universities. I had made it, and of the 100 who took the provincial exams, I placed 59. I would have placed even higher, but at least ten or twenty of them had come from noble families and so influence bumped them up.

Sylvie was, I suppose, my girlfriend at the time. She liked to be known among friends and others as Mona. It was a touchy thing to call a girlfriend a girlfriend because it was inappropriate. That is, it was a declaration of ownership, and because we all read Marx, ownership was sin, another means of capitalist oppression. Sylvie and I attended parties among people who were our friends merely because of ideological reasons. They were not hush-hush parties, and so everything was open. But, I must say, such openness spoke so much about a transparency of character and a veiled sense of repression and ulterior motives. In those days, we all had an *agenda*. Sometimes, it was even political. We were ideologically justified in all that we did, from our most minor indiscretions and excesses to the larger ones... But it was for those minor indiscretions that ideological justification did the most work. I would not be quiet at our "meetings", but would let the vodka poured in the dirty glass speak on my behalf about the things I knew least about: the workers, the working class, freedom, and all those other sloganized things I had only known through books. But this was the same everywhere and I doubt that any of the most vigilant agitators ever knew what it was like to work. The movement was by rich little snots who had become bored with tradition, looking for something to rebel against, some little cause to give their lives meaning.

I no longer care about such things as the working class and the toppling of tradition. These things that oppress us will always prevail. They will prevail precisely because we are very, very stupid, each and every one of us. We need the Law, for without it we just sit there and say nothing. But I did not feel this way back then when I was younger and more driven by desires.

And now a nightmare. I am in my house. I come out. The city people are all outside. I tell them to get off my grass, that they make me sick, that they should all be crammed back inside their mothers' asses! But what do they do? They laugh at me! They laugh and laugh! They mimic my accent like apes! They start yelling at each other playfully, echoing all my statements on this world! *O ho ho, I need more wine, they tease! Go away! More wine! I am so unbearably French! Please! I want to die!* And on and on it goes! They will not leave! *I am Francois, and I want to die, oh boo hoo! I hate god! He is a stupid whore!* They mock me more! And I am too old to chase after all of them, to beat them with something heavy or sharp!

"I do not understand what is wrong with all you people! You come and go like you are madams of the whorehouse, and you

The Vicious Circulation of Dr. Catastrope

talk in all sorts of pointless noise about pointless things! Your movies stink! You all lack passion! Your lives are not precise, but they just wind up and go! Wind and go! *Merde!* You are already in your graves! But you are all too stupid to realize that you are dead!"

I wake up; it is the damn doorbell again. I must remember to unscrew the mechanism and stop its infernal noise! I open the door and there standing before me is another jackass.

"What do you want? Can you not read? My sign says for you to go away! I ask nothing but to be left alone!"

"Um... um... I, I mean *we*... a college paper, doing a... review—"

"Out with it! Don't just stammer like a chimp just learning to speak! Is it that you want to sell me something? Hm? I am not interested! Sell me nothing! If you have silence and solitude, I will buy that! Otherwise, I have no interests at all, and like it just fine that way!"

"I am doing a review of local posthumous authors for an upcoming anthology, and I was given this address, that you knew Leon, and... "

"Leon? Leon? Always with Leon! Now that he is dead, he never gets left alone! And then I am made to be responsible! What is wrong with this country? No, don't answer because I already know! This country is illiterate and full of fat rich liberals!"

"So, I gather that you do not want to talk about Leon?"

"Sure, I will talk about Leon! He drank a lot! He is dead! What else do you want to know? If he picked his ass at night? How would I know? The problem with you people is that you never leave the dead in peace! You always want to fiddle with their parts!"

The boy could not have been older than eighteen. College type, very plain, boring like the rest of them. Avis Pero was coming up the walk... Ah! He would talk sense into these idiots! He knew their language.

"Hey, Francois... I see you have visitors. I can come back later, maybe?"

"No, no, Avis, my friend. I need your help! The city has mistaken my house for a café... They keep coming here! Like I am a mall! Could you tell these fools to leave me alone?"

"We're writing a review," one of them informed Avis.

"A review?"

"Don't indulge them, Avis! Once they sink into you, they'll never leave! It's the Christian way of never leaving anyone in peace! No wonder their religion has a vagabond resurrected! They fear leaving anything in peace!"

"Yes, we're writing a review for an anthology—"

"Ah, I see, I see," said Avis. What a diplomat! He genuinely looks interested! If only they knew how little he cared about anyone but himself... But indulgence sessions like this really made me wonder. This country's constant pestering peoples were making him soft!

"Maybe the three of you can take it someplace else," I said. "Someplace far away. Go ahead! Avis here knew Leon better than I did! Chummy! Best pals! Intimate conversants... artists of the same stripe! Avis has a lot of Leon's unpublished works... You could go over to his house! He'll give you soda pop! Candies! He'll show you dirty pictures! Everything you want!"

"What?" asked Avis. The schmuck!

"Oh, yes, Avis may even give you some wine... You can get drunk! College kids like to get drunk! And look at dirty pictures! And talk about dead alcoholics!"

"Are you, by any chance, a writer, too?" one of the kids asked me.

"A writer? No! Writing is filthy! Pointless! It makes one live longer than they should! No trace visit is best. People only write because they are afraid of dying. And they are so full of themselves! They want everyone else to be as full of them as they are!"

"You do write sometimes," Avis interjected, the idiot!

"No, I do not! I write nothing! Grocery lists and hate letters—nothing more! It is all very boring, of no interest to young minds who want wine and dirty pictures!"

"I like beer more," one of the kids said, trying to continue a conversation I was trying to kill!

"Yes, you like beer... Avis has plenty of beer! He is a beer baron, didn't you know? Twenty breweries! He can give you a thousand beers for you and your friends without flinching, without making a dent in his profits! Avis is a beer merchant par excellence... And he is a writer, too! And he has a phone book of all the dead alcoholic writers in the United States... He knew them all! He gave them beer, just like he will give you if you leave immediately with him!"

"Francois, why are you pawning these boys on me? What have I done?"

"Don't complain, Avis... You are doing your Samaritan duty for me today. I need quiet... If I am not given peace, I will be on the edge of slitting my wrists. Besides, they'll be better company for you than I could be."

Avis said to me in a lowered tone, "okay, I'll take them off your hands, make up a few stories about Leon... No need for it to be true... But you owe me. I'll dump them when I can and drop by later."

"I would rather you didn't. Maybe next week."

"I'll bring a case of Chablis."

"Okay, okay, but why do you need to speak with me again? Did we not go out last night? With that Uma woman?"

"Ah, yes, do you mind if she tags along?"

"Yes, I do mind! I found her boring... She's more your speed. You couldn't stop staring at her like a hot plate of food! Why would you want to bring her here? This is no place for young pretty women, and certainly no place for doctors."

"She enjoyed your opinions last night. She is worried about you. She says you may have cirrhosis. It's why you can't keep anything down."

"Bah! I don't want doctors to attend me with their bandages and big proclamations of disease! I know what is wrong with me! I'm old and sick, and I like it fine that way! Doctors only multiply diseases! By the time they are through diagnosing you, you're suddenly going to die in two days of small pox and consumption! They are harbingers of illness! I have enough illness of my own. I have no designs on her, anyway. I'm too old to fondle and coo! You take her."

"Well, maybe you'll change your mind after a rest."

"Avis, don't speak to me like I am a doddering old imbecile who needs his naps and his potty changed! I know what I want and don't want. Bring her by if you must... What choice do I have? You'll do it anyway!"

"I'll be back around eight or so. Don't bother leaving the porch light on. We'll find our way. Say, have you noticed that your lawn has gone to seed?"

"*Va te faire futre... va chiez*! I've had it today with everyone criticizing my grass. People need something more meaningful to criticize... Why do they not just gaze into the mirror and stop fawning... Look deep, all of you, and find there something to mow and clip! Goodbye, Avis."

"Take care."

Avis took the two college trolls with him. Good. I decided to spend the rest of the afternoon typing something on my computer, the one Avis got for me. What will I write today? Bah! It's all pointless... I have no big ideas! Big ideas are for fat

The Vicious Circulation of Dr. Catastrope

men, and the belief that big ideas mean a damn makes a man an ugly fat man who is comfortable with his wall-to-wall ego!

***

What failure! Everywhere I look, everything I step in—complete failure! Today they sent imbeciles from the electric company to threaten me like a pair of puffed-up gendarmes! They say I didn't pay for this and that... What do I care? They begin like bureaucrats with their threatening letters filled with scary numbers, and then if you ignore that they come like peasants with tools and start cutting wires... They threaten me with darkness and silence, which is no threat at all!

I am told that my account is in arrears, that I still owe them money for all their debt retirement charges, their extra service charges... I tell them that when they cut my power, the contract is at an end and we both walk away! No dice! They threaten collection agencies... Fine! I haven't paid my phone bills either, so they can all go call dead air! If only the postal service could be cut off, too! And the bank has threatened to foreclose on my house! Cut the power, the phone, and then run an old sick man into the street—that is their plan! All of them in cahoots! For what? Because I am poor? Because my lawn is unkempt? Because I throw cans at religious pamphleteers? Because I am righteously rude to telemarketers? Am I in bad faith in this silly liberal country? Perhaps I do not smile enough and care enough about their petty causes. Why don't they all just go and save the whales and leave me in peace? I am called upon to defend myself at the bank...

"Francois, you do understand the gravity of the situation, I trust. We don't take pleasure in giving you this news."

Bah! These bankers, they all stink! All slick and suited up like little princes just waiting to ask the pretty belle to dance!

All they really care about is their stupid numbers. They think their religion of numbers makes them human, will bring them salvation!

"I have no money to pay you! What do you want me to do? I have nothing! I am not hiding gold bars under my floorboards!"

"Let's be calm, Francois. The bank has been very patient. Perhaps you can appeal to some friends or family."

"What friends? What family? Your answer begs the question like a whore! A cheap, washed up old whore! I have no assets! I have no friends! I have no magical relatives with money! I have no collateral!"

"Then you leave us no choice."

"You number-crunching Nazis! What choices did I really have? You make me sign this confusing labyrinth of papers and explain nothing, and then you come and take everything away like some medieval tax collector, like some crooked usurer! You trick me with contracts that are so complicatedly worded that no one can understand them! Lawyers write these for other lawyers! Inside each of these contracts, buried under confusing language, is another right I sign away! And could I have argued on any of these points if I understood them to begin with? Not a chance! It is your way or no way! A contract is a mutual agreement between reasonable men... You do not issue me a contract... You issue me a delayed writ of seizure! An unfair treaty! A war concession! And you take delight in fleecing everyone! You love me for as long as I have money to take, and when I don't, you pitch me away like some chicken bone!"

"You will have thirty days to evacuate the premises, after which time your house will become property of the bank."

"And what will you do with my stinking old hovel? Will the bank come and live in it? Will the bank come and start a family? Does the bank collect houses?"

The Vicious Circulation of Dr. Catastrope

"In these cases, we auction the house at a price that the bank can gain at least partial recompense toward your debt. You are still responsible for paying the rest."

"You take my house from me, sell it for cheap, and then you want me to pay the remainder? What is this? I do not understand!"

"The house is property of the bank. The debt is still your responsibility."

"Take my debt, too!"

"You can declare bankruptcy."

"This is a ridiculous game of Monopoly! I refuse to play or pay! What can you and your bank do?"

"Your case will be put into collections and your credit rating will be ruined."

"Fine! I will love jail! At least there I do not have to deal with banks and their cheating contracts! I get free housing, food, medical attention, exercise privileges, and a free funeral! Your jails are little iron-barred socialist utopias! And you wonder why your country has so many people living there!"

"I'm sorry, sir, but we don't have a debtors' prison. It will simply be remanded to a collection agency to collect the outstanding amount."

"Outstanding amount! Oh, you make it sound glamourous! An agency that will collect what? My outstanding debt? My house already taken over by bank-rats and sold at discount to some other gang of rats! I am rooted here, you hear me? Rooted! Good-bye!"

And with that I ended my conversation with the pushy idiot. Perhaps when the bank comes to pry my claws from the door to my home, they will mow the grass just the way my idiot neighbour wants it. This is the way of America: they seduce you with their gimmicky promises and then stab you in the back once you're in the door!

***

I am just an ornery old caricature. Even my social critique lacks conviction. I am an aborted speech act.

The Vicious Circulation of Dr. Catastrope

Incipit Dedicatio

A book so replete with middling thoughts, that there being laid out end to end would equal one thousand Hook-cerebral miles (contra Newton), or about 49% of any given human life. Crafted in the spirit of a family quilt of metaphors, an atomistic rainfall of analogies, and as a recursive feedback loop among dipso-maniacs of superb taste engaged in the process of promising emesis. As an emetic, this fabulous text chronicles the man for whom ladies in waiting wait for nothing at all, Jonkil Calembour. Written in the cloisters of memory and made public in a closed house where all the servants have been sent away to run im-possible errands devised by a jealous kingly cousin of Heracles.

Printed on this day of Our Lourde, MMX, beside the wooden-key horse of the Inquisition, flying to Roma in fifteen minutes or it's free.

Kane X Faucher

Book 3

Author's Prologue

Welcome again, dear pot-bellied reader and blackguard extra-ordinaire! I wish I could bring gladder tidings to table, but there are two issues that I need to raise that verily enrage me to the point of bilious blackness! My hackles have been raised to the celestial sphere on account of the misprision and codger-stylings of ineptness.

Issue 1: Paper quality. Although we all have had to suffer that most bothersome of garage pet projects by Mr. Gutenberg and his Galaxy of dissolved production quality, I am still a reasonable man insofar as I have since emended my earlier position that all my great cerebro-cloacal offerings be handcrafted by master Persian calligraphers and inlaid with gold leaf. I have accepted this type-setting contraption and its awful homogeny that makes a mockery of the Works of God and their singularities. However, the issue at hand is this: take a very careful look at the paper upon which this book is laid out. Note with scrutiny the deplorable condition and quality of this flimsy paper that could neither withstand the press of an ox or being in too close a proximity with an open candle flame. When I turn the paper toward the light, I can see the other side as if this were more a costume veil or an onion skin than a page! Note as well the poor cutting of the book bloc where one can veritably identify the cutter's mark ripping diagonally along the edges!—as though the lowly labourers had to make their presence known and impose themselves as co-authors of this book! What gall and audacity! Production should neither hear nor see those men who are but instruments and facilitators of another man's great genius. What if I were a great sonnet writer (perish the thought!)? Would it be appropriate to find my marks to be

The Vicious Circulation of Dr. Catastrope

identifiable by the man who would use my poetic apparatus to woo a woman? Should he mention my name while in the act of carnal delicacy? I think not! As well, I find that the pages will not stand the test of time, as my chronicle so deserves. I have turned this same page a mere six thousand times and I am seeing that the grime of the fingers has made the page ends brittle and acidic! Must I suffer *another printing*? Are the printers trying to sabotage my fair and arguably modest claim to posterity? I also have a gripe about the cover, which is set so poorly as to induce disgust in the eyes of the aesthete. The same reverence given the Bible, that Holiest of Works, should be extended in part to this chronicle. For publishing, as we know, is only the domain of the noble and wise, and it is only the nobility that possesses the good breeding to become wise. Should any noble have to suffer an inferior product of his wit and wisdom? Thicker paper stock was decided against by these miserly printers since they had the execrable idea to make my work *affordable for the masses*—How disgusting! The masses, all of whom are the product of tavern liaisons and other mis-begotten lineages, bastards who have not the literacy skills of a piglet! What care I of their ability to have and hold this precious volume? They will only dimly make out a few words here and there, and soil the artifact with their dung-dipped paws!

Issue 2: Counterfeit authorship. Since the advent of my chronicle's popularity, it would seem that envious others work-ing in the shadows around Sargasso have begun embroidering upon my chronicle with their own tales, placing my name upon such deplorable attempts to emulate my brilliance, riding my popularity like stowaways. Of course, history will vindicate me, and my true audience of shrewd and well-educated readers will immediately identify those impostor texts by their incredulous-ness and alarming lack of quality. High end quality of which is usually associated with my name will act as the criteria of detecting the true from the flux of the false, just as one can tell a true Vermeer by which side the window faces; as we know, Vermeer was a lazy man who liked to paint as he read, left to right. It is for this reason that I will not venture to Sargasso to either locate or inform the authorities about this wretched copyist, for I am sure that this "author" who has assumed my name is engaged in less than licit activities I'd rather not be mistaken for partaking in. I would like to dispel any rumours that the identity of the impostor is Dr. Catastrope himself, and would urge very strongly that no one pursue this line of inquiry further.

In closing, dear dimly aware reader, please enjoy this new volume which is an undiluted outpouring of my Olympian genius upon the page. I must confess that when one's only company is the gods, one feels a certain twinge of longing for the amusement of you mortal jackanapes, barrel-sucklers, and organ grinders in the public houses.

(everywhere else is filled with fat jock boys and prissy bitches with their microscopic purses flailing their limbs to top 40 radio like drunken octopi. It's really an urban tragedy.)

DAMN/
/IT

—John 32:12

Your most devoted and faithful manservant.

The Vicious Circulation of Dr. Catastrope

Jonkil Calembour:

You ruthless whipjob fascists! What? Do you want to *punk* me further, you whelpish sot of the new anti-life brigade of near-sighted revolutionettles? O boohoo! Boohoo! I am ever so distraught! Will someone please throw me to the pigs or the dogs or the republicans, or to whatever fiendish jack-jawed party of cabal-swilling tenders that make the grade this week! Let me do a small dance for you and only you—a deadly dance, on a glass shard strewn trapeze amidst psychotic jugglers and little warlord boys with gimcrack plans between their teeth and military expenditure budget files stuffed down their pants. Yes, let's! Join the mob with me, willya? I suppose this is my—or a—story of counter-actualization, of the insurgency that manifests in the bleakest of Reason's abodes and makes an excretion-shit-negativity flight upwards to a surface whose thinness is para-doxical. I guess I will start with more... organized thought... before detailing— or letting detail be sloughed from me in pure virtual expression—the orgiastic unthought. I have never seen such beautiful unchecked metastasis, and I owe it all to the apoptotic tomb of my American beginning.

O lo! I am James Joyce! I am the Pleiades! I am Aldebaran! I am that I am not. What am you? Who are I?—And we are all together, aren't we! The real is the rational, is it? What a fiat exchange that was! I haven't the leather or the credit to keep that check from bouncing. What use is your real, anyhow? I strop it against that little scrap of the rational for kicks, to see how far the Owl of Minerva flies until it hits the black wall and falls to the ground to be devoured by the evil beasts. Counter-actualization makes monsters, they say... but I know that it makes the difference...

There, I said it. Now will you please just *go there*, anywhere but where I can hear, smell, see or taste the likes of you! I do not even want to come across your simulated flavour in a hat, in a cat, in a box, or with a fox!

But you kids are really into grammar these days... Oh, the wrong kinds... the sexual grammar, the political grammar, the satellite TV remote grammar, the internet grammar, the bimbo gear grammars... I know it all too well, but let's do a grammar assignment rather than trot out some kind of genealogy or capsule summary of my person. Throw in some etymology bones to stew in the soup and it will be dandy!

Jonkil Calembour, thrice-celebrated in books *you should not read even IF you could find them* (stay thee away from Amazooey! Crappa-apa-patootie!). He is not the reincarnation of King Nietzsche although he shares many of the same grooming traits.

Ca'lem'bour: Everyone loves a party. To engage in calembour is to tie your tongue to a soon-to-be moving vehicle while you stay stationary and small children hurl empty bottles at you. It is nonsense, of course, and I am king-hell nonsense in a new pair of green jeans!

To Calembour (infinitive, indicative present tense)

I Calembour, you calembour, we calembous, they calembet.

Past perfect tense: I calembourated, you calemsiculated, we calumniated, they calem-bragitated.
Simple Past: I calembed, you cucuteniated, we calembrissicated, they calemgrated.

The Vicious Circulation of Dr. Catastrope

Future mood, broken hypothetical-conditional: I coocoo, you caca, we calendar, they cup.

Past continuous optative future mood banana-split infinitive in new style vocative: You, I will have should calembourized if I and you were in we, We, you could have would should will if and then calembourissipate in us for even if in they we you.

Mid-past subjunctive future partial genitive in a pair of brand spanking new britches as emended by l'academie fran-caise and the great polyglot trust of superior imperative lingual-ist spoonerisms: I can-can, you idiot, we fail, they stink.

Anyhow, grammar is for tin-eared clause-lechers. Let's talk books if you insist. Oh, I see you in the press galley, pumping your arms away below deck with your questions, so many strained oars against the hard current. Perhaps you fancy your-self a great literary reporter, a revolutionary! But I know the principle reason why all revolutions do and must fail: revolu-tions rely on writings, and the people can't and will not read. Perhaps if your revolution was done up in pictures or fancy home décor, diet schemas... well...

I don't think much of many books, and neither does my public. So it goes. I have other things to do. You pester me the livelong day about details, personal histories, my *formacion*, as they say in the Spanish Quarter... Just make them up! I've not the time to shilly-shally with unrevealing personal histories so that you can draw crude, crooked lines across the constellations of my life history! *Why did he write such and such? Ah, he once worked in a retail store, betraying working class sympathies!* Drivel, the whole nut! Shit for brains boiling in a skull-pot! And don't approach me with my views on the working class you addlepated lapsed Marxist buffoon! I have working class, but I could never believe in them as a species... I'm too noble, un-forgiving, and entirely elite—which is to say a highly forgettable creature who just wants to be left in peace. Have I read so-and-so's book on Gramsci or Negri or Althusser?... Oh, go boil your face! Only degenerates fiddle with the genitals of an ailing and perhaps highly fictitious class, on Sundays in the pews! It's all Jesus and punch-clocks, and exploitation is just like complaining about the weather. Spare me the great rallying clarion cry of utopias and classless societies and revolution... All of it stinks accordingly. You want fairy tales? Write a better one than this, better than these worker fantasies where you triumph against a machine that cannot be stopped just because you're indignant.

But my Scholarly writings. Left behind. Even the cats won't piss on them. They are hideous embarrassments only if I pitched a tent of care upon them, tended them, edited them down to the confined needs of the scholastic henchmen who are all about *meaning* and *message* for a *clientele*. Like some sort of confectioner's vision of what literature ought to be! Why bother extending this harangue? You little idiots ought to know better.

It seems that every place has its inveterate coxcombical poopers... I know this all too well. I've been silent myself on a few things, not least of which has been a tormenting last six months of fending off the lies of some little robot of the institution, a system fascist, who has been treacherously damaging my credibility with falsities and spirits of revenge and poisons in ears and all that. High administrators have now intervened, and police, and he cries that there is no evidence because there is no evidence... I would have had to do something for there to be such a thing as the evident. But that is not—evident to this saboteur! Oh, I rioted and yelled, anger and depression, and the thought of little girls crying in courts of back-cottage industries that we call law, cutting figures and poses, while the big galoot can state all the eloquent defenses and still come up nada, or cacademically ruined by the treachery trust. Thoughts of hiking off to Netherlands or Mexico seemed very real at the time, but now the fight is on. The stories he tells are full of holes like a busted old shoe! His continual protests have ceased to solicit the same pities they used to. How yawn! I too was reduced, at least by this debacle, into a poorer state. It is the paranoia of wondering what comes next, every noise and movement recorded in case I need it for the eyes of law and the annals of justice. A veritable psycho and well connected, and I mean that word with all its pejorative flavours and juices since he has done little more than make my time here an endless trial. Resolution will be at hand soon, I hope. The pettiness of others is a violent inhibitor of our play. It seems that so many others are sick-sick, and they want to make us sick-sick along with them. Who needs it? It gets between me and my writerly tablet, and nary a sick-sick should stand between me and my many lovers of the page. Let the system-players cry on command to win their sympathies from fools, let them deal in the rough trade of the low and the base and the servile. To me, they are at the mere penny slots of life, near-life, quasi-life, just a cabal of future bankers in literary apparel and academic drag! They can all go sliding on ice to their midwives. I wait to get the next resounding round when your ally delivers the grace to the suckfish and empties the bog of the bogdwellers that have tried to oust you. Only the loust ousts! And the jouster jousts! This we know, wIth Intrepid flair!

But I should backtrack; give the whole tapestry of context in its ballooning kaboom! But why bother? Stories of my dismal failure among the scholar-kind and unkind are just cutting off the oxygen to the extremities of discourse. It's like what Deleuze and Foucault and Nancy and Lyotard said: an elastic band around the dick does not a real castration make. *They never said that!* Go look it up! Perhaps would be a virgin reading for you! Sure, you own the books, rave about them, but have never even glanced at their contents.

Kane X Faucher

Goddamn ladder-climbing zealot! He was a vile opportunist just like so many Diaspora Belorussians I used to know, and all that. Full of *petitio principii* allegations and a real hard-on for getting their pound of flesh. Oh, he wanted his, with all the hell-stomp fury of vengeance, the pound between my legs to put in a jar as a reminder to others. What a fading little power! A functioning psychotic, the kind of deeply set neurotic that plays at being so normal it is suspicious... So affable, polite, obsequious with authority, but all the while a vile schemer! Everyone a means to an end! If you haven't the means to push his end up the crooked steps of cacademia, he won't bother with you! No wonder he has no friends! What a solipsist! Self-denigrating fascist! He dare say to my colleagues that I'm insane, that I need to see a psychologist? I fancy how the little neurotic with zero friends and zero ability to make or sustain the thought that human beings are not here for his own personal use is going to make these stinky declarations! What a toad!

And what else? My own tight colleague was one of his brood, too... A good man, but a bit naïve or blind or distracted. He played my colleague, an instrument! The toad cried of my cruelties, and my now lapsed friend's heart softened to it... He used a kind of distressed damsel charm to manipulate my colleague's emotional state, trying to play him against me. I haven't much faith in his strength to see through, to see the plot holes, to realize that he is being used like a rag to wipe up some mess and be tossed off!

So what was the crime *precisely* for which I am accused? Long story short, I dared two unthinkable things for which I would be severely punished, both challenging the corrupt authority of the university. I had been embroiled in a full-on war against a new administrator named Martin Schulmann who wanted to deny full-time employment in favour of the fast-food model of casualization! Contract workers! Peonage!

The Vicious Circulation of Dr. Catastrope

All because of "budget cuts" and the "need to make faculties in the arts and humanities more relevant for our clients." Now, one of the main proponents – that sack of useless flesh who hasn't published anything of note in over a decade – was Clive Arkwright, a professor of literatures without substance. It was he who poisoned the ear of the emperor against me! Second crime was daring to challenge the university's stupidity in signing a Faustian pact with a soda company to have territorial rights. And when the soda company didn't sell enough units, guess who had to pony up to honour the contract? If you say "the university", then you'd only be partially correct. Yes, the university had to make up the shortfall, but not before shouldering it on the students who under-consumed the product, justifying by some kind of sick commercial punishment a stiff hike in tuition! Of course I stood in solidarity with the students! Clive made a big to-do about this, too, saying that my "socialist" ideas would bankrupt the university! Never mind that it was the university's greedy stupidity that pushed the pen over that contract in the first place, and then not owning up to their costly mistake! Martin Schulmann was the death of the university as we knew it, and Clyde was his lackey! Keep those names firmly in mind!

Well, whatever! I'm full-bore gypsy indifference! A murder in the Rue Morgue and me without my camera! The word confronts a man the way a banker seizes all my prizes! At the end of the day, I get a slice of myself from the suppurating kibbutz! Group-farmed and groupthink identities that really increase my sour disinclination toward the popular mind that cleans up on inconsequential game shows! What need I of these things?

I am Jonkil Calembour. I am not divided into chapters or bookmarketables because I am pure stream with no break, no fuel-stop islands! The ocean of no mercy, as all oceans ought to be! But, of course, we need to know what kind of creature I am beyond these posturing literary fancies that give eyebrows their workout. I was once a prized cacademic, now reduced to being a roguish flaneur. I once tried my hand at cracking a medieval code, but spun out in favour of dodging bombs for Europe. I spent time with the lunatics to write a great book. I wrote several great books, you see, and that has made me the kicking boy pariah for all those wet-cuffs who want to make a name for themselves by slinging stones at giants. Taking pot shots at the clown is far too easy, which is why they do it. Their public masturbation is unbearable. Bloody score-holes of the Whack-a-Mole trash elite! Fuck it all! I'll respond to all their criticisms with a free mixture of Ebonics and Esperanto. As you are quickly finding out, I am pretty damn hard to follow as it is!

Speaking of the speeches of espers, and all the shadows that are cast, let this be my final Philippic against the imbecilic outrages of all that came before me, all that contest me, all that scrapes along dimly in the night with plots against me on their eyes, all that will take issue with me in the robes of the criticaca, all that attempt to demonstrate their power in the numbers of shoulders they have conscripted to the services of standing against me, all that is descended from the grandfathers of moral slaves, all that engage in the orgies of contempt, all that is ill-reputed in my pantheon of epistemological grace, all that is stripped down to the boring empirical details dolled up like rationalist antecedents, all that smacks of antique derision, all that makes of the earth an ego, all that hatches with the pretension of being solar, all that ripples with the false strength of the derelict legislator, all that displeases me and causes my ire to rise in mercurial fashion.

You are hardly making sense. This just sounds like empty stream of consciousness. Does it? Or are you just a lazy sot, a semi-literate? FYI, this is hardly a trickling little stream, but a treacherously gushing river with fatal undertow!

The Vicious Circulation of Dr. Catastrope

And here is where I must end things, my readerly buzzards, sans tale, sans plotted plant. My rage is nothing but a comedy to you, a parody of myself as the French are a parody of themselves in their current culture vacuum and so many prissy tourist-snatching museums. I have been dubbed a polemicist, a lunatic, a misologist, and so many other labels that are applied to the appellations of my many stations. So be it, and let it be, for my one most polemical outburst that means a damn to your stopped-up ears is only the curdling sound of my wretching, a full chorus-in-one-throat of agonizing vomitus. My final word: in all matters of taste (a rare word that is mistaken for opinion!), *always trust the stomach*. Thus spake Calembour!

Let me quote you from one of my most favoured authors of the week, Catastrope:

> Oh, but they all have come to see me, get their piece, gathering round... shuffling on one foot to the other... waiting for the hangman's rope to be around my neck... Getting a hard-on just anticipating seeing me swing! The whole career, drowned like a witch!... sunk, dead! Yesterday's news!... Hup-two, march on to the next one! That's it! Butcher... in the streets! In the academies... especially there! Another one drops, chop him up into little giblets... just more confetti for the parade! "Reap de bonez o' dat pariah, heh-yeh"... Ach! Fiendish *debaucheros*... Nouveau Bonapartists! With their hate on high in its new vogue! There never was a post-war anything. War has to end for the prefix to mean a damn! The world pisses on your shoes... No excuse or pardon me! Sick jackbooting debacles and slimy spectacles... that's all the people want these days. A

theory? Go hang yourself!... Not a guru or manda-
rin already? Too bad! Suffocate in obscurity!

Well, that's what I wanted from day one: obscurity!... He who
embraces obscurity may reap the benefit of being left the fuck
alone!... Make a name for myself? They counterfeited my signature everywhere... world's most common signatory on all
scandals!

This is not to say that the department took well to me even
despite my hyperactive research and publishing activity... Embroidering more renown unto the department for no personal
benefit. An incident to relate was somehow indicative of their
"gratitude":

"How do we live like you?" Clive asked with much cheek and
thinly veiled derision. I had apparently been overstepping
myself in the department as of late, acting as an advocate for
a fellow professor in search of tenure that the politics of the
department at large wanted to shuffle off with bureaucratic
expediency. I had apparently troubled the waters far more than
just that, but what is the use of a life of bovine obedience?

"You take a dash of critique like a suppository and stick it,
Italian style, innuendo," was my over the shoulder rebuttal.
He was hardly even worth a bad pun. Clyde, may I remind you,
was his name, and he feigned to teach Golden Age Spanish
literature. You'd think he could appreciate a flesh and blood
picaro, but he preferred those safely tucked away in books.

"I'm supposing that you are going to make another ruckus
at the next meeting about your friend?"

"Someone has to. Things are far too quiet, and I am keen on
a policy of noise and transparency."

"Noise is an appropriate word in concerns you, it seems."

"Well, we can't all live off your long silences between publi-
cations, or whisper conspiratorially to the dean."

The Vicious Circulation of Dr. Catastrope

"You seem to harbour a severe case of conspicuous petty mistrust, Dr. Calembour. You also seem to feel as if you have the entire department figured out for being such a new member of it."

I would have launched full-on at Clyde, but I was running late and bored. There is no sense aiming for the last word when the first ones are all the parting shots one requires. A man can hurl as many insults at the one who has triumphed over him while he lay dying, but it doesn't make a difference. In Clyde's case, the ineffectiveness of his career was enough a triumph to me.

Ah! The ferocious indignation and the relentless mockery, the vain deceits and cupped conceits of those for whom ideas fall through their cerebral nets and are not retrieved. Friends busy themselves with betraying me, each of them vying for the position of my 13th apostle, and speaking in conspiratorial tones and codes, coding that reached its acme in the 14th century to exclude non-initiates, and its apogee in the late 20th century in pro-gramming the banal into the portable time-suck machine. They say that hindsight is 20/20, which must mean *watch your ass*, as I tend to read it... but I remain unconvinced of this world's capability to push its own clichés to an extreme until it converts the DSM-IV into a Hollywood movie, and my thesis into a wrestling musical. It is I who dresses the earth, prince of the air, and so the big bang turns out that she was faking it all along.

Anyhow, that aside *aside*, Clyde rushed up behind me all of a sudden and gave me what passed for his paltry frame a mighty push. It almost made me lose my step. What had prompted him to lash out physically, I wondered?

"Bugger you, Clyde! Clyde Arkwright seeks to be clobbered by the truncheon of my reason it seems!" I roared back.

Immediately, an office door on our department floor flew open and there was a sudden rising howl as another professor came at me with a pile of books—big, thick, heavy architecture books—and shoved the whole pile at me.

"Wraahhh!!" he yelled, followed in turn by Clyde who was now trying to pelt my chest and face with his withered fists, fuming and spittling.

"Damnable apish creatures!" I said, fending them off. Another door flew open and another crony joined the fray. I was getting dizzy. "I am the slaughterhouse of language, you inveterate whelps! The abattoir of the Grand Verb! Tremble before my syntactical Might that makes Right!"

"Flush him!"

"Give 'im a chop to the chops!"

"Send him to the Dean!"

One of them drew up a chair and tried to swing it, but the hallway was far too narrow, and so it just collided and smashed against the wall in mid-swing. Another crony had managed to get into my office and was pulling down the bookshelves, hurling my books into the hallway like a mad chambermaid who didn't get paid. I heard the splintering of wood. Clyde was now trying to assault me with his wingtip he had in hand, a Khrushchevian gesture that could not help but make me chortle despite the panic of the situation.

"Enough of your meatbaggery, you oafs! I have a class to teach!"

Which I did. The books I was bringing to the lecture had been knocked out of my hands and were lost in a sea of books on the floor. Every office appeared exploded. I grabbed whatever books I could to bring with me to the lecture. I was trying to flee! I was due to lecture on Kerouac today, and all I could manage to grab was a book by Northrop Frye and a book on Wittgenstein. Oh, well! I'd wing it! Kerouac and the anatomy of the critically atomic fact! Sure! Why not? I was being mauled by my alleged colleagues anyway—I had an excuse!

The Vicious Circulation of Dr. Catastrope

They thundered after me down the steps, trying to pelt my head with whatever books they had in their hands, howling and growling oaths at me, chanting threats and the like. I would have stayed to fix all their little red wagons, but I had to go! They pursued me out the building into the courtyard and all the way to the lecture hall, running in that funny and awkward way sedentary academics tend to.

"We'll crucify you, Calembour!"

"You already did!" I shot back. "Bunch of bad Romans! You managed even to botch a crucifixion, you punks! Mad hens! Fishwobbling freaks! Cantankerous old decommissioned generals of irrelevant wars! Moot monks!"

I was able to reach the lecture hall much to the shock and confusion of my class of about a hundred students. It was quite a sight: almost the entire department howling and trying physically to rebuff me! We tumbled into the hall and now that I had more room I was able to grip the lectern and defend myself against Clyde—heading the attack with ferocious vigour—who had secured a small desk. We were fencing with furniture while the other profs were trying to claw at my face. The students merely watched on in quiet and rapt awe as their cherished professor was being mercilessly outnumbered by a faculty of goons.

"Hermeneutics is the pastime of a lapsed Nazi pedophile!" I yelled at Clyde. "I am here to liberate all of studentkind from your diseased and baggy rhetoric of lies and conceit!"

This merely emboldened and enraged Clyde further. I was able to parry the desk and jab him in the gut with the legs of the lectern. Ignoring the fist-falls of protest by the other profs, I started pummeling Clyde's face and back with a heavy copy of the Norton Anthology of Poetry. "Save yourselves!" I cried out to my students. "The tutorial is still on for Tuesday, but class is by necessity dismissed today! We're experiencing a departmental disagreement!"

"Get that postmodern charlatanical villain," a professor of classic Greek literature charged.

"Choke him with his own deconstruction!" another yelled.

"We'll make him eat all his pages of contemporary language poetry!" yet another joined.

So they wanted a culture war, did they? They wanted a stable, single truth, a perfect interpretation by which all others may be measured? Those Protagorean vending machines! Those etiolating assassins of literature! I'd show them a thing or two about high theory and free criticism!

I felt a book bounce off the side of my head and laughed, "Bah! Was that supposed to hurt, Gregory? That was only the *shorter* Bartlett's Familiar Quotations! How dare you hit me with something abridged! But what am I saying? Your wife knows all about your abridgment tendencies in the boudoir!"

"You insouciant brigand and galoot with no credibility! They ought to can your cavalier ass!"

I was able to aim an obsequiously-written hardcover biography of Hemingway right between his eyes and he dropped. At about this point, my wielded Norton was in tatters with Clyde still blubbering something or other, sounding more like a panicked pig. That was when I decided to unleash upon the top of his head the entire canon of West African literature (anthologized). For another aggressor, I launched *The Pickwick Papers* which I could not resist following up with the comment that it must have hurt like the dickens.

Most of the students had filed out, but were still watching with great interest from the doorway. I was able to smite all my attackers with varying bits of lecture hall furniture and whatever armfuls of books they had brought to beat me with. Once they had all been beaten to the point of exhaustion

The Vicious Circulation of Dr. Catastrope

(books don't tend to cause many fatalities unless the Church is involved), my students overcame their wary shock to let out a cheer. I raised my arms in a gesture of triumph. However, this event would set quite a precedent for my adversaries, and I could expect much worse actions to follow.

Ah, my homespun wisdom, hard-earned and churning within me with the propriety and politeness of a Russian who gets your goat! But, of course. You see, I acknowledge that I am indeed a *phenomenon* par excellence. The state of knowledge is no longer a series of double-treble root canals, back in the time of Nietzsche where one was afflicted, dogged by a question, a problem... You wore it on the body like a throbbing pain, a pulsating abscess, a broken bone! No, today's knowledge workers are like little girls who cajole puppies... They grin stupidly, attend moronic conferences and talk about gas prices! They temper their words so... Something they don't like, they find aberrant and objectionable? Not a peep from them except perhaps a comment of "slight misgiving". There is no nobility in that! Their entire spirit has enervated, the blood all drained, can't even summon up a proper hell-storm rage at something wretchedly atrocious! They lack the fundamental shake-ups of conceptual discovery, the root canals of the soul! Their politeness makes them false, ugly, mere mannequins of Higher Learning. Storefront academics whose reputations make a lot of noise, but they themselves in the flesh make not even one peep or squeak! They have taken "tolerance" too far, so far as to be a kind of cerebral castration! Now that we tolerate everybody's little garnish opinions, their sleepy fireside musings, the true thinker is an unwelcome dinner guest, a relic of yore... No one suffers from knowledge anymore, no one is tormented by problems... thought has returned to the intestinal inertia of high German idealism where rational-based concepts become an anaesthetic... A meso-strata, a Greek limbo!

You'll tell me to pipe down, not make such a ruckus with my complaints. Of course, but you're not being tortured on the gibbet of bad fortune, being born into an age that has lost its sense of irony. Perhaps you think you could be called my contemporary, but that is the mere unhappy accident of temporal coincidence, not a categorical denominator! I'm a comet and you are more than likely a land crab. Upon my feet are pontoons, and so I glide across the water while those like yourself are condemned to be little more than shellfish that vacuum suck the toxins from the garbage bed of the historical seas.

If it were just the dollhouse academics that were the problem, I'd be in the pleasure-pink. But, no, I also have to contend with those who harp on the lack of material contribution thinkers and creators make to society at large. What a flawed measure of value this notion of "contribution", always earmarked on the tyranny of the profit margin. Tell me the value of the telemarketer and the insurance sales poof... the middle management mediocre mumblers, the TV show claques and lavish sports team seat-fillers! Do they mean to say that contributing to society entails contributing pointless services and the multiplication of more commercially produced garbage? A license to harass, to take up space, to delight in the shadowy ephemera of the time? Thinkers: who needs 'em! Right? We just need cheap novelty-manufacturers and more abbots of the reverse mortgage. Integrity of purpose and labour is just a dusty antique these days... The new regime is to eat ourselves stupid.

And here comes our department head, Lawrence Smithwick, with another heaping dose of inanity! Huzzah!

"Jonkil, did you get the email about student evaluations?" he asked, brandishing the blunt edge of semi-pro small talk like the champion chump he was!

The Vicious Circulation of Dr. Catastrope

"Yes, yes. I know the drill."

"Then I suppose you are in agreement with Dr. Schulmann reviewing them."

"I missed that entirely. Why in the bluest of blazes does Martin get to sift through our students' earnest opinionated reflections? By what right?"

"The Dean has approved a change in policy. Schulmann requires the student reports in order to better assess their teaching needs."

"Lawrence, that is an asinine info-grab. Martin can say all he wants to pretty up his plans to conceal his true motives, but he is trying to get the dirt on us, find reasons to shuffle off those stubborn to his diktat. Shift the deadwood, right? A pogrom ought to do it! Student complains about instructor's choice of tie or the shade of their pants? Off with his head!"

"You have a tendency to always suspect the worst, Jonkil. I'm sure this is a legitimate move."

"I'm sure there were some Jews just like you when the Nazis started slowly introducing their rights-contracting policies. Lawrence, don't be such a nonce... Martin won't stop until he's gutted our department, and he's doing it with our blessings, eating us out from the inside. We're just signing off everything to him, giving him the go-ahead to play Atropos with us."

I could see that I had somehow aroused some small buried doubt in him. I could tell when he was truly listening by the expression he got on his face. I was suddenly emerging in his perceptions as something a little more credible than a madman.

"If it is how you say, Jonkil, what would you suggest? I've already given consent to this plan and cannot very well renege. It would look a bit odd and uncooperative."

"Lawrence, you may have unwittingly signed our pink slips. The higher question is why we feel obliged to cooperate with Martin's ramrod ideas in the first place. Chumminess with the

Dean aside, of course. At some point we have to assert our independence, our territorial integrity—or else we are just bending over."

"Granted, his plans are a bit abrupt and far-reaching, but what kind of reading do you get off him? I'm curious to understand your position."

"Spoken like a true diplomat. Let me put it this way: never trust a man who seems to have a perpetual sneer, and never trust a man who needs a pie chart to prove his point."

Martin Schulmann called the meeting to order, and let me tell you by what incident I have landed myself in the trouble I find myself today!

"Bah! You ragabash culdee! You ill tempered relict! I'll fustigate you with vigour, you besotted plagiary! Dare you deprecate me with your soft-pawed swipes? You plunderous rogue! You pestiferous vagabond and painful bowel evacuee! You rivelling malapert! I'm no carrack of your ridiculous opinions, so burden someone else!"

"Pardon me? I think this person is off balance. Can any of you understand a word he is saying, or do you also suspect that he is merely riffing off his own bloated vocabulary?"

"Jonkil, pipe down, now. This is horribly inappropriate. Give Dr. Schulmann his fair due of respect."

"Is that an order? I *am* giving him his fair due! Respect? As much as can be scraped off the soles of my boots! That skullduggering fuckface deserves nothing short of a complete excoriation! With something blunt and painful!"

"Hm, the 'student-appointed saviour' appears to be experiencing a less than moral moment."

"If none of you have the cajones to do it, I guess it's up to me! Martin, you have five seconds before I leap over this table and stomp you!"

The Vicious Circulation of Dr. Catastrope

"Oh, a threat, eh?"

"Jonkil, stand down!"

"Call security! He's got Martin by the throat! Somebody stop him!"

"Jonkil!"

"Dr. Calembour, get off him right now!"

"Kkkghklll!"

"He's killing him!"

"Damnableshitfacedtreblecrossingfascistfuckingpoisonouskvetchomaticshitheelnoxiousserpentsuckfish!!"

"Grfkk!"

"YouDAREspeaktoMEofMORALMOMENTS!! I'llstuffyourVersaillesTreatydownyergoddamnscotchholeyouout modedSassanidempireofgreed!"

"Where are they?"

"I can't... seem to... ouch!... Jonkil!... Help me get him off!"

"Through here, right there!"

"Getoffame! Goonsquadrons of HATE! Gestapo! Hark!"

"Mmmff... Hey! Break it up! I—unf!"

"Jonkil just clocked the security guard!"

"One for each of you! A fist in every face! That is what I promise in answer to your foul and insipid regime! Resistance! My punches are for education, for the students!"

"Clear off!"

"I think Martin is unconscious! Someone call 911!"

"Barricade the door!"

"You clowns clear out before I REALLY dole out the damage! Rargh!"

... Suffice to say, a real hell-zoo, especially for the more mild-tempered academics. That which was rising in me was rising for the good rather than for my usual reasons of abstract and esoteric social critique. I was surging with that thing called Justice, railing against the eternal backstairs log-rolling and invidious policies hatched by those more concerned with accounting ledgers than the spirit of education. I had risen in like manner before, against the corporate-compliant responsibility dodgers that decided to strafe at me right and quick by pink-slipping me for insubordination, followed by a littered trail of their vindictive insults that would insure the end of my career. So I was no stranger to these tactics, for they were in no way properly strategic... Like a child in the throes of tantrum or the passive-aggressive tendencies of a sour lover, they were only capable of the reactive, the tactical, the immediate response to a crisis that threatened their homeostatic lives. Strategy, on the other hand, was the art of those with the true instincts for graft and grift. Schulmann was such a creature, and it was he who would prove the most difficult to unseat. His apostles numbered ever more as the months went by, having won adherents among that most potent and implacable power at the university, its members of the purse.

My outbursts aside, despite their being a mode of my innate excitation and in the register of a harsh and violent truth, there had to be a better way to combat the besotted effects of Schulmann's inveterate policies. I only knew that once these drafted considerations were carved into university legislation, there would be no recourse for dispute.

My story has no happy ending.

The Vicious Circulation of Dr. Catastrope

Incipit Dedicatio

Presenting for your yellowed eyes the stupendous tale of sundry gentlemen as forecasted by that most prophetic and sonorous of voices, Monkane the Greek. Arrayed in verdant bouquet, yet shot through with the bolt of acuity and facticity, a chronicle so vast and pivotal that it compels you to open your purses and pour gold sovereigns upon its humble narrator.

Produced and printed in this year of our Audited Quarterly Earnings Report, MMX, by the United Freebooter Trust, available for purchase in the Albigensian district near Shelby's dilapidated wharf that has been ineffectually spruced up with fresh marigolds.

Book 4

Author Prologue

Ah, my most impatient readers, have I led you all astray? There is but one more voice that desires to express its lively and bon vivant nature, making the fourth in our chronicle square. Why not a more musical tone to the foregoing, like a pleasant and melodic intermezzo? I fully comprehend an impatience I myself would share in presenting three disparate life stories with seemingly no connection. To what end, you may ask? What is the thematic coherence of it all? What threads these voices together? Well, I truly wish to avoid spoiling the ultimate purpose of my chronicles by premature explanation, even if it means keeping you in a state of suspension and anticipation. Do be of good cheer to allow me to tarry with my chronicle, and I assure you that all reasons will be made clear and transparent as a reward for your indulgent patience.

I have a personal fondness for music, I must confess, although it distracts us from moral considerations. I would like to think of music as part of God's bounty gifted unto us that we may better praise Him who enriched our existence with navels and hearty challenges of faith like the Black Plague.

Since last I made my attempt to enthrall and entertain, I have achieved no mean celebrity given the popularity of my riveting chronicle. Not to be a boorish braggart, but I do think my dear readers deserve to be apprised of the winsome fact that no less than the Deacon of Savoy and the Minister of Foreign Oversight have requested an audience of me to pour their sweet liquors of praise upon my modest offerings. This honour has been inordinately flattering, and although I had judged that perhaps I should bring the chronicle to its natural conclusion was met with disappointment that such an act

The Vicious Circulation of Dr. Catastrope

would be grievously premature. What choice do I, the son of the Crown's Pride, but to defer such decisions to wiser heads? I convey this chronicle not out of self aggrandizement, but in humble servitude and deference toward those illustrious figures that bid me to carry on.

You are perhaps rapt in curiousity on how that nefarious affair with my impostors turned out. It would be perceived an uncomely act of boasting to relate how, when the laws of the land had failed to secure my desire for justice, I took it upon myself with trusty sabre and a gentleman's aspect to ferret out that treacherous counterfeiting villain. As I am a Christian man and but a lowly bondservant to God Almighty, the virtue of Mercy was not lost in my feeling of outrage, and so I spared that godless rogue's life, but did so *a point de poignard*. Naturally, of course, for his swordsmanship was as learned as his manners and morals which, if I may say, were somewhat bereft. We can expect nothing more from those who would operate as forgers and thieves in God's shadow. I also received word from sources on high that all his copies have hitherto been suppressed and destroyed in an effort to ensure my illustrious Reputation that still remains without blemish.

These have been preoccupied times, and so I have also looked into the outstanding matter of the publisher's lack of production quality. I pressed upon him the urgency to take more care in the publishing of my books, for they are read by noblemen and kings who would find themselves sullied to hold a book so shoddily printed and bound. Alas, whereas my good nature brought me fortune against the counterfeiter, my thrifty and short-sighted publisher deemed it fit that he continue binding this fine chronicle in whatever rags he had available. I do offer my sincerest apologies for his pigheaded and baffling lack of concern for your appreciation of a book whose immeasurably superior content ought be housed in its appropriate form.

My publisher is quite wayward in his ideas, the sort of reverse Platonist who believes our paltry Art rules Heaven.

But let us move beyond these fetters of quality, for we have no choice but to accept the ragged state in which this chronicle is clothed. Instead, rather, we must consider the last of our quartet, our Great Ensemble. I duly promised something more on the order of the musical, and this is what I fully intend to honour. My chronicle shall relate the sordid tale of a most unfortunate man who had sampled the great heights of fortune only to result in the ruinous state of despair, suspicion, and neglect. But, O, how he shall marshal his Will to mount a valiant return the likes of which are generally beyond the imaginings of normal men!

Be at peace, my readers! I have but this tale to tell for your amusement and intellectual betterment, and then perhaps this will signal an end to my chronicling, having served my public debt, and that I may repose in a most welcome silence.

With much warmth,
Your Virtuous Narrator.

The Vicious Circulation of Dr. Catastrope

Vincent:

Polemical Discharge

1

The pain in my knees is unbearable, so if you don't mind, I'll just lie here on this very nice rug. At least for the duration of this tale I must recount of my beloved yet tragically afflicted former master. Now, I am masterless, as you can see. I'm too old for service, and far too old to learn the idiosyncratic particulars of a new master. I know you, the fireside that flickers, are warm to my story as my fur warms to your light. Please allow me this indulgence, to tell my tale, for I do not wish to be falsely accused for indulging a madman out of some malicious humour... I indulged a man who had nothing much left to him. As though it may seem so to the heartless who hear this tale, I was never comedic relief... even in the objective comedy that our entwined lives seem to solicit.

Bah!

You read me with your beady, jaundiced eyes. Ah!— you sour and doddering parliament of hexed owls hooting whatnots! I'd sell your precious "Freedom" for a song!... For a moment's peace! I see you gathering now... around my house, entire troops of rag-wringers shambling forth in the world's slowest, most agonizing manhunt... for cheap laughs! To torture me with your little disingenuous pebble-pelting! Clawing at my face like a pack of deranged babushki in a flea-market rage!— and out come the daggers in the din of the marketplace, eh? I'm just secondhand textiles to you, rip and toss! The meek shall disinherit me and put me in the hands of wolves! Make a pyramid of my belongings and a pyre for my body! Ravage the whole thing in flames! Auction off the ashes to the sick!

What is this heady rodomontade with its heavy, ugly tempo? A vocabulary of abuse! A lexicon of sabotage and terror! A rhetoric of fickle brats with their swarthy intentions all carefully enameled! I have no time for you backbiters of the national mistrust! Throw me, bones and all, into your bitter soup! Make your hawkish statements... I see it now... all the way up to the UN! "a fatal defect in the plan that prevents its ratification... you'd be ill-advised to push it forward in its current state—at least not without first consulting the amendments in the policy documentation." For sure and certain! Entire realms of policies regarding me... field manuals distributed to even the children on how best to make my life miserable in perpetuity! Even God had mercy on Cain... But these beasts? Not a chance! There he is!—attack! Storm his battered gates and let's tie him to the tail of a horse and, giddyup! You think I complain too much... But you're not the one losing sleep! It's all buttercups and champagne bubble laughs to you! Forty-fifty emails a day! A potential hazard in my mailbox! Serpents in boxes... You don't believe me? Go stew yourself!

All sorts of insinuations and slanders! Hail and bullets! "He's creepy in a Nabokov way, those little young girls he predates on, that filthy brothel of an abode!" A lecher! Pedophile! Sex maniac! Throw him in prison and cut off his balls! Paste his mug up at all the schools! Public enemy number one! Vile beast who deflowers the innocent!—Oh, I've heard it all! It comes to me, you see, through all sorts of channels... people who come around and posture as my friends, confidants... agents of torment trying to slip the poison into my ear, getting a sick pleasure out of giving me the bad news, the town gossip! They come with their sad sack faces, their fake sympathies... give me

The Vicious Circulation of Dr. Catastrope

another dose! All heavy drama, the air all thick with dread! Foreboding! The town is ready to spring on me like a trap, just one more misstep!

No end to my troubles... Every day a new scandal! I don't go out much... as little as possible, but you would be astonished to learn of what exploits I am alleged to be the author of! Brief economic recession in town? Aha, it was him and his sabotage! Tourist turnout low? He drove them away, that fiendish eyesore! My reputation doesn't just precede me... it lives its own life, wild and merry and full of vice! My reputation stays out all night, it seems, boozing it up and crudely propositioning otherwise upstanding Christian ladies! My reputation pisses on all the walls!... It needs to be put in a cage! A ravenous satyr with cloven hooves and the devil on its eyes!... A derelict! A scheming villain! It's always such a disastrous surprise to find out what my reputation has been up to... I get the regular updates, my "friends" who come and confide in me the ugly gossip of the town. To torment me further! Drive me around that awful bend and into the ditch!

"Oh, my friend, what the people are saying about you today... It hurts me to relate this..." Bullshittery and knick-knackery! Ballyhoo! He likes to crawl around and watch me writhe in fury! Loves to give me the newest atrocity! For kicks! And me, powerless! Another round of awful, baseless accusations! What now? Did I throw an old lady under a train? Molest some children? Cheat the local butcher? Steal from the collection plate again? Poisoned the water supply? Shredded glass in the baby's milk? Never a moment's peace!

But please don't let me paint you a mono-chrome portrait of a life... There are happier times, or at least quiet times when the town's vicious mockery is spent... I'm not always everybody's kicking boy, their little monkey. A little time to myself, maybe take my dog for a walk... read the papers, a few books, anything that doesn't tire me out too much! Let it be known that fatigue kills. My little factory of a brain, of a body—all abandoned now! Hardly standing on its wobbly stilts! The towns-people were no help in that regard, either... always suck-ing what was left right out of me... But I live for those quiet times, just me and my faithful dog, Frederic, part wolf... Some-times he howls, right at the moon like a postcard from the taiga! The neighbours complain, but don't come near. He can growl, too! Big teeth! A trespasser is as good as a walking raw steak! But Frederic is getting old and tired, too, like me... The town wearies him just as much! Spends his time moping beside me everywhere I go. A man doesn't need friends, wives, children, cousins as hangers-on... a good dog is all the company he really needs! You feed them, walk them, pet them, they don't pester you with any more demands than that! Dogs don't play manipulation games with your overheated head... they don't ask for money to buy some bijou... they don't torment you with their banal woes or harangue you about your "bad habits". No judgment! No endless, maundering preacherisms and moralistic blather! No gibbering that the house is too small or about the latest crooner-sensation! Completely honest: they get angry, they bark and growl... they need to make their "fait", they paw you to get the leash... they want attention, they nudge you with their cold noses. They eat, shit and fuck without making a big scene about it, without all the ceremony and patter, without elaborate contrivance!... A dog is far superior to a man!

***

Ok, I have to quit clowning around with you... I was called in for questioning by the police over various matters, idle gossip being the muse for the heavy-handedness of what passes for the law!

The Vicious Circulation of Dr. Catastrope

Oh, they don't like me right from the start!... Wordy bastard! But that has passed now, and so where's my t-shirt, ass? Perhaps you would like me to recycle some old love letters! Encomiums to the great service of the badge!... The sergeant, a complete ass as well, his wife a calliope!... I only know this because she lurked around the station... Well, the walls may have ears, but the wife has a mouth... an unbroken line of chatter and communiqué... before I even give my testimony, it's already on the other side of town! The pig-farmers preparing their pens, grumbling about my moral turpitude, feed me to the pigs! A special place for me where no one would bother checking! This town is a cage where one can neither stand up nor lie down!—always caught in mid-erect posture, hunched over and aching! Damned if you do or don't! Ten times worse than Abu Grab-bag!... This wretched mothball justice! And over there, my so-called "lawyer"... nothing more than a moral charlatan, a carpetbagger president, a weathervane when it comes to allegiances—like everyone else in this town!... the wind changes direction and so do they! Ready to see me hang... already has the *tricoteuses* on speed-dial! Sell my severed head on eBay! My lawyer, the wannabe politician, avaricious eyes on the mayor's comfy seat... speaking out of two mouths at once! Thinks himself all glide and glow with the girls, all stylized and sexualized... Nothing more than a purloin steak, a rotting carcass nobody with a store-bought legal diploma, alma mater of the University of Online! Fourteen easy installments $29.95! Couldn't tort his way out of a paper bag! But I'm disgusting... my lawyer doesn't dispute that! In league with the rest of them!... Erect some kind of enclosure around me, some public decency sanitary cordon of the blue kind! Keep the children from seeing the satyr! Moral guardians every one of them!... In a place like this, my "public acts of indecency" are everybody's alluring private enjoyments of sport! They dare impugn sickness to me?

Moral failing? Never better than a twisted sadist to play the ethics police!... Nice way to play the reversal, a kind of psychological projection... mediate the inner guilt by crucifying the other guy!... If they put me up on the cross tomorrow, they'd all laugh and mark the event with a joyous festival!... They'd all get liquored up and bugger each other right under my bleeding, writhing body, all nailed up as they nail each other! You'll see... it will be an animated blockbuster put on by Disney! When it came to sins, Christ didn't die enough... a botched job! Oh, he did fabulous in the Disney adaptation, though! Go ahead and write a bible, but let's see you enforce it!

But the "questioning"... more like a Soviet interrogation, a vicious community intervention, a job ripe for a Grand Inquisitor in training! Torque-madas! "Where were you on the night of...?" They know exactly where I was... at home with my dog, Frederic, him grumbling away at the proximity of all the community spies creeping around in the bushes... tired of it! "Witnesses place you at the local sex shop" this or "peeping in keyholes" that! Who are these witnesses? Thirty-odd silver pieces for their pains?... A bunch of fiendish collaborators! Getting fat on ali-bribes! Rogues of the new mendicant order! No choice for me but to go hide up a tree, like skittish King Charles! Might as well be the tree I'm hung from! "Yeah, why don't you go up a tree, you lout! You smelly pervert! You nuisance termite boring into the foundations of our Christian family town! You pile of flaming feces! Put you in the poke, we will!"

Witnesses... witnesses... Frederic is mine! Too bad he can't speak! He growls! Barks! Not much for the witness stand! They'd sooner beat him off with sticks than even let him get anywhere near the possibility of my defense! Like they did to Cellini's dog in the Papal apartments! Yeah, you're welcome, too... the welcome we give your dog will be how we welcome you, too! Sticks to the noggin! We crown you, king of the

The Vicious Circulation of Dr. Catastrope

deviants! Thwack!—oh, they don't need to pin and staple a rood to my back to drag that through town... they'll just nail me to my alleged reputation, watch me hobble... You stagger and fall? Nuts to you! Proof of guilt! Why not pin some scandal and legal charges on that gorilla on your back? We saw you masturbating in the park! All over the swingsets the children use! Disgusting! Peeking up little girls' dresses and hunting for rabbits, eh? Full, triple castration for you, punk! You slobbering bridge troll! Oh, stop your bleeding on the cross, you cross-eyed bastard! We'll staunch that bleeding with a vinegar soaked pair of panties, you licentious git!

Now even the town trash has been given a bit of a boost because of me... all of them circling around my house with their taunts, in their beat up old '90 Camaros... A new pecking order has been established! Them and their trailers... black-eyed wives, filthy children... Even the Mullet-brigade has someone they can look down on, finally! But that's the thing about the Western *chadras*, the lumpenproles, the untouchable-unlikeables... the most vicious and snobby lot if they get the chance! You'd think they'd show pity to those at the bottom, but—No!—it has made them mean-spirited, finally an opportunity to treat others as they have been treated!... They suddenly become emboldened, complete reversal, just as soon as someone displaces them from the bottom echelon... welfare crack mothers suddenly gain the affectations of well-bred queens! One-toothed pickup yokels are suddenly members of the Freemasons and MENSA! Now they all have someone to spit on!

So there I go again! I get up to say my piece and —*plop!*— ham-smacked down by the community's moral avengers! They'll have a volcanic picnic over my remains... a volcanicnic... whatever! It's all dust plumes anyhow!... You should see the diarrhea gushing out the church door with every spicy sermon, with me playing the devil, the icon as a window right to the anti-divine!

Kane X Faucher

The laity fuck-laughing themselves sick, my guts as the main course. The neon frolic of cinema, a pan-hatred for the one afflicted with *pariahsis*!... watchmakers setting their wares to my inevitable execution!... Oh, you'll read all about it... in the papers... the great triumph over evil... maybe it will be part of your childrens' history lessons in school one day, in the text-books. Marched up to the banks with a mighty shove and *sploosh!*... no more problem, but not before they load my pockets with my own bricks! Believing I pinched some tyke's bottom they pinch my belongings, my organs, my bones—for deviant science! The new phrenology—no need for an ethics committee! This is not time to quibble and parse out the pronouns... me, you, them, the great worker's "us"... I'm the one left holding the big stinkbag of guilt! Throw a blinding spotlight on the fucker! He's the one with all the town's naughty giblets! Charge! Hurry before he has the time to return all that we foisted upon him! Clam up, you clown! The accused wants to speak? Drown him out with the air horn of moral panic!... wailing mothers and outraged gentry calling for me to be quartered, pronto! The din of their complaint, the courtroom stuffed solid with screeching, yelling, accusations by the boatload imported from abroad! Outsourced allegations... why not borrow a few from history while we're at it? "He killed the Czar, JFK, John Lennon, Richard the Weasel-Hearted, and every pope that went mysteriously missing... "What's that you say? Innocent? Shut up, you abortion! You addlepated poof! Dickering buggerist!

All of it—sawdust and rainbows! Might as well be dreaming in colour if I think I can prove my innocence! Everyone waiting for me everywhere... they know my quarry-value increases every time I evade their clutches, their endless fox hunts... I become a more enticing prize, a wildly sought-for hunting trophy par excellence. Whoever bags me at top dollar and mounts my

The Vicious Circulation of Dr. Catastrope

mug above the mantel gets all the bragging rights and more! Every day my "monstrousness" increases, the bounty goes up! "We got 'im! Mission accomplished!"—all that to cheers and yelps, picnics and parades, flag-rallies and the sock-hops get wild again! Finger-banging with more gusto! Maybe for good measure they film my scraggly face being inspected by the army veterinarian like I was some sort of feral jungle boy or a rabid raccoon! Then they'll put me through a show-trial only to hang me in botched fashion... a spectator with a "hidden" cell phone cam who " accidentally" leaks it to the press and the web! All for jollies! A websplash! Exclusive footage, unfairly obtained! Most downloaded video on boobtube! See the crooked huckster swing!... Nowadays, the circus is always in town, right there online... the guts are still hot!... the voyeurs get to stay home, all dusty with cookie crumbs! In their holey socks and gravy-stained PJs!... no action here? Go click yourself! Go Google yourself, too, while you're at it, Jack! A fickle finger... if we don't give the people their circuses, they get ornery, restless... maybe they pick the nits from each other's fur... maybe beat the wife and webcast that!—DIY circus! Even the corporate bozos do everything from home... Is that a pleat in your pants?—out to pasture, you business relic, you corporateer in bad faith, you heretic of the virtual!

It is always this way with the gutfest. New media tech is always accompanied with new ways to broadcast the circus to the maximum number, the great cull of actual talent!... Perhaps some outmoded ex-Soviet client state author could write the rejoinder in happy yellow, "The Infinite Snarkiness of Being". Who knows? I don't have political afterburners on this craft! I am merely the State itself, the whole of it, the whole pie, the big stinking enchilada of ideology, right?

"Volunteers are priceless treasures."—are they? Any time I volunteered for anything, a heavy rebuff, a hard slap to my snout! I cough phlegm upon my computer screen these days, oozing, itching, bitching, full or sores! The people don't want volunteers—they want butcher-bloc satori... None of my boring lojinx! I may have the lateral torque to spin a few lines here and there, buttress the community with my benevolent services, but they only come out in stronger force to dub me some sticky-dicked fondler! But my bones can carry the mass... quite a load! Crushing tragic sentiment... heaps of abuse... You should see what this body endures—I outwork them all!

Ah, but you have had quite enough of my hive-bonnet of complaint, all abuzz and pestering you! No word of a fib, no little icing of despondency, but my life has been a phosphorous bomb, perpetual burning even after the explosions!... But that's just boring, morbid, bad faith in spades, hook him off the stage with all his little existential antics! Give us singing woodchucks— that's what entertains us... and excoriated virgins, mammoths of entertainment! Not you over there, you with your "culture" and "books" and fritter-away "art". Not practical! Not enough blood gushing out every cornice! Well, it's hard to appear valiant guarding a bone-palace, I admit... and hard to appear modest when you make your coin as a professional howler... Just ask the talk show hosts, ambulance chasers, ham judges, politicians flirting with reelection, the televangelical pontiffs, the radio punditocracy! You have gonzometric flourish?— yesterday's news! You're a waste bin of creaky old sentiments, an anachronism! Yesterday's wilted lettuce! They'll chase me around with their swords and snarls, screaming "Yulla! Yulla!"... You'll see! It's in the works... my ruin a factor in the next town budget!

***

The Vicious Circulation of Dr. Catastrope

"Ok, shit-for-brains... show us what you got! Stand up and deliver your washtub of grey water!" Ok, ok, I'm working on it! Patience! Unlike the late Robert Palmer or the current Ghaddafi, I don't have my own fleet of Amazonian-sexy all-female security entourage! I can't just say nor do what I want... that's a luxury that is shared only by the crookedly rich and all those booze-shellacked by good fortune! Beat me in the street? Beautiful! These days, even the ghettos and shantytowns turn me out... And this town—you can tell who had money in the way-back-when... Stately homes, now surrounded by chic refurbished barn houses. Top of the hill and near the river, a real Victorian throwback! Half of them carved up into apartments for frat boys... rimed on all sides by clapboarded and aluminum-sided semi-dwellings! A meth lab here and there for good property value measure! You think they're just reliving the old chem-lab school days? Finding a cure for cancer out of the nobility of their good citizenship? Who is the idiot now? Me, the hub of all arcane negativizing value? Please!... I'm only quilting a few things here for you... lifting a few episodes from our "dear town", mere reportage of the blatantly obvious!

You aren't just kidding me... I see how things work around here!... Some nubile tart just jiggles her tits... red carpet treatment! Bowing and bribes! No, madam, please, you don't have to pay... They'll break your balls for the hell of it! No elixir will do, boost up the public appeal... no vitamin regimen to make my teeth look pearly enough for the cameras! My polished words? Pure retrosonic echo-grade returns!... archaic! Dummyspeak! A discourse among mannequins! Bad puppet show—boo the fucker off the stage with all his Bach cello sweetness, pure scale-exercises. Not a jot or a mote of justice in all of it! Hack! High dudgeon of the dead frontier! The people only gather—not to get your autograph—to pelt you with rotten tomatoes. That's how it goes! Break a toe or a leg while tapping soft-shoe? You're finished! Retrosonic becomes retrograde, so pitch it in the dumpster and let the rats take their share!... After the lions take the choicest morsels... and then the scavengers, bubble-headed taxmen, licentious preachers, scrap ironists!... Then they sign the next act, another rube!... Here, brother, you have talent! Light up a cigar! Let's do business! The contract, pre-pressed already! Just sign here and there! All glitz for the Schlitz! A scrolling neon marquee with your name in bold letters!... in every town! You're a sensation! Tomorrow's household name! All swooning to your crooning!... But not me! They've had just about enough of me. Better to wipe the shit off their heels on the unwelcome mat of my mug! Who the hell are you again? Ah! Yes! The contract breaks up, dissolves, it was all written in magic ink!

You see, I was something of a singer on stage many years ago. Maybe you heard me? Came to a few of my little soirees... Jazzy blue and marigold-glint of the brass band! Beloved in this town... Before me, people wouldn't dip off the highway to even gas up or take a quick power lunch here... I still have a photograph of our town sign before they "revised" it... I remember! "Population: 2000. Home of the Pelvic Prowler... " My old stage name! When I fell into disrepute, they took it all down. Pass the peanuts!

The Vicious Circulation of Dr. Catastrope

2

*His grackle-voiced brogue, the half lisp and barefooted accent
of an enfant terrible, engaged in no half-measures to be as
vituperative in his sideswipes as possible. Bolstered by the
buoyancy of self-righteous privilege, he bore in on attack against
a bulwark of alleged phonies. At times he would defend himself
with a leatherneck offensive, a war-horse of spirit backing the
maverick of speech... other times he would recoil into himself,
buckled, bewildered, and dispirited as all he could muster was
some semi-amicable and antiseptic response. His mood was
pendulous, and it was in those moments when he was alight in
the fulgour of his polemic that his thoughts became cancriform,
garishly gangland, lodging his assault of accusing another of
horse thievery to another's imputation of being a liar.*

*I had been his reliable companion for nearly a dozen years
which, for my kind, is akin to a lifetime of service. Half his claims
against the town were confabulation, phantom episodes that
were derived from the ether of a terrible mental affliction. Yes, it
was a veritable certainty that he was once a mildly well off
crooner having submitted his musical specimens to the equally
mild and lukewarm approval of a fickle audience that more
came for the alcohol with a musical backdrop. I know my master
is ill, and it is by no mean pity that I tend to him, even if I depend
on him so much to fill my bowl.*

The whole town stinks of failure... It's contagious! And so much
ill-will... dripping of it! Can't get decent service, be it from the
butcher, the baker, or the candlestick maker! Well... the butcher
has psoriasis and a harridan for a wife who keeps the books on a
barely licit operation to begin with— I've seen the make of cars
that go in and out of that place all hours of day and the night!
And the baker is a short, bald ogre who slaps the yeast out of

his hands on your face... always shorting everyone, putting bricks in his loaves! And the candlestick maker, too, but he also moonlights as the pharmacist and impromptu philosopher like he's papa doctor Descartes eating up his own candles and refusing to believe anyone but he exists! And did I tell you that the baker named his dog after me once, and then he mysteriously "disappeared"? Probably hanging up as links in his window! Juicy dog chow! Chihuahua cutlets and poodle pork! I wouldn't touch his tainted meat without gloves! We all know it is a front! Mr. Albioni is his name, a real greasy wannabe Cosa Nostra type. He has a jumpsuit! I've seen him wear it and never take to the trails on a jog. He has far too much gold for a butcher. A butcher, right! A butcher of what and whom, more like!

And let me tell you more about the town baker, Mr. Eigen. Never a kind word unless some young tart jingles her way in... Serving you when some young adolescent fox comes in looking to buy a loaf of rye for her sick mama?—he drops everyone else with his fatuous and lecherous "Oh, let me help you. Oh, no, madam, for you it is free! I have just the loaf for you in the back... come see... baked just this morning—no, just an hour ago! What am I thinking? Just for you! Of course, no, it is no problem! And may I say that you are absolutely fetching in that little summer dress number!" For sure... and his wife sits at home, fat and crippled. I've seen Mr. Eigen prowling the night. He's a mean drunk. A satyr from hock to hoof, too. He gets his kicks and pinches many a fresh loaf, if you catch me!

And the candlestick maker and pharmacist, Mr. Brown. A presumptuous bully! Proud that he speaks his mind, but some people's minds are like gurgling, open sewers that need to be capped! He may be brutally honest, but he is actually just honestly an idiot. He reads a little and applies right away, like how a fool attempts to assemble a complicated machine after

The Vicious Circulation of Dr. Catastrope

reading just the first page of the manual. And what surly attitude he takes with me! I've no choice but to go to him to get my prescription, and he'll just as sure as shit toss the pill bottle out into the street and bade me to fetch it, and there I am, scrambling after it and on my knees picking each little pill up from the filthy sidewalk. Some philosopher! A goddamn Caligula, more like, with control over our medicine cabinet. I have to watch him carefully so that he doesn't give me some nasty mix-up in prescription. He himself suffers from irritated bowel syndrome, or something, and pops whatever pills he likes... probably hooked on an alphabet rainbow of substances, judging by his eyes and pallor. Of course, we had been friends a few decades earlier, but he witched me by burdening me with his secrets, and then stealing off with my belle. Hard words were exchanged, me holding up my end with some very heavy thrusts, but he countered with his own kind of slow revenge... and so now he tosses my incorrect prescription in front of the buses.

This inveterate, slavish raillery of those pharmaceutical marmalade dukes and barons of that other, sick end of the medicinal ticket! He knows I am desperately ill and need my medication! But, oh, he relishes the fact of my deep pain, masturbates in private to the sound of my burning cough! He'd finish me off with just one mix-up, one lethal dose to make my organs buckle in agony and death if he could find some way to evade detection... But I am sure he is working on it! In cahoots with the coroner who will just bag me up after a perfunctory autopsy, claim that I had it coming... Not long for the earth and we didn't like him anyway, that bum who lived so aggressively alone!

My doctor refuses to make house visits anymore... He tells his other patients in less than clandestine terms that I am a stink and live in absolute squalor. "And that dog! The poor mutt should be put down, but I fear it is his only friend." He tells anyone with the ears to listen all my most private medical details. They laugh over them! Heaping lies to boot! Impotence! Aphasia! Bowel failure! Schizophrenic!... Oh, yes, he spreads such things as wide as his tin pot voice will reach! He can't get it up, shits his pants, and talks to his hutch! A real stinking loon! Forceps injury? Early onset senescence? Thinking of prescribing something that will level him out to make it easier to transport him to the funny farm! There the nurses and orderlies can deal with him, get a few laughs!

Sure! Do I have any autonomy left, being spied upon all the time, the reliably inexhaustible punch line? Scapegoat? Pariah? "He was a famous vocalist at one point, now he just croaks, or tries to entice young girls into that filthy den of his! And that vicious old dog of his, maybe they both get in on it!" Such slander I have had to endure! Such discredit and dishonour! I know Frederic feels it too... He's given up barking at my tormentors... as resigned as I am now! Skulks off to a corner and just grumbles. In no mood for fang-based quarrels, Frederic just nests his head down low between his two big paws and patiently waits for the idiots to leave and peace to return. Who is at my door now? Why do I even bother answering that lovely barrier to the outside world? It only brings more grief and vile reports. My joints kill me every time I have to get up and welcome another acidic swindler!

"May I come in?" says a neighbour from up the street.

"Sure, why the hell not?" I say. "It is just my home, a common exhibit, my rugs worn raw and bald with everybody tramping in to poke the bear in his cage."

"I won't keep you long. I'm just going door to door with a petition to City Hall."

"I sign nothing if I can help it. Everything I have signed has always resulted in theft or grievous harm at a later date."

The Vicious Circulation of Dr. Catastrope

"Oh, it's nothing like that. I'm just rallying up some signatures to convince the mayor that we the citizens are opposed to the proposed tearing down of our heritage building, the old fire hall."

"That crumbling layer cake hasn't been in service for twenty years. Out with the old, I say! Soon it will be me, you'll see. I can be pinned with all sorts of badges that declare me a heritage citizen, and that will invite all the developers to tear me down and build a new, more affable man. The place has been abandoned and neglected forever now. Let it fall! Tinderbox! Rat condo!"

"I would like to persuade you otherwise. It is a very important piece of our history. Did you know that in 1923—"

"History belongs safely in saccharin textbooks and town records, not standing like a rotten tooth in the town core. What, will we make a little tourist museum out of it? Charge entrance fees to make the fat councilors even fatter? What do any of us have to gain from this? Old things can go to rot. In with the new. Demolish it and erect a brothel or another ooh-la-la coffee shop. Who cares? People like you get all anxious and concerned about dead buildings, but smile blankly about the water quality!"

"What's wrong with the water?"

"Full of poison! It is a sick-maker, but unlike you, some of us cannot afford to buy bottled water from far away mountain springs! We are forced to drink and clean and cook with it. My poor Frederic can barely drink it either, and he's a dog! I say that if the dogs get sick from the tap water meant for human consumption, then we have a very big problem! Where is the accountability? Is there liability in all of this? Save a crusty old fire hall? Pfah! Treat the water!"

"As far as I know, our water meets national standards for safety. I don't know what you are talking about... "

"National standards? To live by those is to accept too little! The nation is cheap with us and cares only to have expensive luncheons and smiling idiots with gold tie clips to tell us all is well. Standards are unacceptably low... It is bare minimum life! Unless one is rich, and then all is milk and honey."

"I would like to debate this with you, but I would more like to urge you to add your name to this petition. If you won't, then I have to be on my way. We are trying to get a thousand signatures by tomorrow."

"You had my answer right off! I'm not budging! I would tear the ugly fucker down myself if I had the right tools! Nothing is immune to progress. Heritage anything is a cash-suck. Vox populi and the hoi polloi all the way! Right up to the gates where work will set you free! Who cares about the damn fortalices of the past? Grind those old bricks into powder, heavy-down the bread!"

"I am sorry that you feel this strongly about tearing it down. I'll leave you to the rest of your afternoon."

Didn't even dare cajole or upbraid me in any way! An even-toned and polite hysteric! But I know he is itching to tell his other cronies all sorts of lies... Whips and chains on my wall! Or that he saw proof with his own eyes that I am a boozehound dipso and a worthless old cadger! But you won't see me begging on the corners or even touching one drop of the idiot grape... I despise alcohol, too acidic, makes for too many miscarriages of judgement, makes idiots of all who guzzle it! And I know just about everyone in this town is an unquenchable fire for the stuff... their carnival balloon livers... pocket flasks and fireside binging... even the children steal away and get pasted at the bottom of the slides — I've seen it myself! And I'd be blamed for it, too, if that wouldn't compromise the hush-hush policy of the volk!

The Vicious Circulation of Dr. Catastrope

A trip to the mailbox always seems to be a funereal march to another disaster, another catastrophe in letters... Bills and threats: amount pretty much to the same thing! Late payment claims that are false, or maybe another town letter from some cagey onanist threatening me with murder. And so what if I show any of those fan letters to the police? They'll say I made it myself and just looking for attention and special treatment! But today's letter is a bit different...

My old talent manager, that huckstering ass with his fat belly full of pelf! He is writing me about the possibility of my reprise... cuts right to the short of it, not much for the polite palaver and how-are-things. Fine... I hate the conversational dance. He wants to cash in on something retrogenic, exhume my once gleaming talents to croon a few old songs, squeeze the last drop of cash he can from me, me the singing ape! And where are my royalties now, you dope? Thief? Workshop operator?

Oh, here they come... the whole tipsy town, all hollering on some bent Ouzo frenzy. What now, what now... Have they come with a petition from the ASPCA, take my dog away and put me in shackles? Banding together to throw me down the well? I'm so exasperatingly tired of their workshy jingoism and bad town council special causes brinksmanship. You posh community action seat-fillers with your one million forged signatures on petitions that make the Treaty of Versailles look reasonable! You flower cushions of middle-class crotch rot on parade! I'm ready for them now... some choice words! May I cut each and every one of their mewling cavils and complaints, slander and blackguarding dither with the sharp gilt-edge of my verbs! All action verbs! Hardly a static noun to slow their river rush flow!

No, no, they're passing me by – more important quarry? Another hapless victim of their collective "concern"? Perhaps they are en route to take down Bill Preston's scarecrow because it resembles Christ in some sacrilegious way. We won't stand for agricultural blasphemies on our town limits, no sir! They'd rather crucify the innocents, the ones that can still scream... For sure! "You: rumour has it you are an inveterate pedophile, and in these parts, rumour is fact! Ipso facto! De jure! Something or other! Up on the stick! Light the tinder around his feet and let's watch him dance as he dangles in mid-air! Invite the kids; let's make a town picnic of the affair!"

Oh, but I'm tired... If Constance were still here — if only! Constance had her way to keep my mind off things, a good woman, sharper teeth and a harder backbone than mine if the opportunity called for it... Protected her man with incredible zeal. An iron fortress, a daunting cathedral door against the vicious throngs with their hungry claws looking for my face to peel. Dr. Brown tried to pluck her from me, too, but Constance was wise to him! A disgusting lout, a Seconal addict! No doubt! She knew all about it, could see it in his half-loping gait, that beady look of narcotic hunger in his eyes, all tales told just in a glance! With Constance, there was no need to be sore with Brown after all – he did me a favour without realizing it, I'm sure... and back then, when I was on top of my career as a crooner of love songs that oozed and melted so delectably, well, I had plenty of admirers... In the mail, what a pile! Long written mash notes, sonnets, requests for marriage in beautifully poetic script, all hand-written, some scented with luscious perfumes! So many pictures of Bettys, Matildas, Heidis... autographed, wanting one of me in return... gorgeous cameo shots in black and white – I still have a few boxes in the attic with all that memorabilia. I find myself humming the old tunes whenever I go through them, but I don't do that often.

Constance was a real woman compared to all these teenage lust queens, those puppy love sentiments as they swooned with

The Vicious Circulation of Dr. Catastrope

what they thought was love. Frederic here was just a pup then, hardly bigger than a spaniel... I bought him from a reputable breeder who wasn't keen on the pedigree. Frederic took to me instantly, and even growled at the breeder when he tried to take him away, show me "more appropriate dogs." That's when I knew Frederic was the one I wanted... that innate pro-tective instinct. Would come in handy, certainly, and has! Constance loved Frederic, too. They were inseparable. He would wait by the door in the late afternoons for her to come home from work. I think her death shook him as much as it did me... He wouldn't touch his food for days, would mope around, let out a sigh. I was in the same way, but had to focus on all the respon-sibilities... no grieving allowed just as yet! Funeral arrangements and all... I sank what I had left of my modest fortune into giving her what she deserved, or as much as I could afford. It was the second big purchase of my life, the first being this house, which I paid for flat out with royalties, no mortgage sentence for me. But cancer took Constance too soon... You wouldn't have known it to see her, kept smiling strongly right up until the end, even though it was ravaging her body, dulling the sparkle in her eyes. A terrible struggle all the way through, passed away at 51, leav-ing behind a broken man and his dog.

With Constance gone, my dear Connie, that was when the town went into a feeding frenzy. Oh, they gave me a mourning period of about a weekend, just to adjust to their new policy of decrying me as a public menace. Those damn Torquemadas! The town inquisition started in earnest just days after the fu-neral. First it was the state of my house exterior, my garden, my lawn – all of it unkempt. Well, from where was I supposed to draw any will or desire to play Gary Gardener? The love of your life dies, and you're expected to go out and plant tulips? Prune the hedge? Put a fresh coat of paint on the garage? To them, I was a shambling eyesore, a wretch worse than an alleyway abortionist! Why did they suddenly decide to turn on me, I'll never really know, but I have my suspicions...

The Vicious Circulation of Dr. Catastrope

3

The sickness that eats from within my master was a sad thing to behold, especially for me who would fain to alleviate his suffering by any means. But the illness of my master was infectious, and all of his accusations – many born of his own delusion – installed themselves as matter of fact among the townsfolk. If one perceives oneself as being the object of hatred and suspicion fervently enough, it may come to pass that all those who encounter such an individual may come to believe it... subconsciously at first until it takes root, blossoms into something heinous like belief, and belief has a way of forcing one's hand despite the intervention of cool reason.

But some of my master's unending lament did initially have their claim in truth. Perhaps it was his brusque and abrasive nature, doubtless cultivated during his minor bout with fame in dealing with irksome hangers-on (although I would presume that this, too, was overcompensation for the fame he would have liked). It was perhaps this, and his somewhat aloof style of personal comportment that others found distasteful – for even they did not think his minor fame should accord him any more special attention. Certainly, there were a few moments of envy among some, but this was eclipsed by what seemed to me to be a growing campaign of ridicule. If there is one thing I know about human beings from my lowly perspective as a dog, it is this: people take a certain cruel delight in the downfall of those with large egos unsupported by any measure of real importance. This Schadenfreude the people embrace is mistaken for a kind of justice, a reckoning where-upon the inflated ego is taken down to a more suitable level.

Suffice to say, my master did not fall from grace with any ease. Strangers treated him unkindly on but the vicious circulation of hearsay and rumour, pronouncing their judgements from second-hand information. The process of his alienation was indeed fairly rapid, and he succumbed to it by becoming increasingly bitter and distrustful. The only truly beneficial moment in my master's life after his retreat from modest fame was in meeting Constance. I cannot bear to linger upon my fondest memories of her without lapsing into an irrevocable fugue. However, she leveled him out considerably, and it was perhaps her positive – albeit brief – influence upon his life that made me love her ever more. It was a time when the three of us were at our happiest; my master was downright convivial with the townsfolk then. Surely, not all, but more so than his previous plummet into caginess and sullen isolation. The stigma of his amplified ego would not disappear, but it was muted for a time, and the townspeople began very slowly to accept him, which is a sign of the beginnings of forgiveness. The insult the people felt they had suffered by his holier-than-thou attitude was starting to abate. Perhaps my master would have been better off if he could have developed this temporary armistice and brought about full acceptance to fruition, if not for the untimely passing of his dear Constance. With her demise, everything seemed to return to status quo ante, if not worse, as if Constance was but an ephemeral phantom. My master reverted to bitterness, but of a more twisted and caustic variety and the townspeople became more vituperative. Constance's death stole away the last vestiges of my master's reason, I believe, and with it any hope for his redemption in the eyes of the town.

With his own eyes turned inward, he began to harbour more ill feeling toward the town and its motives, fuelled by terrible and impossible fantasies that his feverish mind conjured into fact. Suspecting everyone of malice, he projected unto the people more reason to treat him in such manner. The more he ratcheted up his hatred for the people, the more they returned their hatred in kind, a fatal build-up of detestation.

The Vicious Circulation of Dr. Catastrope

What else could I do? I was honour-bound to protect my master from any and all harm. I would growl at intruders – not fearing that they would do him any physical harm, but more that they would incite his madness further. And now I am guilty by association, it seems, since the people declared that my master trained me to be disagreeable and feral. My reputation as a dog has been besmirched, and I have been declared a filthy mongrel menace... But I care not how others perceive me given that my loyalties always lay with my master, even after his death. Let them take me away to that sterile room that smells of masked urine and pain, and let that person in the white coat palliate me cautiously with a few perfunctory strokes behind the ear as they steady that lethal needle into me that will make me drowsy and weak. And, what then? I die, and the last vestiges of my loyalty, service, and dignity will flow out with my own urine as my bladder releases it upon that cold, hard tiled floor. I am far too old now to fight against my inevitable capture. I have no regrets, and I lived my life in accordance with honour. But this is morbid, and surely I may have just a bit of time left to spare to relate the saga of my dearly departed master.

Ah, my little iniquities, right? Never an end to the flak I get thrust in my face, the blowback of their little half-baked cruelties like little flecks of foam spraying... I just wish they would spread their shit where something would grow, a field somewhere... enough shit to make the cornfields thrive! And I know it is their boredom that makes me their target, that, and pettiness... That's all the fat ladies talk about in the town salon as they get their perms under those nosecone rocket contraptions, flipping absentmindedly through Cosmo, denouncing me in conspiratorial tones, trying to outdo each other with their zeal for fiction and melodrama. No, it is not enough for one to tell a tale of how I diddle three local schoolchildren, so her neighbour ups the ante to twelve! Throw in some bestiality and grave-robbing, too! Godless! Head of an international terrorist network! A vociferous and committed anti-Semite and a member of the Al-Qaeda hate-mongering club! An organs trafficker and the head of a child pornography ring that stretches from here to Sri Lanka! Let's not forget my predilection for prowling the streets at night, naked, capturing people's beloved cats with fiendish traps and boiling them, making kinky sex attire with the fur!

Bah! They should all go and choke on their own bones for a change! They must think that I am without my sources about all their own little intrigues... Some canaries do sing just loud enough for me to hear them! I'm a repository of all sorts of heinous gossip, mostly against my will! People talk and talk, sinking all sorts of ships... The hatchet jobs they perform on each other's reputations – sick and damning! But do I launch back, get down in the dirt and squalor of their savage antics? No! Who would take my word for it anyway, discredited as I am, never mind if what I know about each and every one of them is true! I have eyes and ears, and I don't change anything a jot... Objective reportage, for sure, intimate details of their craven appetites, infidelities, tortured neuroses, child abuse, theft, sabotage... it's all here, all crooked, in this sleepy town with its plastic grin of welcome. Only a fatal epidemic would correct the wrongs of this place, the ultimate natural course of mercy... nail the boards up all over town, declare it condemned, keep outsiders away lest the disease spread, and then burn the whole place down to cinders and ash! What's worth saving here? The inept mayor with all his corrupt and incompetent councilors? You want to talk fiendish designs? Go ask him about the skim on the budgets! Town in a deficit, my ass! Nice new black Mercedes, Mr. Mayor! And is that a new pool in the backyard for all your niece and nephew brats? The shit spreads fast in

The Vicious Circulation of Dr. Catastrope

water, it seems, and here we all are drowning in the lies, malfeasance, and homilies of those silverback barons of pelf! But what should I care about the mechanics of backstairs politicking? All I know is that there is a very real reason why our streets are rarely ploughed in the winter, and it has nothing to do with any of the fatuous, palliative excuses City Hall dishes out wholesale.

Well, if all this doesn't make the junior high barn social crepe paper princesses all wet and randy! Our future gossip-mongers and baby-poppers... The children learn early... What great role models they have in their parents – they get all their prejudicial cues from the inbred hatreds of mummy-daddy! If I lived to be 300, each generation would inherit their unfounded distaste for me... hatred 2.0! It would just snowball!

I could've been bigger than ol' Blue Eyes, but I lacked his mercenary business acumen... I just wanted to share my voice with the world, the velvet and velour melody with soft suede lyrics... the kind of music you throw on the radio for beach-bound teenagers in love... My voice, eddying from a parked car's speaker on lover's lane, something that may prompt delicate caresses, fumbling hands, deep-felt sentiment, a hand slipping shyly into another's while the moon lets off its soft luminescent glow... Nothing complicated... the same themes: young love, sweet and tender times. I still have a bit of the old voice, a bit of huff and puff left in these lungs, but it's been near forty years since I've had the kiss of stage light. In my day, the golden age of dapper and clean crooners, our sentimental songs were *de rigeur*. Things were simpler then. Singers had talent, presented themselves with aplomb and good evening attire, no animal antics... no guitar smashing or indecent grotesqueries or sex carnival acts. Something happened... Golden voices went raspy. Tailored and crisp tuxedos were traded in for the casual rags of dipso bums and muck-rolling clowns. Musical talent all but disappeared, replaced by the schizophrenic hollering and bedlam screeching of caterwauls. Hippies, drugs, sensationalism, tits, rag-tag three-chord wonders, industry-made human jukeboxes... Ugly songs, offensive lyrics, a jangle of random notes amplified and distorted to sound like metal scraps caught in a lawnmower... No soul left, pure cacophony... Now singers need a veritable army of studio producers and sound wizards to make their voices follow a recognizable tune, modulating pitch here and there on a cold mixing board... We never needed the technological razzle-dazzle post-production whatzits to sound good: we had talent, and even our rawest talent was leagues beyond what passes for trained and refined today... We had dedication, discipline, vigour, spirit, craft, complete devotion to melodious voice. Sure, we were all handsome faces, but it was our voices – our voices! — that made our handsomeness shine with real expression. How we sounded made us beautiful, made young ladies swoon at our feet! We didn't croak ourselves hoarse at the audience with songs about smoking up or Satan or uncontrolled shopping sprees! We sang songs from the heart, real melt-in-your-mouth ditties that had the girls swaying, hanging on our every note!

And then it hits me... Yes, why not beat a return to simpler times? Why not stage a comeback, a small one, give to this wretched community what it doesn't deserve but what it truly wants? Show these invidious buffoons that I have *grace*, that I value my art over the petty squabbles and so many bent noses... to show them all, once and for all, that I can still give no matter how much they take... I'll warm their atrophied hearts despite themselves! But, oh, I will need new songs, a new repertoire... Won't do to just sing all the old classics, the reliable standbys... no, throw just a handful in for nostalgia's sake, but not more!... Fresh material, show development, artistic evolution... Hook them in with some familiarity and then blow them away with a

The Vicious Circulation of Dr. Catastrope

whole new barrage of songs that would have been chart-toppers if times could be like before. And perhaps this is exactly what the curmudgeons and backbiters of this town desire but don't know how to express it, like a small and lost piece of soul missing from their lives, misplaced for so long that they forgot what it was that was lost. Then let it be done: all hail the grand return of the Pelvic Prowler!

The musical reprise enjoys its place in the music scene today, as if somehow there is a subconscious undercurrent of ambiguous dissatisfaction with the garbage marketed today, and so there is a deep yearning for the talents of yesteryear – something that I fully intend to exploit. Reunion acts are fashionable now... It should prove easy for me to make my return debut... I may be a venerable seventy years-old, but I can still carry a tune and belt them out! With all the miserable yelling I have had to issue against the people of this town, it has kept my lungs and voice in top form, a de facto vocal training. Despite, and because of, this town's untoward treatment of me, they need this overdue dose of nostalgia and saccharin words... The mind is a murky, tricky thing... perhaps they didn't once realize that their hatred of me stems from my having violated some unwritten covenant to keep on singing... They just don't know how to express their feelings of loss. How can anyone excuse the sensation that puts a damper on his god-given voice? No wonder they find me abominable – I let them all down! Icons are never given leave to retire. The only acceptable exit is death. The pricks were just afflicted with negative atten-tion-seeking disorder. It all makes sense now... those loath-some, vile moral cripples and personality-deficient poltroons reciting their clumsy litanies of disgusted complaint upon the table tops in their beer halls... Woe begotten accusations puking forth in a grand emetic chorus in the dog parks... jeremiads and awful philippics at every town council meeting... brush-rolled ink on the newspaper gossip columns and op-ed pieces... Well, it's time to heed the intention of their grievances, their abuses... I will sing again!

I don't have many friends left in that alder bog of leeches known as the music industry. Most of the honest and good-natured kind dried up or were eaten alive.

The Vicious Circulation of Dr. Catastrope

4

In that notorious book by Cervantes, Sancho Panza states that sadness is the proper dominion of animals, not of men. I would come to this conclusion independently, but in belatedness. We must all do the impossible; namely, to assume responsibility for our capacity for sadness, and not try to cover it up with muddied ambitious plans that only briefly obscure the inevitable truth. As a creature not disposed with ambitions beyond the rather quotidian and necessary – to eat, to sleep, to evacuate my bowels – there is room enough to discharge my mundane pleasures to allow sadness' reign. It is not the absence of Reason that renders animals sad, but an overabundance of it. We, the silent watchers who cannot traffic in the same language as men, can only act as distant chroniclers recounting a story that none can hear or read – not even among our own species. My linguistic repertoire is limited to the bark or the trace of urine's scent on a tree as I choose to inscribe myself in space. And what folly and redundancy that is! To think somehow that my identity is confirmed through a baseless act of marking territory, something so ephemeral as it is covered over by stronger urine or the next rainfall. Such acts will not redeem me any more than my bark will be understood as anything more than threat or annoyance. Making a map of the world does not bring anyone closer to possessing it – and even if one could, we only lease space before another cartographer of the human will comes along and shuffles the people differently, according to another set of distinct values and beliefs.

But there is a measure of grace, if not resignation, in acknowledging one's limitations. Yes, this is rather banal and commonplace wisdom, so well-worn and hardly profound, but it is the hardest lesson to internalize. My master, rest his confused and warring soul, was powered entirely by ressentiment... and so his answer was that if he could not attain to that level of respect he felt entitled to, he would destroy history itself. And what is a revision of history, courting a belief that what one constructs is true, but history's destruction? And what, again, is a plan of action based on this revised history but a confabulation of error?

I was waylaid by a few stuck piano keys. It was as out of tune, having fallen into disuse, as my voice. But this was only a matter of practice and correction. Even the songbirds of spring issue wrong notes after a long winter. By evening, I was nearing top form, but it would still be a few very intensive weeks of training before I could set foot on stage. Plus, there were calls to make, letters to write, announcing my glorious return.

"Orpheus Talent Management, Yolanda speaking. How may I direct your call?"

He went for the cliché classicism, didn't he? Orpheus, no less. Look back to see if Eurydice is in tow while he picks your wallet, inserts hidden clauses after the fact.

"I need to speak with Paul Temple; he was once my agent, long ago."

"Mr. Temple is out of the office right now. If you'd like to leave your name and where he could reach you, I'll make sure he gets the message."

"I'd rather make first contact. I don't want to give him the option to let this lie. He owes me a great deal. When does he get back? I'll call then."

"Mr. Temple is very busy. I can relay the message when he returns."

"Yolanda, you work for a crook, and I'm not about to mediate my demands through his secretary."

The Vicious Circulation of Dr. Catastrope

I continued into a long harangue, doubtless her finger on the button that would end it. But she was being drawn into it, propelled by some mysterious desire to play this exchange out, or perhaps too polite to end a conversation so abruptly, even if the caller was justifiably irate. At one point, I was yelling, laying out the whole besotted affair of how he cheated me, left me for dead. She must have been visibly distraught, unsure of what to do or say, sputtering excuses that were running thin. I had caught her off guard. I knew Paul was in the office, and probably saw Yolanda in this state, probably hearing the shrill cacophony of my angry voice blaring through the receiver. I heard Paul tell Yolanda that he would take the call in his office.

"Hey, hey, now, what's this all about? Berating my secretary. She's new. How is that a way to conduct oneself?"

"You expect me to adopt a conciliatory tone after you left me in the lurch, you gold-screw?"

"Still as much of a firebrand as ever," he said with a defusing chuckle. "How long has it been? Must easily be thirty years or more? I didn't know you were still alive... I mean, aw, hell, you know what I mean. So what can I do for you? We should meet up and have a coffee – it has been forever. How have you been keeping yourself?"

"Keeping myself? In a state of vicious self-protection! I've learned from you what people are capable of!"

"Calm yourself, old friend. The past is the past. Let's not go over this again. The industry was different back then, and I was a bit of a novice. No, I didn't always conduct business very well, or even very fairly, but that was the reality of the biz at the time. The ethics of the thing was still in its infancy, and I can hardly be called to account for the decision I made when everybody else was doing the same thing. It was all the ne-ce-ssi-ty of being com-pe-ti-tive. But, seriously now, what can I do for you?

If you've called to get your pound of flesh, I don't think this is such a good idea."

"Ok, let me get to the bare bones of it. As much as I despise what you did to me all those years ago, you are my only in. I'm coming back!"

Silence.

"Coming back?" he asked as if it were preposterous. Take the wind right out of my sails! It was supposed to floor him, and instead I could tell that he thought the idea absurd and was trying to find a way of dissuading me. "My dear old friend, are you sure you've thought this through? I mean, the landscape of the industry has really changed since you were on the bill. It's tougher now – "

"Bullshit! I see what comes out now! Walking jukeboxes that sing what they are told to sing, vapid songs written by silver-haired hacks in the marketing department!"

"Well, now, that's not such a fair appraisal. But these days it isn't just about talent... There's a whole mechanism behind it now."

"Yes! Profit mechanics! Legal intermediaries! Merchandising deals! Corporate bedfellows! PR splash! The support network has ballooned at the expense of real talent! You execrable goof, I wouldn't be talking to you if I didn't know what you were after, how you work, what you want. I am not naïve. I know daddy wants his sugar at the end of the day, and I have just the act to give it to you."

"My friend, you know how many performers try to shill themselves to me, promising all sorts of lucrative return on investment? I have to side with realism here. Let me be blunt: you're washed up. You were washed up long ago. No one even remembers you, no one buys your songs. Maybe it's unfair that time forgot you, but that is just how things pan out sometimes. This is not to say that you weren't a talented modest sensation in your time, but things move fast now. A comeback is just not feasible, really. I urge you to enjoy your golden years, delight in fond memories and forget all this return to glory... It will only result in disappointment."

"You're stonewalling me, Paul, and I know you owe me. You are honour-bound – if you have any shred of that! – to represent me. I've got new songs to mix with the oldies. It's the perfect storm, a blast from the past, a return to order and quality in singing and songwriting! Let the public decide. You'll see... A good bet!"

"Representation is very complicated and expensive now; we can't just invest in anybody with a dream, even if they were once good in the ears of the listeners. But those listeners are gone now. We have to appeal to the youth."

"When I started out, I had no audience. Remember? There was no fan base, and no precedent. I *created* my audience. Think of it, Paul: a whole new generation turning on to the old grooves!"

He was not convinced. "There was a precedent. The genre had already been in existence before you set up. The Zeitgeist was ripe for it; it was the type of music people came, and paid, to hear. But that genre is gone. There's zero market for it now."

"For once in your life, Paul, be brave and take a damn risk! We could reinvent the genre, can introduce it to the young crowd... They may love it!"

I could tell that he was exasperated. He perhaps thought that he was speaking with a lunatic... But there were signs of him yielding, if only to give me a condescending bone. "Ok, ok, listen: I don't want to argue market realities with you. I still think at your age this would be arduous, not to mention disappointing. But I do know that I owe you something, and it is out of a feeling of debt and nostalgia that I'd be willing to give you a shot. But I know that whatever financing I provide for this will be at a loss for me, no matter how you sell it. But I'll do it for old time's sake. And if I do this, then we will be even for all past wrongs, *comprende*?"

I wanted to retort that nothing could settle such a debt he owed me, but thought better of it. "Of course! You won't regret it, Paul."

"Never say that – those are the famous last words that usually jinx the whole thing to result in regret. But let's be clear: no big splash. I'll only finance up to a point – small shows, modest coverage. We're not talking packed superdomes and pyrotechnics. We are talking small out-of-the-way clubs. You have to work your way up from scratch since it's been more than an eternity since an eternity in the music biz can be as short as a five-year fallow period these days."

"Thank you, Paul. I never expected to make top act right away. I know I must struggle from the beginning, like any untested artist."

"Here's what I'll do. I'll give you the name of a producer friend of mine who has studio space. You bring your songs when they're ready and we'll cut a few tracks. Let's be clear, though: I am not financing the pressing of CDs, but we can produce a sampler for a little bit of promo radio play. Not big radio stations, either, but local, wherever you'll be slated to perform. I'll call in a few favours at a few small town bars and the like and see if they can fit you in on an off-night. Fridays and Saturdays will, of course, be out. You might have to do the weekday performances. Small crowds, but it's less of a risk for the owners. Maybe I'll try to line up some light hotel gigs. Do you have a band?"

"I'll have to rely on you for that one."

"I'll see if I can rummage together some kids for it. They'll have to learn the old licks. We're talking kids who are as old as rap music, though, so don't expect miracles. It will be very likely boring for them. Grandpa music. But they want cash. I'll sub-sidize a bit for whatever door won't cover. Can you be ready in two months? I'll need the time to arrange everything. I won't make you top priority, you understand, so things might be a bit slower and modest. Are we in agreement?"

"Yes, I can be ready in two months. I'll agree to this and – who knows? – I may surprise you."

"I won't build up any expectation. As far as I'm concerned, I'm doing a favour for an old client. That's all this is about. Come in sometime this week and we'll hash up a light contract, nothing too binding. I want to ensure that either of us can pull out at any time. If this flops, then we should both be able to shake hands and walk away from it, ok?"

"Ok."

Ok, we'll leave things like that. I am, after all, a "just no-body" these days, so at least I was spared his usual sanctimo-nious claptrap airs... his peevish exhibitionism so rife for the mockumentarian circuit! I knew he had his cabal of market flacks all too busy shilling what passes for popular music these days: ridiculous t-shirt activists and their off-key neo-hippy caterwaul, frcoked by li'l missies who squeeze their daddy-bought titties together, going for the lootbag and their song-lyric ellipses lasting for infinity!

Don't let me lose you hear, but I do recall when music was music. Johnny Mathis... Bobby Darin... Belafonte, Vic Damone, Patti Page, Tony Bennett... chart-toppers all! And justifiably so. All thriving in the spotlight of the industry's salad days, before the boostership of it all came before the talent itself. And where is our jive and bop nowadays? Everything now sounds like it is being decanted through an angry, broken machine!

Oh, but my old manager, he wasn't a runner—heaven forfend! No, he was about as mobile as a heaping mountain of construction debris! I can tell you that it was a hard dollar—

always! Sure, he wanted to manage the biggest acts, the real shekel-earners, the jumbo stars!... I signed on with him, bought his entire shill, how we was going to promote me throughout the whole damn solar system.

But what am I now, now without my lovely anchor? Just a feuterer—a dog-keeper... And a pariah, no less! At least I know the origin of the term, how it fits... A *parai* was part of the Tamil caste, the one sentenced to beat the village drum. My duty? So be it. Someone needs to keep rhythm, just as the jester has to be the voice of reason when the reason of the court nobles fail. I beat the drum, the great performer! Spat upon, of course, a lowly task others feel far too noble to undertake... The people of this village could not soil or blister their pretty-soft paws thwacking skins.

The Vicious Circulation of Dr. Catastrope

5

My dear, doddering master took it upon himself to attempt a wily comeback in an era weary of such things, and with no appreciable appetite for the genre he believed would come back into higher musical fashion. He began to obsess upon his newly self-appointed task with a mixture of revenge and as a means of filling that void of purposelessness that marked his listless days. He would brook no naysaying on his chosen direction, and although I could most likely predict the sour outcome of all his vain efforts, I also knew that for the moment this would provide my master with sense of purpose enough to regain that old fire in the belly. Like a trusted old blanket, it was hard not to love him like a living anachronism.

The phone was cachinnating from the living room, disrupting my rigorous vocal routine.

"Vincent, I may have just the right sort of thing for ya as a starter... You know, get your feet wet," announced Paul Temple.

"A gig already? But I'm not ready yet... I need more time. I'm not scuttling, but I just need a few more days."

"Don't matter if you're croaking a little—bound to happen being out of practice. But while I was taking drinks, I heard through a friend of a friend that someone needs a wedding singer. You game? Would be a hoot to do all the old favourites. Can you do covers?"

"Covers? What's wrong with the old repertoire? It was good enough to jerk a tear or get people into a jitter."

"Yeah, I know it *was*, but people want the other stuff. Sinatra, Avalon, Darin, that kind of thing. It's a pretty retro affair, and they're really stuck on the entertainment side. I know you'll work for a reasonable fee."

"Would I be allowed to insert a few of my own ditties?"

"Well, I dunno. I dunno. Maybe? Add them like a spice, though, ok? Let's just get Vinnie the Voice back up to snuff with covers before we start with the personal artistry. No 'death by back catalogue' business. They want a straight shooter, a singer who can make the day extra special, a -"

"Jukebox. They want a human jukebox. Plug in a nickel and get an oldie favourite. I know this kind of gig, Paul. It's the last refuge of the washed-up... the Vegas sideshow carpetbagger, the kind of shit that floats. I know, I know."

"Don't take it like that, Vinnie. It's just a little get off the ground gig. You know, the kind of thing that can generate a little positive for you, put you a bit more on the radar. A little cash, too, can't hurt. We all know what we would really like to do, but we sometimes have to bow down and give the people what they want until what they want is what you choose to give 'em. How the biz works. Show off a bit of your talent; doesn't matter whose song it is, really. No, wait, I'm serious... Yes, don't get me wrong: you're a massive talent at songwriting, but we gotta warm the crowd up a bit, belt out a few tunes they recognize. It's easier to convince an audience when you've softened them up with something safely recognizable first... more willing to listen."

"It's still a sideshow gig, Paul. A for-pay, song-on-demand kind of gig."

"Aw, c'mon, don't get down in the mouth about this. I promised I wasn't going to coddle you. I'll carry, but not coddle. Got it? You have to see this as a good opportunity... Build a client base, and all that. Don't worry: you won't be consigned to stuff like this forever. We just want to get into this slow. Yeah. We want to come on slow and quiet and then ramp it all up. You're a hard sell these days, Vinnie, you know that. If you want to stand on principle, you go ahead, but that isn't audience-building. Look at this as an opportunity."

The Vicious Circulation of Dr. Catastrope

"I understand."

"Does this mean you'll do it, give it the ol' whirl? I have to get back to my friend soon-soon."

"Yes, yes, I'll do it."

"I think this will be a real breakaway for you. Gives you a chance to cook the pink out of the meat, really, clear out the vocal rust and all that. I'll call you back in a few days with all the details. Thanks a million, Vinnie—I knew I could count on you. Ciao!"

Reduced to the on-demand, just like that. Pfah! Well, no sense letting that put anchors on my sailing ship... No, I'll give it all I've got.

I took a stroll today for the first time in a while, beating the dust out of my pants and refusing to live in the fear that the locals promulgate. I took it on slowly, the walk, touring my old haunts like the decommissioned grain silo, the now for lease apple farm, the former court house. Despite how much I despised the town, there were always some small pockets of solace and respite. A few quiet zones where I could let my thoughts course across. I remember when she died, it was all I had... getting out of the house, so morbid, so agonizing. To live in a home where once one experienced such marital bliss... It is like living in a constant reminder, a memory tomb. You feel as though you died alongside them, and perhaps in many ways you did. Good to get out, some air, blood circulating in the legs reminding you—albeit painfully—that you are alive. Alive, alive, and... why? I sometimes gaze at that crepuscular horizon from my porch just as the sun has tucked itself behind that jagged and happen-stance wall of distant pines and think that, *soon, Constance, I am coming soon*. Most times, it feels as though I am just idling, wasting time until I can be reunited with my Constance. When she left, she took all the mooring with her.

Adrift in a life without any kind of drama, really. She used to tease me about being so grumpy, so critical... perhaps cooling me down with a kiss or a few caresses. "You'll be a grumpy old man before you hit fifty," she used to say. She kept snapping my attention to those things that were more positive, optimistic, happier things... Without her, I seemed to have defaulted to this weak position of perpetual anger and bitterness, perpetually poring over all those experiences that amounted to zilch or worse... What was it that Wilde said? "Experience is the name we give to our mistakes."

I fell into a dream. The scene opened up on a hotel lobby as a slightly distorted lounge music was playing in an adjacent room, the kind of music that is supposed to be soothing but usually comes in a falsely over-lit room and conveys loneliness and eeriness. I saw myself there, about forty years of age, my hair Brill-creamed with a few errant wisps come undone and trying to merge with a bit of forehead sweat, and I was wearing a rumpled tuxedo, hunched over on a stool at the hotel bar, idly swishing a gin and tonic. A voice from behind and a few peals of laughter from an obviously drunk woman. I turned around to find that I was now in an immense parking lot, still sitting on the stool, the bar now an unattended island. A figure in the distance that looked like Constance was just standing. The music swelled and its genre slipped out from beneath it, only to usher in a kind of cacophonic punk.

I was rudely shaken from my reverie and sank into another one. Words, heated ones, lobbed angrily back and forth between what looked to be me and some unknown conversant...

"You know what life is? Piffle, beginning to end! Nothing more than a long queue without filigree, a boring terminal where everyone gathers round, irritates you!... pelts you with rocks... You sink into delirium, but not so fast! Bad faith to do that... lock you away, a whole gang of cronies with their institutionalizing cordon sanitaire... Dissolves all your credibility... a Kook! Nutbar! Maybe they'll cover you with sanctimonious well-wishing, pump you full of meds... a chemical lobotomy... ward of the state, and then who'll care?

Enough of all that... I was overheating. Losing my focus. I had a wedding gig to warm up for.

6

Despite how forlorn I might have been to see my master's denouement, there were moments that were less woeful. And, as much as my master was a bit starch-collared on tradition, there was at least one thing that would tug him into the present, and that was when he saw his former youth reflected upon the faces of others. Indeed, he was a hard man and a bit of a bitter and ornery sort, but in his heart of hearts he was also generous, warm, and kind.

Some sort of wayward youth, no doubt, at my door, the look of an Oliver Twist gone rotten and spoiled.

"What is it?" I barked. The boy was no more than fifteen, but sheepish unlike his irreverent and rude contemporaries that felt a sense of extreme entitlement. I noticed a very familiar object in his hands: my second record – and my last one.

"I'm sorry to disturb you. Are you the Pelvic Prowler?"

The boy knew my stage name, but I was suspicious. Some maligning sack of crap in this town must have put him up to it. Taunt the old geezer! Drive him batty, torment him until he says uncle! Well, I'd have none of that, but I wanted to hear the boy out anyway.

"Yes, I was the Pelvic Prowler, baron of the ballad and cream of the crooners... but that was very long ago. Who might you be? Where are your parents?"

"My name is Thomas, Thomas Kirkwood. My parents are at work."

"I don't know the Kirkwoods."

"Mom's a nurse, and dad works at the cannery."

"Working people, eh? Good. A very good example to set for children. Everyone should cultivate their talents, take up some

The Vicious Circulation of Dr. Catastrope

kind of trade. What can I do for you, Thomas? You may already know that I am not very friendly to visitors."

"I was going through my parents' old record collection and found one of yours. The sleeve said it was produced not too far from here, back in 1957. I Googled it and didn't find anything. Anyway, I listened to it and thought it was really cool. Old fashioned-like. I sing for a group at school, and I think I could learn a lot from the past."

"Googled?"

"On the internet... Y'know, Google?"

"I'm sorry, Thomas, I am not familiar with those contraptions. Why don't you come in for a little while. Would you like me to autograph your forty-five?"

"Oh, that would be really nice of you!"

I waved him inside and we went into the living room.

"Hi, puppy!" he said to my companion. He began playing with him a little, and the boy's youth showed. Frederic let the boy pet him.

"His name is Frederic. He is my guard dog and best friend."

"How old is he?" Thomas asked, playing with Frederic's ears.

"About as old as you are, Thomas. So you've developed a real taste for the good old tunes of yesteryear? You know, Thomas, that was when music was truly *alive*, made with passion and performed with real vigour... Days when the talented poured their entire souls into a single song, in each catchy measure. Today... Today? Pfah! Music made by and for robots! Not a shred of soul in any of those tinny things they call music... Just endless repetition, sounds sampled from the factory! They throw a pretty tart on the cover or gather a bunch of steroid-poking choir boys on the cover – instant sales! Gold records and award galas... While we – we, the pioneers of songwriting – end up dropping dead, wasting away forgotten and ignored. There's justice for you, Thomas. Talent means squat these days to your generation... Oh, of course, there are exceptions, and you may just be one of them. That's why I am staging a mighty come-back, but keep it on the down low, if you know what I mean. Mum's the word. I don't want all the sick and twisted saboteurs crawling around, those so-called denizens of musical progress. No, this will start as a quiet, subtle affair until I can mount my real offensive!"

"You mean you'll be cutting another record? Will it be available online? My friends are in a band and they put their stuff up for free."

"Music for free? I agree that music ought to be free, but everybody ought to be paid for their labour. Once they hear my new act, people will *want* to pay for it! They'd feel guilty not to, they'll feel it in their blood... they'll want to pay tribute, do me the highest honour for having rescued them from so many sour decades of musical decline and decadence."

"My music teacher said you had faded away, were washed up."

"Your music teacher is a buffoon and has no faith in the strength of the human will when it is coupled by the power of creativity. Creativity never dies, Thomas, and I've always been – always will be – an artist. It makes no difference if the public turns its back – the audience is a fickle thing, and rarely has taste. It makes no difference if the greedy producers won't bankroll your ideas because they are myopic, can't see over their ridiculous bottom lines."

"Aren't you a bit old?"

"Bah! Good music is timeless, forever young! As soon as I start singing, it transports me, breathes new life into these old bones. I'll show all the young upstarts! I can still prance and pace, better than them! I don't need any gimmicks, either. I've still got lots of juice."

The Vicious Circulation of Dr. Catastrope

Oh, but the memories come flooding back... Nasty ones, and no way to keep them from overcrowding me like some on-slaught of ugly painted ladies... Paul, that Grand Poobah of fools, chiseling me out of every dime he could. Some manager! A downright cheat, and him sentencing me to do the beer hall circuit... claiming that I just wasn't a commodity anymore. Unsalable! An entire warehouse of stacked wax with my name on it, just not moving... "Oh, but Vincent, the market is fickle." Fickle? If anything, the level of active PR under Paul's command was what proved fickle! And so were the trickle-royalties... High handedness! Big promises of stardom this and that, forever unfilled... And him treating it like the whimsical promises of a teenager in love... All it was worth! Love you forever and ever until you don't sell... Contracts being torn up – rip, rip!— consigned eternally to the back catalogue! Why was I even considering working for that huckster again?

Oh, but times change... Things get patched up everywhere... Enemies become friends in the end, but some of us are cursed with long memories. I know I am. It's not my fault... Good genetics, a grand evolutionary trait... But why was I setting myself up to be burned once more? Ok, so here we go... one step at a time, retracing the old steps up that wobbly staircase of fame. In much need of renovations as I look around. One more step and I look around... Who are these young faces and how did they avoid the crooked old steps? Some magic escalator, perhaps, from nobody to icon with one wave of the marketing wand... Poof! And just as quickly – poof again!— back to nobody. Up the staircase again, or just wither away in the basement, back catalogue, a quaint piece of trivia on a gameshow... "Whose one hit wonder, 'Baby, Baby' topped the charts in year x?" All it amounts to! Oh, maybe a retro tribute, a resurrection of the dinosaur on a reunion tour – for giggles, kicks, squeezing out the very last dregs of a career that is more laughable joke than talent! Refried kitsch, in the end, served on the warming plate for a tune-deaf fickle crowd who want you to jukebox their memories... But you're past your prime. You croak something awful. Something gives way beneath you, another rotten step gives way – poof!—and back to nobody and worse!

And Paul... Fat now, blood pressure problems... He's gone all holistic, organic, au naturel. Snuffling his wheat germ by the bale-load. Not for his health, no! For the kids, his "image" as a being "with it." Not for just any kids, the old lecher... For the girls. But there he is, on the side, exhausted from licentious nonsense, doing a chaser of pork fat. Doughnuts cached in his sideboard, cakes in his desk drawer, cookies and sausages and butter tarts in his filing cabinet... A little nibble here, there. But, oh, still the wheat germ – especially if anyone is looking! Controlling his weight... doing his part for the poor farmers, a real sensitive hero! He talks up a storm, denouncing in stentorian voice genetically modified anything. You should hear it! Meanwhile, he's nipping out, maybe to the closet to nibble on his hoard, his secret stash! He'll come back, no worries... Where has he been? Oh, oh, oh, he'll falsely deprecate with his two fat hands, just on the phone with the Natural Rainforest Collective, gave them my full support... signing every one of their poor Brazilian farmers to lucrative music contracts, spreading the word! And then? Then he'll pop one of his Witch Thistle or Eye of Tiger-Lilly pills right in front of you with the label of the bottle showing... What a conscientious supporter of natural remedies! All hail Paul and his homeopathy, his enlightened sense of medical well-being! But that blood pressure... up and up it still goes, soaring with the weather balloons now... Wheezing his bulk from one cookie stash to another, scarfing up all that bacon when he thinks no one is looking. Our great all natural health hazard! Our organically grown fatso! Our holy holistic clogged artery! But hip as all git out, no less! Paul cares... cares about

The Vicious Circulation of Dr. Catastrope

the environment and the bean growers and especially the young and pert hay-haired girls who will sing about it! What's that? You want to produce an album on the endangered urban rodent? Here's a million signing bonus! Meanwhile, as Paul taps into the topical, he comes off looking clean... caring... a corporateer with a heart. A big, fat, overworked heart that palpitates that much more when he sees his quarterly earnings! Another few zeroes added to the end of the cheque and *thump thumpity-thump!* That is now...

Back when I was being mismanaged by him, he was nothing of the sort... A greasy little shill, nothing more! By then, the peace & love bullshit was just starting out... small pockets here and there, stuff Paul said was just an excuse for bored rich kids to bonk themselves stupid. I saw it as a portent of something more... "No, don't you worry, Vincent... A fad! It'll pass. Most kids have some taste, and they go in for quality. You're top shelf." And for all that, all his telling me not to worry? Paul bolted with the fad and never looked back, leaving me to rot! I'm older now, hopefully a little wiser... People who tell me not to worry make me worry double-time. Every time a doctor tells me "it isn't serious" or a politician with his polished public face tells us "the recession will be minor," I know what to really think. "Oh, this won't hurt a bit"... Sure! "It's only a temporary slump in sales, nothing to break a sweat over." Keep going! The last straw was that bungling ass of a doctor whose negligence and incompetence took my Constance away! Oh, but fortified by malpractice insurance no doubt, an enshrined license to practice no matter what your body count is! He wouldn't even let her die... Her agony was a living-dead torment, and her wishes to be unplugged unheeded... For me to do it? Attempted murder is what the courts would have handed down, that and all the slanderous testimonies from the neighbours... Wouldn't stand a chance! When they took away her dignity, they took mine along with it. Decency is the first real casualty in a war of idiots. Oh, but I'm losing myself here... The Kirkwood boy in my house.

"Are you going to do a live show?" he asked.

"As live as alive, Thomas.

The Vicious Circulation of Dr. Catastrope

Book 5

Where the four voices enter into a most toxic yet bracing exchange, a mosaic of polemic...

You see, dear reader, if you have your doubts about the veracity of the Hereafter, if it be a God or Demon that runs the afterlife, if such a place and time exists at all (should you be more of an empirically minded being), let this stand as my modest speculation. Let it not be of any offense to godless nobles that I freely speculate so, for you may read this as a correction of life's injustice. That these four voices have been separated by their circumstances of geographic distances, and that they perhaps would have no means to engage each other even if they were in immediate proximity, let this be our hypothesis that we arrange the conditions so that they may in fact converse together.

I do hold fast to this very idea, that there has been such a miscarriage of justice in God or Existence (pending your faith) in preventing these four men from colluding in their bitter acrimony, these four men bearing a similar streak. Bet-placers on pugilistic events would perhaps be the first to signal how unfair it would be not to bring these four together into one verbal contest, the great combat of whose anger and disgust may come to outshine them all. I do confess my own appetite for a particular brand of violence, and it is – thanks be to God – of a more verbal and mental variety than it would be of that rather vulgar fisticuffs that our more ill-tempered tavern patrons indulge. I also do not care much for that type of middling combat common among husbands and their wives, for woman renders us impotent in matters of conjuring up the best defenses.

I do beg your pardon that I engage in this somewhat frivolous act of fictionalizing, for this speculation is designed to right a cosmic wrong more than it would be to exercise some degenerate capacity to tell tall tales that distort the True in this perfect world that God has fashioned for us.

We have in the offing four disaffected men, each for their own patent reasons we need not reiterate here. That they should be brought together is a matter of merging dynasties of acrimony together to perhaps demonstrate the legacy of bitterness that adheres to the human condition.

As I shall no longer be making my noisome interjections that merely over-explain and staunch the narrative flow of this chronicle, I will bid thee adieu with but one last personal anecdote if it may be allowed. You see, the Keeper of my Heart whose shrill ululations ensure that home and hearth are well maintained, with a steady supply of dry black bread and loving rebuffs of my general behaviour, will most likely be in a bit of an emotional tempest this evening by the time I conclude my chronicle. With hands on her billowing haunches, she will make insistent inquiries as to why I have been so thusly detained, and how deeply the draughts of demon grape have affected my wobbling gait and slurring manner of speech. With caring chides, all manner of sweet expletives will seep through her bulbous lips, expressing her marital devotions by alternate means. She will bid me, in strong and loving terms that portray her concern, that I take my gadabout self to take my slumber in the barn instead of the marital bed. Amidst her usual beseeching clatter about the nettlesome matters of finance, my negligence as a suitable provider, I do know that she secretly appreciates the noble function I have carried in disseminating this vital chronicle.

Francois — And? So what? You say you tell my story. Do I make a centime off this, for your telling my story, making me look like an idiot?

The Vicious Circulation of Dr. Catastrope

Narrator — Now, now, my good sir, I mean not to exploit your circumstances for the sake of telling a tale, but I thought it would be an invaluable service to the Public as an educational moral lesson.

Jonkil Calembour — Bah! You pelf-eating graft machine! What makes you think you can represent me? Are you an attorney? I ought to get a real one and launch him and his fourteen rows of shark's teeth right on your ass!

Catastrope — What is it that you are saying about me?... I have a right to know! Post haste! Serve it up! I have enough of you little fiends knocking on my reputation!... I'm a good doctor! Have I not suffered enough libel and slander?... Perpetrated by experts, I assure you!... Real pros!... Character assassins, presidential bagmen, muckrakers with degrees!...

Vincent — Your type is worse than my agent... What are we doing here?

Catastrope — What was this? This gathering of yammering freaks? And me among them... A madhouse. But what's that? the economy? Oh, the economy! Now there is something in tatters! May as well burn for another few decades, policies handed down where the cash goes up – zoom!—into either. Ok, then!... Times are tough. It's harder as a politician to justify the regular lunch hour facelifts and spa sessions when the cameras are in your face, asking those Hard Questions... A hundred thousand more on the dole, a million more unemployed by the end of the quarter... three million filing bankruptcy... A cancerous national debt, deficits building up steam. And how long until they cut everything down to the bone, "Save the Cent!" A penny earned? Pfah! Every dollar in ten times more out! Bailouts for troubled industries and fiscal stimulus? Not much of what is promised on TV and radio ever gets out the door... speculators and consultants take their fat skim – slurp, slurp!—and then there's barely anything left to spread around! Amounts to a band-aid on a gruesome car accident victim! And my industry? *Social spending*. That will go up in smoke, too! And the politicians? Oh, they'll shrug their shoulders... Oh, well. Oh woe... it's this global economy, so slow, contracting... For sure! Certainly, and then it's no more medicine and pensions for anyone! Schools? Make do with whatever you can steal from the public library. I won't get a dime for my practice! And the government will blame the Chinese, the Japanese, the Russians, the Moravians, the Fatimid Empire – anything but take responsibility! I've lived through one of these "recessions" before... Those greedy jackbooters on Trade Street speculating on overinflated stocks, borrowing freely... Not that I can do that!... And the banks just giving it away, no questions asked! And if I want to get even another couple of bucks on my line of credit? Oh, like being interrogated by the KGB, my finances and assets scrutinized with extreme meticulous zeal... hemming and hawing... No dice! Declined for being too much of a bum risk! My fault for asking to get a little more credit to make it through the lean holidays... Should have asked for ten million with the guarantee that I'd blow it all away in six hours at a Las Vegas casino... Oh, then they'd dish it up right away! They'd even escort me to the casino, the bank manager in tow sweating with a wheelbarrow overflowing with gold bars!

Francois — Who are these blablablahing men? I feel as though I am trapped in a stupid neighbourhood committee. Perhaps this is where we are all to complain about complaints against us, how we do not cut our grass or that our window sills are rotten. And this mustachioed man over here, telling me that he is

The Vicious Circulation of Dr. Catastrope

writing a story about my life... As idiotic as those college kids who want to make bad films about Leon. I do not need any help to look like an idiot. All I want is wine and to be left alone! Alone! Is that too much to ask? I am looking around, yet there is no door. What kind of prison is this where I am stuck with a bunch of loud oafs?

Jonkil Calembour — Hm... O ho ho, so this is the ticket, is it? Trapped among some plainclothes Stasi, quiet cameras nested in the wall? I'm sure this is the ticket they are going to punch: mine! Informants all, no doubt. And that fellow over there with his antique get-up... Looks a little like Rabelais. Did he just say something about being our chronicler? Like I need one of those! I've been distorted and had my protests of innocence served up as snacks to wolves for long enough – I write my own damn chronicle! Only a Calembour can portray a Calembour with any convincing flair! Who is that man over there, the one who calls himself a doctor? Would that be my beloved and most favoured author, Catastrope? Let me ask:
"Are you Dr. Catastrope, author of *The Corpse of Opinons?*"

Catastrope — "Why? Have you come here to dump more shit on me?... I've had enough!... Can't carry any more! Drowning in it!... Oh, go ahead! Have another complaint? Another criticism?... Heap it on the pile! Burn it and me along with it, a big pyre for your pleasure!... Yet another agitated reader who buys my books only to hound me with their grievances!... That I'm some decrepit monster... a beast! Throw me in the drink! With all my books! Have done with it already!"

Jonkil Calembour — "No, it's not like that... I'm actually a fan -"

Catastrope — "A fan? What's wrong with you?... Another sicko? I have no fans! Anyone who claims to be a fan of mine must be bent in the head!... Oh, I know your kind... real sadists! Belonging to some religious or racist group... finding whatever you want to find in my words, some kind of justification for hate!... I am not an advocate for your lifestyle, your interests, your misogynist secret clubs!... Fans? Pfft! People just take what they want, tear out all the words they need and dump out all the context!... Revile the rest... I know what my fans are... Wackos! Degenerates! Only a degenerate would read me and actually derive pleasure from it!"

Vincent — "Don't begrudge fans, no matter what their reasons. Take it from me: when musical talent was taken over by three-chord dilettantes and sampling machines, I lost every one of my listeners."

Narrator — "I suppose, dear gentlemen, that I can count my fans not only in their sheer quantity, but the quality thereof. The King himself is a loyal fan who has beseeched me to continue on in the telling of your plights. Of course, I am stickler for facticity in every regard, not embellishing one mote, not covering over one blemish, and so demonstrating only the most noble fidelity to Truth. Adulation and praise has come like a tide to the feet of your most humble and modest narrator, and it is to them I thank for attributing to me all manner of flatteries such as pensmith, grand chronicler, weaver of fresh yarns, quilt-master of the unforgettable saga, deft laureate of the sophisticated bombast, vox formalis, magniloquent fellow of the classical word -"

Jonkil Calembour — "Ok, can it, you list-monger! Sufferer of logorrhea! I've heard just about enough of your ridiculous and

The Vicious Circulation of Dr. Catastrope

undeserved self-praise, you profiteering life-pirate! Arrogance! Your sorry rendering of my life makes for page-burners and penny dreadfuls! Drugstore poet! How can you compare your pathetic literary attempts to my major metaphysical opus!"

Narrator — "Metaphysics is balderdash! You dare accuse me of logorrhea, to malign me with an attribution more befitting of yourself? May God see fit to dispel this fog of confusion you reside in! And, as for the rest of you, do pay respect and tribute to the one man who has rendered you all so fairly and justly, bringing your mundane personal tragedies to the attention of the reading public. My pen has immortalized each of you, and so I believe I am owed a considerable debt for soliciting the pity of the public in concerns your miserable little lives.

"And, may I add, that I take issue with each of you, how you choose to squander the amazing gift of life that God and his great Bank of Investment Generousity has given you. For shame that you do this when the interest rates on the human soul remain adjusted at the prime rate! The Good Lord hasn't considered raising the rates – as is His prerogative and will – since the Deluge! That each of you take to airing your sordid grievances against life so shamelessly... If it did not provide some measure of amusement to my reading public, as well as function as a moral object lesson on how not to live, I would spare no resource of my words in castigating you severely!

"Let us take you all in turn, shall we? You, Catastrope, calling yourself a doctor – a noble title – who claims to minister to the sick and unwell: you are perhaps the most afflicted of all! Imagine the hypocrisy of a man so ill in treating the infirm! It is a blight upon your profession! Certainly, I would agree that you have suffered at the mercy of circumstances that He has designed for you to suffer – how better to test your faith!—but that does not grant you the liberty of defiling His Creation with your gibbering complaints. When you were falsely accused and sent to prison, this was Justice writ large, doctor. It was His way of telling you to live your life properly, according to noble moral precepts.

"And you, Francois, also an inveterate nag! Your moral crime is sloth above all else. You fail to see the value of being neighbourly, and would rather be selfish by rigidly sticking to this shabby artifice you call your principles. First of all, you chastise honest God-fearing call centre serfs whose dedication to their corporate masters is a direct reflection of the heavenly hierarchy and that great chain-link fence of Being. Secondly, you fail to understand that a well manicured lawn is a reflection of a well manicured soul. Do you not see that it is vital to our thinking species to maintain a neat face to our homes, to trim our shrubbery to avoid offending the delicate aesthetic sensibilities of cultured gentlemen and women afflicted with fainting spells?

"What sour grapes grow on the withering vines of your life, Vincent! I cannot bring myself to sully myself in listing your character crimes save for reliably reporting what is the truth in my popular books. To think that you were entitled to prosper in your chosen profession, for as we all know music is just a tootling artifice that numbs the spirit and sickens the mind. Respect is accorded those more honourable and necessary professions like woad-dyer, local tavern slattern, egg-checker, and persistent tax collector. All those noisome lute players and caterwaulers have no place in our moral world but in gracing us on Sunday mornings in His churches, should we not be too hungover to attend. I do profess to a small measure of fondness for music, but not as a profession on par or exceeding that of a carpetbagger. For, as the wise Plato says, 'the musical arts only cause our beloveds to be taken away to Hades where we shall follow them, and so we will lose them there once we turn around, and our parking will not be validated.' For you

The Vicious Circulation of Dr. Catastrope

uncouthly unread individuals, that is a direct quote from passage 56 in the dialogue entitled *Socrates versus Mothra*. Vincent, you would do well to avail yourself of this profound piece of classical wisdom to better redress and direct your moral self.

"Jonkil, he of the sputtering, infernal, *perpetuum mobile* of nonsense... Your mind runs like a pen of agitated pigs and your mouth runs faster and fouler than my Beloved Wife in the worst of her lunar moods when I have been too tardy at the tavern. You are in desperate need of a lesson in obedience just like our intransigent and indolent friend here who refuses to demonstrate due diligence with the sward of his property. I ask you, which is the wiser? The selfish rabble with their discontent and their inarticulate mess of opinions or the head of state who introduces reforms for the betterment of all? It is a travesty the way you treat your senior affiliates who have clocked far more experience than your youthful temperament can comprehend. Ah, but youth is always pure fire without the coolness of reason, forever proposing little whimsies and revolutions that are so terribly confused. Imagine a world where every youthful fancy was indulged? It would surely collapse into chaos, anarchy, and barbarism. No, we need cooler and wiser heads to govern our affairs to prevent against the reckless and foolhardy ideas of youth who have not yet gained the wisdom of the world. If I could counsel you on anything – should your fiery stubbornness permit it – it would be to keep the organs in their proper perspective: with one mouth and two ears (barring genetic mishaps or the loss of anatomy to disease or sword-related violence) you should listen twice more than you speak. This compulsion you have to natter endlessly on nothing makes you little better than Woman whose proper domain is to obey her spouse."

Catastrope — "Who does this anachronistic oaf think he's fooling?... No, I know an opinionated schoolmarm when I see one!... brandishing that moral ruler and rapping our knuckles with it!... A bitter old nun enforcing catechisms!... What right do you have to represent us and then add insult by scolding us with your silly opinions? To what end?... Oh, but you've profited from telling our tales of woe on our behalf! Have I seen penny one? My story, my money!... Pay up! My story doesn't come cheap... No, it comes with heavy debt... Just ask my publisher! The more of my story I roll out, the deeper down the debt-hole I go! Can you hear it? The sound of a dead body down an empty elevator shaft!... Debt for you, too!... For every word of my story you've told! Why should it be different who is telling the story when it all comes up snake eyes?... Besides, I won't just sit here on my thumbs while you leverage my life story for moral points!... I'm used to thieves like you, insufferable jackasses!... My publisher, the banks, the 'moral smudge-ority'!... Peddling the underfed ass of my stories, for profit!... And I get? Bumpkiss! Squatso!... You could work for Furlonghetti, too... Oh, I'll set it all up!... Polite introductions, organize a little salon with crustless cucumber sandwiches!... On my word, I'll hail you as the emergent voice of no generation that has yet to arrive! A futures investment... That's how I can shill you to fat Furlonghetti... And then you, too, can become one of his sweatshop scribblers, like me!... Every bestselling triumph adding another ring of blubber around Furlonghetti's globalizing middle, yanked right off you! Write yourself into debt, endless debt... Him and his 'deficit spending' on us, his little slave genii! You, too, can become a dope! Another weaver of small tales toiling in a flat with no heat!"

Jonkil Calembour — "You dare say that I belch nonsense? What know you of nonsense? I am the absurdist supremo! The great mullah of the incomprehensible – but whose fault is that? Not mine, I assure you. I only make sense to those who are at least a few strokes up the river of literacy and thought. You, on the other hand, are yet another sour pragmatist, and we all know where bottom-line thinking gets us: right down to the bottom where human value is sacrificed to expedite the money machines, the celebrity jiggle-tit machines, the simplicity uber alles! You can't represent me! I can't even represent me!"

Francois — I do not know any of these men, and I do not choose to know them. What is that funny skinny man saying? The nonsense man? He is very mentally ill and should be in a hospital, mummified with drugs. I do feel sympathy for the doctor, but he is very loud. And what of this oaf who says he tells my story? Him and his many lists, like Rabelais, a very silly liberal. What I need him to tell my story for? I do not want my story told! You see, I cannot be left alone... It is the liberal fear, so much that they cannot even leave you alone in words. No, they want to pester you from afar, too! They want to make a big *fait* with your life, which only invites all sorts of people to harass you, asking if this or that reported thing is true. And then the interviewers come, in a horde. I am certain this is what killed Leon — not being left alone, just hounded every moment, no peace! I want to go home, be left alone. This is not the place for me. But where is the door? How did I come to be here?

Vincent — "Okay, I've had enough of the yelling already. Listen, this man is probably not to be believed. He says he is our biographer, so let's just ignore him. I have enough enemies already! This cretin will only multiply them, have them at my door, ready to settle my hash right and quick!"

Francois — "Yes, this man speaks the truth! I do not need more idiots coming to my door!"

Jonkil Calembour — "You think you have enemies? You should see mine! Dangerous types with all sorts of nefarious secret service connections, a list longer than the Church's crimes against humanity! I want no part of this. You, alleged biographicizing miscreant, desist immediately! Make ready with the delete keys, scrubbers, mops, gum erasers, and all and remove any trace of my mention! I don't even want to see a citation! Zero references! You foul-mouthed hobgoblin of distortion! I'll have twenty lawyers chasing after your blood trail by sundown! I'll get my piece, you'll see!"

Catastrope — "And I'll join with him!... Armies, mongol hordes of lawyers! I will not be dragged down yet again by the likes of bad reportage!... I also demand erasure! Absolution in absentia!... No mention is the best mention of them all!"

Narrator — "Gentlemen, gentlemen, please... There is no need for this pointless squabbling. Do keep in mind what joy and delight your lives have bequeathed my readers. Think of posterity, all of you, and be humble servants to the craft of narrative. I may find each of you morally repugnant, but let us reasonably assay the higher and noble purpose of this task to which we all play our part. As your narrator, I have not altered one fact. I have not falsified or embellished a thing, gaining my purchase among those high ranks of biographical historians to whom I consider myself on par. And I am quite equal to the task of representing each of you under the light of truth, fairness and justice."

Francois — "You speak to us about fairness and justice? Justice is being left alone! Fairness is in keeping your dirty words out of my life!"

The Vicious Circulation of Dr. Catastrope

Narrator — I could see that these men were an intransigent lot. O how facile it all seemed from a distance, chronicling their lives, but in having to confront them thus in person has turned out to be a trial! They continue to heap abuses, these philistines and anti-knowledge barrel-runners, and I do think this commits grievous Insult to my readers – one of whom is none other than the King Himself. To spare my delicate readers further offense, yet to reliably detail the sorts of abuses my moral armour must endure, I paraphrase their attacks as declaring me:

A grid-system reductionist
A mendacious disfigurementationist
A low-born pisspot
A cauldron of gypsy stew
A ribaldricator
An empiricist

How am I to reconcile my noble deeds in portrayal with these unfounded jibes? It is upon Hermes' winged feet I glide, but these crass, uncouth and bafflingly ungrateful defilers of good intentions choose to spew their vomitus upon me, to perform their ritually beastly castigations upon your Dearest and Most Heroic Narrator. It is only my devotion to Christian mercy and peaceful piety that stays my sabre hand, I assure you all. For, it must be understood that I endure these assaults for *you*, dear readers so that *you* may not have to. No need to give me your tearful thanks, for I am far too modest a man to receive such adulation, having learned this becoming trait from the humble autobiographical work of Benvenuto Cellini. What would you, my dear readers, think of me if I resorted to the barbarous act of responding in the knuckle-dusting act of fisticuffs? Why, you'd lose almost as much respect for me as I would forfeit myself! One must keep crucially in mind that in matters of Reason, it is pure insult to commit physical atrocities where well-crafted arguments would suffice. It is absolutely pardonable to cuff a wayward goat or a stubborn cow, and perhaps even entirely justified to toss a pickpocket carnival midget off a steep cliff – but none of these beasts are God-gifted with the faculty of Reason, and so it does not engender good sense to treat your dealings with them reasonably. No, it is best to respond in the only way they can understand: brutishly. But, please, let me not saw the air with my giving forth on matters of appropriate versus inappropriate conduct, and let us resume with this vicious circulation of voices...

Narrator—"Gentlemen, I wish to make amends for any perceived insult. Do let it be known that what I now offer stands in absolute opposition to my integrity as a truth-teller and factual being. However, my compromise is this: that I may mask your names so you may preserve some shred of personal dignity. For although your reasoning is barely more than that of dumb, servile beasts, this obfuscation I will grant. Let us be at peace with everything and make to part ways now. I do not make this offer lightly, so your consent is requisite."

So I must leave this Chaucerian Tabard and allow you, dearest reader-who-reads-while-his-mouth-moves, to ponder the meaning of my little circulation, the circulation of these voices that seem to go into overtime catharsis and hyperborean Ciceronian histrionics the sort that launch into crescendo immediately with no gentlemanly sense of cultivated preparation. The circulation of my winsome books, the circulation of litanies and laments, the circulation of a coin burred and harshly struck as the token of vituperative speech. That I must end things here and bring us back to the narrative port of safety from whence

The Vicious Circulation of Dr. Catastrope

we first departed may be an abrupt closing, a disappointment. And, how I endeavoured to keep this collection of chronicles well-heeled, organized, well-ventilated in the louvered dome of my narrative arrangement. I did it for your amusement, a little amusement to make you laugh just a little, but most of all to inspire self-reflection on the grander questions that burden the soul. That I have lightened your burden just a touch with the grace of some risible tales will enshrine me in your future favour. However, to those who can never have done with hearing tales, where I must now fall silent shall be taken up anon in the future by others. Of this, I have no doubt. However, I must release my charges, consolidate this series of tales in their shrink-wrapped moral lesson made in China, and obtain a few pounds of ox feet to bring to my lovely harpy who will grace my post-tavern night with her own nagging melodies.

Adieu, fair semi-literate readers, and may God be your eternal beacon and moral compass as you pilot your dinghy across the tempestuous seas of the flotsam of life.

FIN

Kane X Faucher

A final word or two

This was not meant to be a definitive demonstration of all manifestations of literary polemic. It was but a vignette, a few casebook examples. Polemic is more than just religious, judicial, ideological. Despite impoverished readings of whatever makes the theory runways these days, not everything is ideological. Is this true? Everything can be said to be ideological as all things can conform to a preset numerical pattern if one imposes the limit of a personal fiction upon it (conveniently forgetting that the fiction is arbitrary and infinitely substitutable!). Literary polemic, as we find it in the saturated rhetoric of Cicero with his amusing character assaults on Verres or Antony, or in the works of Henry Miller, or Mencken, O'Rourke, Hunter Thompson, Céline, Gunter Grass, Hemingway, Bataille, Rabelais, Zola, Voltaire, Nietzsche, Baudelaire, O so many others, *must be redeemed* – or at least revisited. But first it must be salvaged and then raised up from its subaltern literary heritage. Some blanch at the prospect of either reading or endorsing (is to read an endorsement?) polemic of any kind. But what kind of spirit is that? *An oppressor and a suppressor*—a veritable censor in language. It reminds me of a title by Raymond Federman: *Take it or Leave it*.

I do not speak of the mundane polemic either. Hate speech that bothers itself with ethnic assault is patently weak-minded, hurtful, and just all around ridiculous. Okay, of course I can be held accountable for some slightly anti-Christian utterances here, but it is hardly incendiary enough to earn me a place on the Vatican's Index. We must also remember that these are characters, and they speak in the voice appropriate to their constructed natures. My opinions stay somewhat veiled, but according to Dr. Catastrope, opinions aren't worth much anyhow. Perhaps not even this one in an afterword.

The Vicious Circulation of Dr. Catastrope

What is needed is a polemic of tomorrow, a raving that is both a cultural critique and a recipe for how the new can gain purchase on the now. Polemicists who rage against the Now are perhaps the most illustrious optimists, for their doomy-gloomy speech is so sorely mistaken for an inveterate pessimism. In fact, they show such fidelity to an optimism for tomorrow that their complaints ring with a hope—a fundamental hope—that things can be better. The polemicist attacks an object with such fervour in the hopes to provoke change. We would be naïve to think that real change occurs in those polite, quiet regions of reasonable discourse, as if we could appeal to people with softened adjectives and careful logical deliberations. Patient arguments only hold sway over those who agree to the terms of giving attention to the rules of argumentation... and, as history has shown us to the point of monotonous repetition, the people will more likely appeal to a prose of reactionary lunacy than they will to a carefully embroidered treatise of societal emendation. Maybe the UN will not save the world after all.

Then, you will object, the solution to the problem that would wipe polemic from the table of options is to encourage more people to adopt the rules of polite and logical argumentation. This takes a wider program of education, a centrally planned sort that dogmatizes a people to adopt rules of appropriate discourse. But this plan, beyond being hopelessly utopian, labours under the terrible assumption that polemic is aligned with the negative, that we morally ought to scrap polemic entirely as being an obstruction to new forms of discourse. Can we so carelessly toss away a very long and shadowy heritage of polemic? Do not many of us gain a secret pleasure from reading invective? Do we not titter in private over a good jibe here and there, especially when it is true? We may in fact be a species that enjoys a good fight now and again.

Such verbal sport, such verbal jousting, is both light on its feet and laden down with its own genitals. A speech with *cojones*! A world without polemic may be wimpy, populated by graying relics, without *esprit*, a world of narcoleptic discourse. Although a good argument done up in careful philosophical style may be enough on occasion to stir the masses, it is not enough to truly cause sweeping changes. Even Rousseauism, in the mistaken paternity of attributing to him the genesis of the French Revolution, could not have really become inflamed without a few good fiery rhetors and polemarchs pamphleteering in their own way. Rabble rousing? Perhaps, but sometimes to good end. We already know historically what happens when that goes tragically sideways, from the beer halls to the camp walls.

Not all polemic is good polemic. But let us not get bogged down in questions of good and evil. Let us stay with good and bad, and on that order, an order of style and taste. That some polemic has inaugurated many foul and insidious political and cultural programs that have darkened the portrait of human progress, blemishing the face of Enlightenment, it is of the utmost carelessness and neglect to eviscerate polemic from our speech on account of a few bad apples. Polemic in itself, as a concept, has nothing to do with the ethics of what occurs as its result. In some instances, a poem has started a war, but we are more adroit in not discarding all poetry on account of it. Those who rail against the use of polemic are suspect, and many of them have been Christian. But do they not realize that the same ferocity of rhetoric can be found in the assaulting and prescriptive epistles of Paul? Is it not polemic when the religious Right are belching hellfire on the airwaves or on television? Is it not polemic if what one says one believes to be true?

To polemicize is to speak as a god. It is a speech act that goes well beyond the minor confines of body and ego. It is

The Vicious Circulation of Dr. Catastrope

to speak as if from something larger than oneself. Hopelessly romanticist notion? Perhaps after a fashion, but the wellspring of a vivacious and puissant polemic can almost be said to be in a mystic domain. A polemic that intoxicates its listeners as much as the speaker can be said to be of a transcendental nature, of a sense much higher than can be corralled within any linguistic apparatus. So many have bothered themselves to become combatants against polemics, to efface it wherever it lives, to sanitize speech, all without *understanding the exact nature of polemic to begin with*. And, should it also be understood that what we call the vaunted palace of Reason is motored by polemic, too? Reason is a polemical act as it wages its crusade against the irrational. Logic, the Vienna Circle, Pure Reason—all of it built with the bones of revenge! Hatred! Calumny! That it speaks so eloquently is but a disguise. An enemy of true, affirmative difference! A poison pill dipped in sugar! What vicious circulation!—ok, pardon my little polemic there. But it may come down to pathos and catharsis. If you can't go for reason, go for volume, but why not go for both? I think a good polemic can achieve that.

The exuberance of language, impassioned to the point of rupturing its own bounds, can sometimes lead to toxic, inflammatory utterances that form a contour for a speaking to come. Following that tangential vector from reasoned discourse to its extreme limit, a literary polemic devises new zones of speech that unapologetically emancipate expression from the demands of order, logical sequence, and rational repartee. It is language becoming-mad, the vicious decentralization of sense.

There are only points of departure in polemical speech. When inner experience goes into crescendo, into those perilous domains of the highest pique and pitch, this is where these five characters can be said to spill over the fragile constructs of selves by means of becoming discursively febrile, martial, or-nery, a critical assault that lashes outwards like an explosive object. This is the very core of "voxplosive" language.

But, we must face what will be the case for perhaps gen-erations to come: the linguistic gift of fire that those of the polemical stripe have brought becomes the tragedy worthy of Prometheus. The others—critics and legislator-rogues and soft-hearted do-wells—will continue to pick at our organs as we are chained to the high rock of polite sodden values! Perhaps there is one among you who will be our Hercules... And there I go again, seduced by my own fondness for polemic. Inflicting my preferences upon the reading public may be considered bad taste, but I fully affirm it, and it is a mode around which so much of my work will continue to orbit.